D1218756

VOICE-OVER

Voice-over

Carole Corbeil

First published in 1992 by
Stoddart Publishing Co. Limited
34 Lesmill Road
Toronto, Canada
M3B 2T6

Second printing June 1992

Canadian Cataloguing in Publication Data

Corbeil, Carole (Carole Cecile)
Voice-over

ISBN 0-7737-2572-5

I. Title,

PS8555.072V6 1992 C813'.54 C92-093275-4
PR9199.3.C67V6 1992

All of the characters in this book are fictitious, and any resemblance to actual persons living or dead is purely coincidental.

Typesetting: Tony Gordon Ltd.
Printed and bound in Canada

For my mother
and my daughter

CONTENTS

Claudine
June 1984

IT IS LUNCH TIME. THE WAITING ROOM SMELLS OF CABBAGE and institutional disinfectant. In her steno pad, Claudine writes: Everything gouged and scarred and worn but spic and span. You can still feel the huge grey mop that has gone over everything, wiping out cigarette ashes and grief.

Claudine is waiting for Cindy, a "young offender." She has given offence, has been taken out of the group home where she was living and put away in a correctional institute until the courts decide what to do with her.

Most of the young women here, Claudine has noticed on many visits, have had themselves pierced or tattooed. They are like a tribe with roses, hearts, lizards, snakes, devils and spiders on their limbs. Words, sometimes men's names, are laced into the designs.

Cindy stands out from the tribe. No tattoos, no make-up, she looks lost and unprotected. When Claudine saw her working in the kitchen garden of the institute, foot pushing down on a spade, digging a hole for a tiny tomato plant, she thought of her sister, Janine. Cindy had that faint air of having given up a long time ago. In the garden, she was doing what she was supposed to be doing, but she wasn't really there; the air around her was soft and syrupy. She had freckles on her shoulders, her hand left a print of sweat on the wooden handle of the spade.

Most of the footage Claudine had shot for her documentary was of women in maximum security, and she'd come to the correctional institute looking for something else. Following the women around the penitentiary in Kingston was like trying to decipher a code. They lied, they exaggerated, they wanted to shock. Claudine figured she needed something else, something softer. She needed a Cindy.

Cindy is to come to the visiting room after lunch. Claudine has already set up the lights and the tripod for the videocam. She will warm Cindy up for fifteen minutes, and then Anne, who does all the camera work for her documentaries, will show up with the camera.

Claudine writes, Don't fucking blow it, then scratches it out. My god. She's started to say fucking this and fucking that about everything. Last night, when Colin said you're disappearing into them, she wanted to say it's not true. She thought, it's his way of getting off the hook as usual. But there's truth in what he said. She is disappearing, becoming what she's watching. She's got to be careful. It's starting to make her sick.

"Yeah, sometimes," Cindy says. "Sometimes I remember her." She's wearing a grey T-shirt that covers her big breasts, and jeans.

"What do you remember about her?"

"I don't care."

"Did she hurt you?"

"She wasn't there, how could she hurt me?"

"I thought she was there for a while. I thought she left when you were six."

"Fuck. My mother didn't leave. I told you she died. She up and died. Get it?"

"Your father?"

"He kept me for a while. It wasn't his fault, eh. I was lots of trouble. Sometimes he said I was like her, kind of born crazy."

"What do you think?"

"I'm trouble. I'm dumb, eh. Kind of thick. Cindy's thick. Can I have a cigarette?"

Cindy pushes the bangs from her green eyes and starts to bite her fingernails.

"Here." Claudine hands her a cigarette.

"Next time can you bring me some chocolate. I'll talk for the camera, but bring me some chocolate, and what do you call those things, those licorice things with colors, you know, in layers?"

"Licorice allsorts?"

"Yeah. I like those. I really like those."

Claudine lights Cindy's cigarette with her Bic lighter. She can't stop staring at Cindy's nails. She hasn't seen nails bitten to the quick like that since grade school. Who did she know with nails like that?

"I can't help it," Cindy says.

"What?"

"Biting my nails. You bite your nails, too, but not so they show."

Claudine laughs. It's true. Not so they show. She stands up, smoothes her short skirt and walks over to the window. Where's Anne? She's supposed to be here by now. Things are about to turn. Claudine can feel it, just like an animal feels when a storm's about to come. That's what you want the camera to catch, when the subject's about to unwind with such force that they turn the camera into the thing that hemmed them in.

"This place," Claudine says, "reminds me of Catholic schools I went to. It has the same smell."

"You have a funny name. How do you say that?"

"It's French."

"I know that."

"Beaulieu. It means beautiful place. I'm from Montreal. I grew up in French."

"You don't sound French."

Claudine wants to say when I drink a lot I sound French.

Cindy flicks ash into the little aluminum plate that serves as an ashtray. "He said my mother was French. Her name was Lucille. One time I said I was gonna go look for her. That's when he said she was dead. Do you think she's dead?"

"I don't know."

"Do you think he's dead?"

"I don't know."

"Do you know why I'm here?"

"No." It's a lie. Claudine knows why. She just doesn't want to get into anything tricky, without Anne on the camera. People don't give themselves away twice.

Watching the back of Cindy's head, her wavy brown hair, her rounded shoulders, Claudine realizes that she wants to be in Cindy's place. She wants someone to ask her questions.

"Say it." Cindy turns in her chair and faces Claudine at the window. "Come on, big shot, say why I'm here. Big shot with the miniskirt. You think Cindy's thick, too, don't ya? Well say it, say why I'm here."

"I don't know, Cindy."

"I don't know, Cindy."

The mockery is perfect. Claudine looks at the blue sky through the opened window. They're in the middle of an industrial park, but this building is made of old, pink granite from some Ontario quarry, an imposing old building with a drive lined with poplars. Claudine can't move. Her body is trying to hold on to the moment until Anne gets here with the camera. She's got to hold on now, a little while longer.

"Cindy, I don't think you're thick," she says. "Don't say that about yourself." Then she sees a Citytv van driving into the parking lot. No wonder Anne's late, she's been chasing ambulances again.

"French, eh? What you doing here?" Cindy says.

"I don't know."

She can feel Cindy getting angry because she keeps saying I don't know. But she doesn't know. It happened, that's all, she moved here with Janine in the seventies, and sometimes wakes up in the morning and thinks I want to go home.

"I hate the name Franco-Ontarian," Cindy says.

"Yeah, I know what you mean. It sounds like canned food."

"That's what I'd be, eh. Franco-Ontarian. On my mum's side, anyway."

The door behind them opens, and Anne comes in, apologizing. There was an accident on Islington. A transport truck and a mini. "It's going to be all over the *Sun*," she says. "I don't want to know what happened. I had to take a few pictures for City. They'd kill me if they knew I was in the area and I didn't do anything. Never mind. Hi, Cindy."

She's all out of breath. Her short hair looks wet and slick as if she's just stepped out of the shower, but you can smell the gel, something just a cut above Dippity-Do. So efficient and brisk, she is, with a vest full of mikes and wires. Anne always wear vests, or something sleeveless to show off her slender, muscular arms. She pumps iron every day.

Claudine sits down in front of Cindy.

"Claudine, give me a voice check," Anne says, all husky, smiling with that big gap between her front teeth.

Claudine goes into her automatic voice. "Citytv Is Everywhere. Citytv Is Everywhere. Testing. Testing one, two, three. What a slogan. So comforting. It's like saying Idiots Are Everywhere."

"No," Anne says, and moves behind Claudine. "It's like saying Pretty Idiots Who Blow the Boss Are Everywhere."

Claudine turns. "An-nie."

"Ooops, sorry. Can you say something, Cindy? Are you okay? Are you comfortable? Pardon my language. I'm very crude. That's why I'm crew. The crew's always crude. Makes the boss feel refined."

Claudine laughs. Anne starts adjusting the lights around them.

They are quiet now, watching Anne work. Cindy, who's sitting across from her, looks fascinated by Anne.

Anne flicks a switch and the visiting room is suddenly flooded with bright white light. Cindy's hair takes on an auburn lustre, her eyes are shiny. Anne nods, the camera's on.

"Cindy, I'm sorry I lied," Claudine says. "I know why you're here. Can you look at me. That's it."

"If you know," Cindy says, "don't ask me." She's petulant now. She thought it was going to be different.

"But I don't know why you did what you did."

"You know that, too. Everybody knows about Cindy, but they pretend they don't, so they can feel good about askin'."

They stare at each other in the blazing lights. Cindy's mouth is set in a straight line, her cheeks are flushed in the heat of the lights. There is something beautiful about her that she won't allow. It's like looking at a lovely view through a smudged windowpane.

"Cindy?"

"Yeah?"

"We don't have to talk about it right away, if you don't want to."

"I didn't know what else to do."

"You could have told."

"He was like my dad, eh. He said I was pretty, the prettiest."

"Who?"

"All the time I'm screaming it out of my forehead." Cindy's got her chewed-up index finger on her forehead, and she's jabbing at it. "In here, I'm screaming, I'm screaming." Her teeth are clamped, she is breathing heavily, still jabbing her forehead. "Do you see it?" she says.

"What do you see?"

"I can't tell. I'm gonna die if I tell." She's yelling now. "She doesn't do nothin' for me."

"Who?"

"Fuck you. I don't want you. I don't want any of you." She brings her face back down on the table, cradles it in her hands.

Claudine looks at Anne, who seems to be in a trance behind the viewfinder. The light bounces off Cindy's hair, bathes her lightly tanned arms with radiance.

"I don't want you," Cindy mumbles. She looks up, face wet, a strand of hair stuck to her cheek, and then crumples back on the table. "I don't want you."

Claudine finds a kleenex in her bag, touches Cindy's hand. After a while Cindy looks up, takes the kleenex, blows her nose.

"Fuck you," she says in a feeble voice. "Fuck you all."

Claudine gets up, smoothes her black miniskirt and kills the lights.

"Bring me those licorice things," Cindy says. "Next time."

Claudine is shivering, even though it's hot in the van. The sun-dappled green of trees whizzes by. Clusters of sumachs by the roadside fan out to tall maples and locusts that almost meet in a green arch in the blue sky over Rosedale Valley Road. The van windows are open. Claudine sticks her head out, and almost loses her breath. The heat is so sudden this year, the season's moved from light lacy green to full bloom in a couple of weeks.

"We can do it in voice-over," she says.

Anne gives her a quick look. "Sure."

"You were late. It threw me off."

"I told you what happened. It wasn't my fault."

"I didn't say it was your fault."

Anne flips the radio on, pushes the buttons to find a station. Aggressive static, then Bruce Cockburn's "If I Had a Rocket Launcher" comes on.

"I love this road," Claudine says. "It's the greatest road in Toronto."

Anne sings along to the radio, going into high gear with "Some son of a bitch would die."

Claudine looks at Anne's profile. She looks so fresh in her short, cropped hair, her face is like a kid's.

Claudine thinks, I used to like what I did. Or maybe she just liked it that other people liked what she did. Critics called her work tough, unsentimental, uncondescending. Over the last four years, she's done a documentary on prostitutes, a documentary on drug abusers, and for the last year and a half she's been working on this women in prison thing.

When she started she wanted to push people's eyes into what they didn't want to see. She wanted them to see the damage, to see where the damage ended up. But seeing is not believing. The response she got was admiration for her form, for the pitfalls she avoided, for what she — and the she part was important at that point — was able to take. It was men who praised her. How did you get that stuff, they'd say, shaking their heads, how do you do it? Most of the women didn't like her detachment. They wanted her to go soft in the middle and slap on a moral at the end. Maybe she just imagined that. Maybe it wasn't true. Maybe those voices were closer to home. Her sister wanted to know when she was going to do something nice for a change. And her mother, when they talked, once every two years or so, well, Claudine could feel that Odette was proud of her, but she seemed ashamed as well. As if what Claudine did had ever had anything to do with her. In spite of, she wanted to say, in spite of you, I am making something of myself.

"So," Anne says, "what did she do?"

"Who?"

"Cindy."

"She set fire to this guy's room. The guy who was supervising the group home she's in. She poured kerosene around his bed and set a match to it. He was sleeping. He got second-degree burns."

"Yeah?"

"The guy almost died."

Anne stares ahead at the road, then gives Claudine a quick look.

"And then she took some pills. The usual." Claudine swallows. She's heard worse. There's just something about Cindy that gets to her, the way she bites her nails, the way she sucks the tips of her hair when she's crying.

"You're having a bad day. That's all."

"A bad day? I'm having a bad day? Citytv Is Everywhere, no doubt about it."

Anne's laughing. They're both laughing now, hysterically.

"You're used to gruesome," Anne says. "We're the gruesome ghouls, the girl-ghouls, remember?" That's what they called themselves back when they worked as editors in local news. Before they went free-lance and Claudine started to win prizes.

Claudine is suddenly all choked up, and she doesn't want Anne to see. Anne will poke and get her unravelling, then give her some cheery advice. Claudine looks at her legs, and wonders if she should shave them for the summer. "I'll take the tape, okay?" she says. "I'll check the sound out. See if there's something I can use. See if there's something I need."

Anne is turning left, going up Park Road to Church Street.

"Can you let me off? I'll take the subway."

"Where's your car, by the way?"

"It got towed away. Colin parked on Adelaide. Right in front of the sign that says from four to six."

"What a drag."

"I'm not getting it. He can go and get it."

"He did it, he should go and get it."

Yeah. But in the meantime she doesn't have a car.

"I can drive you home," Anne says. "You don't look so good."

"I want to walk, Annie. It's okay."

Anne stops the car by the Ontario Association of Architects building. The building reminds Claudine of Ben, the architect she lived with before moving in with Colin. It is such a simple building, a yellow brick box that says I am so much more than a box. Ben was like that. He kept saying you don't know what you're throwing away. Claudine reaches into the back seat and takes the tape out of the video camera, puts it in her big black bag and steps out of the car.

"I'll talk to you later, Annie."

She slams the door and looks down at her black sandals. She is standing in the leafy shadow of a maple. Up ahead, the sun bounces off the flat top of a privet hedge. The sky is achingly blue, with clouds that look like fish scales. She pulls her skirt down and starts walking towards The Bay as Anne drives off.

Then she changes her mind. She wants to go and sit in the green grass by the Architects building.

Claudine sits under the first tree she sees. There are sugar maples all around her, but she's sitting underneath a honey locust with thin lacy leaves filtering the sun. She puts her bag down on the grass, crosses her ankles and looks around.

She is in a sea of light green. The grass is prickly, it was mown some time ago and there are little mounds of yellowed, dried grass floating here and there. She watches the intersection of Park Road and Rosedale Valley Road for a while, how the cars pause for the briefest of moments before moving on, and then she stares at a silver maple rising tall across the street. The wind bends its branches, flips the silver undersides of the leaves. It strikes her as such a sad sound, wind through trees.

Yawning, she watches ants crawling on her legs. It is ticklish and annoying but it feels like it's happening to someone else. In a trance, she watches stunned bees bend the heads of clover blossoms with their weight. She stretches, lies down, and uses her black bag as a pillow. She can feel the corners of the videotape, so she shoves it over to the side of the bag.

Safe here. As a child she wanted the whole world to be like water so she could dive into the earth, swim up tree trunks and feel the sun on her face among the leaves. She's always looked for safety in a patch of green.

*T*hey both shook when they first met. Shook and stopped eating. Of that time, Claudine remembers the taste of capers, which she could eat, off the fluorescent salmon, which she could not, and the feel of a salt-rimmed bloody caesar on her lips.

She doesn't know why she had to match Colin's drinking, drink for drink, but she did. It wasn't so much a need to drink as a need not to miss anything, to be equal on all fronts, equal meaning the same.

She doesn't remember much of anything lately. Her memory is reserved for working. When she's putting other people's lives in documentary films, she remembers every gesture, every line that comes out of her subjects' lovingly photographed mouths. Living with Colin, on and off, has left her in pieces, pieces that know nothing about the other pieces. Colin keeps her so insecure that she spends most of her time thinking about him. It doesn't matter where she is, her little wheels are turning inside her head, turning and pounding and grinding. In her steno pad, she occasionally writes things like I am a forehead figuring him out, and then scratches them out.

She hardly remembers the Claudine Beaulieu of three years ago, when she met Colin. That Claudine had just turned twenty-nine. She'd been staring at her black, salt-stained suede boots in a Queen Street booze can when she felt someone gazing at her. Looking up, she thought the guy was familiar.

He tried to lock eyes with her, but she wouldn't oblige. At first. She was too tired, her eyes too blurry from watching the same images over and over again in the editing suite. Besides, she'd recently settled into unhappiness with Ben, in his blue apartment with hand-painted clouds on the high ceilings. She'd ended up there like a stray. Was doing that a lot in those days. Moving into men's lives and treating their apartments like hotels. Nothing was supposed to matter but work and wearing black. She did both vengefully. What looked like botched, haughty indifference to others was, to her, something more profound. She was going to take the bad-boy artist myth away from men and shove it back in their faces. See how they liked it. Waiting up. Waiting for phone calls. Sitting through artistic tantrums. Being the doormats of female genius. Trouble was, she always ended up feeling sorry for the men and wrapped the pity around them as if it was love. And the men always thought she was frail, no matter how she behaved.

"Are you angry?" sweet Ben asked about twenty times a day.

"No," she would say. "What makes you think that?" And her voice box felt squeezed, as if someone had slipped a choke-collar around her neck.

Their romance had been very compressed. He'd rescued her

from a messy apartment with ringed coffee cups in every room. After three weeks of intense lovemaking and lyrical outpourings about her beauty — he did portraits of her that looked like architectural Mount Rushmore renderings — he asked her to move in with him. He had a beautiful profile, soft eyelids, clean-shaven cheeks. She liked to watch him sleep. He was so open when he slept.

Three months after she moved in, Ben started to complain about her housekeeping. "It's an aesthetic thing," he kept saying as he followed her around, picking up the clutter she dropped in her wake. She tried to pay more attention, but she couldn't keep the apartment the way he liked it, tidy with things in rows. He lived with his eyes. The apartment had to be the clean showplace of his architectural soul. After he tidied, he would sit and watch what he had done, like God contemplating his creation.

Eventually, she pretended not to hear the scolding in his voice. And then he started telling bedtime stories about previous lovers, and Claudine, a voyeur by profession, listened and folded the jealousy away somewhere; she couldn't use it just now, but might someday need the force of it to pry her out of a stalemate.

The man who wanted to lock eyes with her was standing by the shuffleboard, thumbs hooked into the belt-loops of his jeans. Christmas lights blinked above his black leather jacket. It was snowing outside, and the people coming in to the booze can, the ones who'd manoeuvred two doors and a bouncer with membership cards or contacts, had rosy cheeks and snowflakes melting on their coat collars. It reminded Claudine of Montreal, the way people sparkled there with innocence anytime snow framed their faces. Odd how in Toronto there is no romance of snow.

Of anything. People came from all over Canada to do the Toronto huddle, sneering in insecure bunches not at what they'd left behind, but at what they found. It was a way of making themselves feel better about ending up alone in a city they'd dreamed about. For years, Claudine sneered, too, the special Montreal-to-Toronto sneer. Now she was looking for a tribe. Any tribe would do.

For outsiders, the pickings were slim. There were the people she worked with and Ben's designer friends, that was all. Ben's friends wore wonderful clothes and lived in wonderfully weird places where people sat around like props approving or disapproving of the other props. You had to behave as if your life were a piece of performance art.

Between shots, the guy in the jeans and the leather jacket was pushing against the shuffleboard with his thighs. He was tall and lean, with longish straight hair he kept pushing out of his face. He seemed to like his face, and liked his hands, but he didn't like the rest of himself much. He was playing against a guy with dreadlocks and a great, warm laugh. "Yeah, mon," the man said every time the guy in the jeans overshot the stone. "Dat's more like it, Colin." And every time that happened, Colin looked for Claudine's eyes, and she looked back, just a beat, before looking away.

She hadn't drunk quite enough beer yet to want to play with that, even though the music was loud enough, her black jeans tight enough and her black suede boots just high enough to give her the illusion of being bright and apart from the small, frightened rhythm of herself.

She finished her beer. To Marianne Faithfull, inhaling a cigarette, mouthing what are you fighting for, what are you fighting for, it's just an old war, not even a cold war, Claudine walked to the shuffleboard and parked herself by the middle line. Say it in broken English. Broken English.

"You want to play?" Colin asked.

"You've already got a partner," she said. Colin's friend laughed and said, "He's getting slaughtered. Why don't you give him a hand?"

And so she did. Sawdust sticking to the sweat of her hands, saying zen to the stone, she slid the stone, pulling back with her pelvis at the very end, willing the stone to hang back on the lip. It worked almost every time. She played out his game and won it for him. His friend, Rocky, pretended to swoon with masochistic pleasure. "She's a killer," he kept saying. "A killer."

"I'll buy you a beer," Colin said. And Rocky winked and disappeared.

It wasn't until much later that Claudine realized that Colin had drunk a lot more than she'd thought. He held on to her hands and said where have you been, and while it embarrassed her, it also pulled her out of her tiny self and plunked her down on the huge stage of his hungry eyes.

Colin was a writer, a novelist and a poet who was beginning to get a reputation. That's where she'd seen him before, in the newspapers. There had been interviews lately about a book he'd written, something about guys on a druggie escapade in northern Ontario, bonding on Nembutal in the bush.

She'd heard of him. He'd heard of her. They talked. He had a remarkable ability, it was a gift, really, of making people's lives interesting to themselves again. It was a form of flattery and it was bewitching.

It was five o'clock in the morning when they left. The light was greyish blue, Queen Street covered in snow. He guided her to the entrance of a barbershop. "Let's get a haircut," he said. He turned her collar up. She was leaning against the glass, her back pressed against the faces of men in short, slicked-back hair. She kissed him. For a long time. The city started to come alive with streetcars and snowploughs as they held each other and kissed and read each other's eyes. Their breath rose around them like smoke.

Finally, she pushed her hands against the skin of his leather jacket and said oh god, what am I doing? And laughed, because she'd told him about Ben, and the thought of giving in to what she was drawn to made her feel guilty and wicked.

"Come home with me," he said.

"I can't."

Ben was pretending to be asleep. But he sat up in the dark room and screamed, "Where the fuck have you been?" It terrified her. She could almost see a rolling pin in his hand. She said I was walking, I needed to clear my head.

Two weeks after this, she was out of the blue apartment with the hand-painted clouds, out on the street where Ben had thrown the six green plastic bags of her possessions.

Colin lived in an apartment above a dry cleaner and a bakery. It had a sharp yeasty smell, very little furniture, a mattress, a desk, an antique chesterfield and two chairs, heirlooms, he called them. He had no chest of drawers. Piles of clothes on the floor completed the decor. He took her in, even though he said not much of a dowry when he saw her green plastic bags. She laughed. They lived together, or rather they slept together, and he wrote her into his next book of poetry. She was the you, she was the she, he even called the collection *She*. He wrote about everything. He wrote about meeting at the shuffleboard table, he wrote about what she called the melodrama of her parents' life, poems that named them, Odette and Roger, for the world to see. She felt robbed and anointed both at once. When her sister read it, she said he got one part right, the part where you say you don't remember anything.

Standing in front of the United Cigar Store in the underground mall by The Bay, Claudine reaches inside her bag to get her wallet out for a subway token, but instead she grabs the tape with Cindy on it. She wants to hold it in her hand as she walks towards the train. In the mirrored columns, she can see herself walk by. She would like to have the courage to stop and really look at herself, instead of sneaking these partial looks and trying to put these patches together in her mind.

But she must never look vain, like her mother, who could not walk by a shop window, a toaster, a kettle, a mirror, the chrome of a car without twisting herself to sneak a look, who sat at kitchen tables facing windows so she could look at herself talking, who took her compact out in restaurants before dinner, in between courses, after dinner, furtively looking for food between her teeth, who looked at herself in three-way mirrors, lost, in a trance when she took the girls shopping.

No, Claudine can't admit that she wants, with all her body and soul, to look into that mirrored column and assess just how awful she looks, as Anne so kindly put it.

She is hugging the tape to her chest now. Walking by a white moulded plastic trash can attached to moulded plastic chairs, Claudine feels an urge to throw the tape in the garbage.

Her arm goes out, she is holding the tape, ready to let it drop. She almost drops it. She wants to drop it in and then retrieve it. She imagines dropping it in the garbage can and walking away. She wants to do this so badly, as if her hand had its own life, at the same time knowing she won't, couldn't, throw such irreplaceable footage away.

Still clutching the tape, she goes through the doors leading into the subway, walks to the turnstile, puts her token in, walks through, faces another garbage can. The impulse again, a twitching in her fingers. She imagines dropping it in, going down the stairs to the southbound platform, running back and getting it just as an old man in a grey uniform is starting to empty the trash.

The tiles are very yellow by the platform. The Bloor trains have come in, a crowd of people is coming up the stairs from the east–west line and gathering on the southbound platform. A woman with blond hair steps in front of her. She smells sweet, it's a familiar smell, Lily of the Valley by Yardley. Claudine stands right behind her. She wants to walk in this woman's wake for the smell. The train clatters into the station, the doors slide open, Claudine follows the woman into the car. She walks to the centre pole. Claudine stands behind her, leaning against the doors.

Her hands are sweating on the tape. She puts the tape back into her bag, closes her eyes as the train pulls out of the station.

Lights
1950

ROGER WAITED FOR ODETTE IN FRONT OF THE BELL TELEPHONE building where she worked as an operator. She knew he was waiting, so she took her time about getting ready. She changed her blouse in the green staff washroom, splashed Yardley eau de cologne on her neck and wrists. The light coming through the glazed windows bounced in the mirror over the sink, threw back a fine-boned face framed by a blond pageboy. The fresh blouse she'd brought with her had a wide pleated collar that made her feel open and summery, as if a breeze followed her, as if she were made to float in warm air, and she needed that, to draw all the voices asking for numbers out of her ears.

Odette hoped that Paulette and the rest of the girls would be standing at the bus stop when she came through the big revolving doors, so they could see Roger open the car door for her. They were. That felt good, to come out revolving, collar fluttering in the late afternoon sun and feel them gawk a little as she walked towards Roger's new Studebaker. She imagined her blond page-boy gleaming in the sun, her small waist cinched in a pale blue skirt with a little flared pleat at the back.

Roger opened the car door for her. She smiled and got in, taking her time to settle in the big seat. Her nylons made a little *whoosh* as she crossed her legs. The car door sounded like the clapper on a movie set. She rolled the window down and gave Paulette a little wave. The other girls pretended not to see her, but Paulette rolled her eyes and blew her a kiss. And then Roger tried to kiss her, leaning over in the car, but she avoided that by bringing the visor down to shield her eyes from the sun. Just the same, he wore the girls and the work off of her by the time they turned the corner of Saint-Antoine Street. All he had to do was say, "Mon Dieu que t'es belle aujourd'hui, mon pitou." And touch her knee.

It wore the work off her, but it made her shy.

After a seafood dinner at Pauzé's, where she felt ancient and sophisticated from sucking on crab legs, Roger drove up Côte-des-Neiges, and along the Boulevard, all the way to Summit Lookout. He seemed happy in his new Studebaker with silver sparkles on the upholstery, and when they parked and they looked at the view, he was amazed at the lights everywhere, as if he'd never seen them before, as if he'd never thought about all the "juice" it took to light up the city like a Christmas tree. He said he wanted to put those lights on her fingers, in her hair, those tiny lights twinkling below the Westmount mansions and around Jacques Cartier bridge, and all those lights spreading beyond the island. He said, "C'est-tu beau. Je veux te faire un collier de lumières."

She smiled. He was so fanciful. She wanted to say that would make me look like a statue in front of l'Oratoire St-Joseph.

He sighed. The lights were like garlands to him, he said, strings of lights binding the city together.

She waited. He turned off the ignition. He looked at her profile and shook his head. Ma belle, belle Irlandaise, he said. He unscrewed his silver hip flask and took a long swig. She looked at him, curious now, and he shook his head again, as if saying I can't get over you.

She was tired of waiting. She could feel him swallowing like a fish out of water. She reached for her clip-on earrings, dropped them in her lap. Her ears were sore from the earphones she wore all day, saying may I help you sir, may I help you madam. And now the pinch of these fake pearls on her lobes.

Roger picked up the earrings. She said oh, for the grazing gesture that shot feeling into her legs. He looked at her and shook the earrings like a pair of dice.

"Odette," he said.

"Oui," she said.

"Odette, tu es tellement belle."

"Merci." She couldn't get used to the effect she had, even though she expected it now, and when she didn't get compliments, she would rush to the ladies' washroom and find consolation in the mirror. In the last few years, she'd lost the gawkiness in her limbs, she'd filled out in what her mother called all the right places, and she'd lightened her hair, bit by bit, with peroxide at first and then with a bleaching compound she got at the drugstore, and that made her blue eyes really stand out.

Her father, Béribée, called Roger un flatteur. Un maudit de nouveau riche. Which Roger was. Smelling of Brylcreem, looking spoiled around the edges. Roger called himself too sensitive. "Ma mère a toujours dit," he always said when he'd drunk too much, "que j'étais trop sensible."

Odette didn't think a man could be too sensitive. But sometimes she wanted Roger to look through her, the way actors looked through actresses in the movies before they kissed.

The giving in her knees subsided. She looked at the view. She said, "C'est beau." He looked right through her. "Ouais, c'est beau, mais c'est pas New York."

She was quiet after that. If only he could bring himself to pop the question.

*W*hat if she said yes to him, what would happen? And what if she said no?

She always thought she was going to miss something, whatever decision she made. It drove her father crazy. When they played cards and she couldn't make up her mind about what to set down, he said, if you were a horse, Odette, you'd never get out of the starting gate. And then he shook his hand in the air, cracking his finger bones like a whip, shouting: Go, woman! Go! The more he pushed her, the more confused she became, and then she'd play anything, and go off into a trance, watching the flowers on the worn Oriental carpet in the dining room where they played.

The wind blew in lilac from the yards below, and rustled the pale leaves of poplars above them. It was like a shiver, this wind, as it danced over their soft, young faces in the dark car. Odette's hair rose from the back of her neck. Roger leaned forward, took her chin in his hand. "Je t'aime, Odette, si tu savais comme je t'aime." She jumped out of her skin to hear it, repeated it to herself, but couldn't say it back to him for fear of raising expectations she had no intention of meeting just yet. If she said je t'aime too soon, he would end up pushing himself against her like he did that time at the swimming party at Pierre Leduc's place in Sainte-Adèle. And she felt dread in her belly, remembering how the sand on his thighs had pressed against her legs, how everybody had laughed at them later on.

He said, "Viens," and got out of the car and walked around to open the door for her.

They leaned together on the stone parapet. She imagined the currents of the St. Lawrence flowing under the bridges. He put his arm around her shoulders. The lights twinkled in the warm air, the wind blew her pleated collar over her mouth. "Dis oui, Odette." She started to shake, felt choked by the desperate way he held her. She couldn't say yes. She couldn't not say yes. She closed her eyes, lost the feeling in her legs, her knees almost buckled under her. When she opened her eyes, she felt herself falling into a net of lights, falling and choking with a non from a long time ago. She smiled as best she could and, feeling tiny and apart from herself, said oui.

A mosquito had landed on her neck. Odette crushed it absent-mindedly, smearing her neck with her own blood.

Le futur was going to be glorieux, everybody said so. Everybody said les années cinquantes vont apporter la prospérité au Québec. Everybody being Roger's father, Eugène Beaulieu, and Roger himself, who thought the war had solved all human misery. "It's a new world, baby," he said to Odette. "Maintenant l'argent va tomber du ciel."

The shame of being conquered, a shame handed down, swallowed, spit out with the stringy guilt of Catholicism, that shame was going to disappear, dissolve in the bright lights of machines never before imagined. The past, everybody allowed, had been a torture for le peuple canadien, who had been stretched on the slow rack devised by the English, sinews contorted by inferiority, tongues burned to conform. But that was over now. The future was going to be glorious. The future was being invented by physicists and engineers who had recently conceived of the atomic bomb. It was a future that would dwarf all human concerns, that would find its apotheosis with Expo 67, where the sun blazed on the treeless site, where slides dissolved to the sound of cymbals and xylophones in disposable pavilions.

Roger was always telling Odette that they were going to be part of this brave new world. They were going to be special. That's what Roger said all the time, "On n'est pas comme les autres." He was proving it by wanting to marry the half of Odette that was Irish. Irish, English, there was no difference, he was marrying the blood he'd been bred to hate. He saw himself as brave, as new, as willing to take huge leaps. He was not really French-Canadian on this account. No child of Duplessis, he, no descendant of tight-fisted, narrow-minded habitants.

Roger's grandfather had made a fortune by selling his land, and then other people's land, in what they now called Montréal-Nord, but that didn't count as habitant. That farmland was now sprouting duplexes and triplexes. The Beaulieu family had gone from habitant to rentier in two generations, and Roger hated any mention of his origins. He could never let anything be, was forever asserting his identity as an Outremont playboy. "Baby, ça, ça fait habitant," he'd say to Odette about anything that looked old, used, worn, real. And she laughed, very citified, very Montréalaise, hiding her surprise at the bitterness behind the words.

Over time she got to know that the bitterness was directed at his father. Over time, she got to hear the stories of how Roger's father loved to talk about manure over dinner, after ringing for the maid with his foot on the buzzer underneath his chair. He did it to get to his wife, and to annoy Roger, to rattle what he called les grands sensibles. As the family sat down to chicken en cocotte, he talked about the honest smell of fumier, or about the blood flowing from the bodies of butchered pigs, and les beaux boudins you could make out of that. Eugène Beaulieu called his farm talk la réalité. Roger didn't want to have anything to do with la réalité.

At twenty-five, he had no idea what he wanted; he swam in a warm sea of possibilities, tried not to crash on the narrow rocky shore of his father's plans. His mother, Louisa, read the poetry of Chateaubriand, Lamartine, Musset, and quoted dripping alexandrines as if she were eating chocolates. She took the train to New York every two months to seek the services of a Freudian analyst, and between those visits took to her bed in fits of what was called neurasthénie. For as long as Roger could remember, his father had hammered everything his mother thought or felt into tiny boxes he called les folies de Louisa.

Roger didn't want much. He wanted to have du fun. Pourquoi pas, he said, all the time. He wanted to party with his generation of rich French-Canadian youth who affected American slang, who said ben swell, hunky-dory, no flies on you, who danced to swing music, who swooned over Frank Sinatra. Sometimes he thought he wanted to play the drums for big bands. He imagined pounding out the feeling of loss that never left him into the bodies of dancers filling up the big ballrooms of English hotels. But that would never have been allowed, Eugène's son, playing the drums, mon Dieu Seigneur, c'est pas possible.

He wanted to take Odette to parties, to skating parties, and costume parties and carnaval parties, and watch her face when his friends said, "Y est donc l'fun, Roger, y a donc de la personnalité." He had lots of personality, that's what he had. He could make people laugh, had a way of telling stories that told a bigger story. He had no idea where the stories came from. They just came out of him, and when he drank, they came even more easily; he could give himself up then, to all the words and ideas and fantasies that welled up inside him. He liked not knowing where things were going to end up, he liked how words opened up into other words, into puns and innuendoes and pictures that made his friends laugh.

"Arrête, Roger, j'en peux pus," they said, heaving, tears in their eyes.

Being a party boy, walking the tightrope of what other people thought of him, that was his true métier. But now that he wanted to marry Odette, his father was going to give him a flower shop to run. And so he was going to do that, too. Be liked, be loved, and run a flower shop. Until other possibilities galloped in and kicked dust on la réalité.

When she finally said je t'aime on the grass that stained her pale skirt green, it was to slow him down. They had walked around the stone parapet and down the little path that led to a sweet-smelling grassy slope. He had spread his jacket on the ground. And now she was going numb from the heavy breathing in her ears.

She didn't want to lose him, but she didn't want to do this either.

A clump of grass dug into her shoulder blade. She tried to ignore it, tried to chart her body through the effect it had on Roger. He was sighing and moaning. He was so heavy on top of her, she could hardly breathe. Her whole body wanted to heave and shake him off, buck and send him flying.

She opened her eyes, lost herself in the night sky full of stars.

When he hiked up her skirt, and she felt his hands on the skin between the top of her nylons and her underwear, his whole body went stiff and then collapsed in choking sobs. "Odette," he moaned. "T'aurais pas dû faire ça." What? She hadn't done anything, just imagined the soft skin of her thighs, felt the beginning of something warm between her legs. That was all. And now she was ashamed.

He stood up and tucked his shirt into his pants, rummaging around in there, so that she had to close her eyes. She didn't want to see his face. Sometimes, looking up from a kiss, she was shocked by his features. So dark. Black hair, black eyebrows, brown eyes with furry eyelashes, so defined for a man.

"A quoi tu penses, là, Odette?"

"A rien. Je pense à rien. As-tu mes boucles d'oreilles?"

"Sont dans ma poche, pitou."

He sat down again, adjusted his jacket around her shoulders. She said merci. He said de rien. Traffic sounds rose up from below, a squirrel clawed its way up a blue spruce. Roger lit a Sweet Caporal and inhaled deeply.

"Tu m'aimes, hein baby, tu m'aimes?"

She wanted to cry. She took his hand and put it on her cheek. He stroked her face, then reached into his breast pocket for the silver flask he always carried with him. His hand grazed her breast on the way out. "Pardon," he said. "Un p'tit drink?"

"Oui. Non."

"Oui ou non?" And he took a long swig. She watched his Adam's apple go up and down, and suddenly fell in love with his neck, the soft skin there, the skin without stubble.

"Oui," she said. If she was going to be kissing him some more, she'd better taste the same as him.

"A nos fiançailles, Odette," he said. "On va avoir du fun, ma belle Odette. Tu vas voir, ben du fun."

She brought the flask up to her lips. He said ready, set, go. Before she knew what she'd done, she'd gulped down the rest of the brandy.

"Woa, woa, pitou, pas si vite," he said.

She coughed. She felt warm as toast. She laughed and liked her laugh. It was like a great ringing of bells. She couldn't stop laughing, seeing the disappointed look on his face because there was no brandy left for him now. "Tu devrais te voir la face," she said.

"Tu fais ton Irlandaise, hein Odette?"

"J'avais soif, Roger," she said. She pulled at a tall piece of grass and bit into the soft succulence of the stem.

*I*rlandaise. What a joke. Every year, on St. Patrick's Day, Odette's mother bought pots of shamrocks wrapped in green aluminum paper. Ceramic leprechauns sat on spotted toadstools. That was all, and her uncles sang old songs that made their bloodshot eyes water. Keening for something over the water. What? What in heaven's name were they going on about? Odette had no idea. That whole side of the family, the Irish side, wiped tears from their eyes all the time, from laughing or crying. It didn't seem to make much difference in the way they looked.

They liked the French because the French hated the English as much as they did, and because the French were good Catholics. Not one of them had ever learned a word of French, though.

The English took our food, that's what Odette's mother said when they talked about Ireland. The English took our food. As a child Odette always saw her brother Eddie's face when her mother said that. He got the second helpings, and the thirds, Eddie did, because he was the only boy. Nothing. Nothing to eat, she said, blue eyes fierce, twisting her apron as if it had all happened yesterday.

Odette couldn't give two cents about the past. They weren't hungry now, so what was the big deal? It was a way of liking to be sad. Her mother liked to be sad. That Irish sadness had seeped into her feeling of exile as a child, when her mother had left her at her grandparents' house for two whole years. She must have been five or six at the time. Her mother left her there and went back to Halifax. She didn't even say goodbye. Granny Mattie had stood in the steamy bathroom while Odette took a bath in the biggest tub she'd ever seen, and said, "Your mother's gone now. She took the train back to Halifax. You're going to stay with us awhile."

In her grandparents' house on Rachel Avenue, Odette cried herself to sleep, face pressed to the glazed pillowcases sad Granny Mattie had starched. Granny Mattie yelled stop crying, stop crying, so that Odette half-cried, a twisted feeling in her belly, corkscrewed on the bed.

She was left there, and her sisters stayed behind in Halifax. No one ever said why.

She couldn't start caring about that.

What she cared about were the big faces on the movie screen

of the Loews Theatre, what you could do with your pale eyebrows, what you could put in your brassiere for the perfect silhouette under tight sweaters. Odette knew how to put things together so they shimmered, how to bring people's eyes in her wake. It was a gift, like divining. She was possessed by it. She knew how to create the Look. The Look could make you as big as a screen face in other people's eyes, so big that people shrank, thinking they were the only ones with butterflies where their stomachs should be, with chips where their shoulder pads should be.

She day-dreamed her way through her cours commercial at the Reine Marie convent. In classrooms smelling of chalk, she dreamed about Alan Ladd and Gary Cooper and Clark Gable. She modelled her kisses on their lips, lips bigger than her body. Watching those movies, transfixed in the dark, feeling the ridged velours of the seat under her hands, she wanted to melt into light.

She wanted to be a movie star or a nun. She didn't want anything in between.

"Maybe I should be a nun," she said to her mother one time. Her father, who'd been listening, said, "Odette, you'd be a nun with two pairs of slippers under your bed." She didn't know what he'd meant until later when she was doing the dishes. She blushed then, looking down into the soapy foam of the dishwater.

*T*hey were so quiet now sipping brandy on the slope of the Mont-Royal. She was feeling the brandy. "Embrasse-moi, Roger. Embrasse-moi," she said.

He kissed her. He tasted of vanilla and sugarcane, sweet as Christmas pudding.

*S*till in her bathrobe two hours before her wedding, Odette wanted to finish her toast and tea before her father got going on something he'd seen in *La Presse*. The world was being divided in two. Les Rouges and everybody else. The headline in today's *La Presse*, which Odette's father was holding out with disdain, was "Le Communisme Menace L'Asie Toute Entière." Anything to do with le communisme was bound to remind Béribée of his brother Jean, who, Béribée said, was one of Duplessis' white-collar goons. All that meant was that Jean made his legal living hunting and prosecuting reds.

"He always was a squealer," Béribée said about Jean. "Now he gets paid for it."

Not today, Odette wanted to say. Please, not on my wedding day. Dear God do not let what is in *La Presse* travel through my father's face like an invading army starting with a twitch around the mouth and ending with a throbbing vein at the temple.

She wiped the corners of her mouth with her fingers and pushed the crusts of her toast to the side of her plate. Béribée sat at the head of the dining-room table, the rest of them ate in silence, clustered like refugees at the other end.

Odette's sisters, Kathleen and Doris, were already made up, looking dusty and waxy-lipped in the white, milky light of the dining room. Snow had fallen all night, piled high on the windowsills and flat roofs of the houses on Sainte Famille Street.

Calculating now, Odette figured that Kathleen and Doris had already used the bathroom, her father had his own sink in his room, Eddie was shaving. The bathroom, when she would get to it, would be steamy and uncomfortable, the door flimsy against the collective will of the house, because they would all want to get in again and again, that was for sure. You could never get any peace in there.

"Are you excited?" Kathleen said. "I'd be excited." There was red lipstick all around the rim of her coffee cup.

"Mum?" Odette said. "Mum?"

Special, she wanted to say. Special day. My special day. Could you get rid of them?

"Yes, dear," Julia said.

"Can we go now, Mum?"

Odette looked at her sisters. She was trying not to smile. If she looked too happy, it would invite some teasing.

Julia took her apron off and folded it. "Yes Mam'," she said, winking at Kathleen and Doris. "Yes Mam', your highness bride."

"There goes the bride," Doris said.

"All dressed in pride," Kathleen added, and both of them laughed.

Odette threw them a dark look.

"C't'une joke, Odette. Voyons donc," Doris said.

"Regarde-moi ça," Béribée said, "un autre speech sur la race. Le maudit verrat de Duplessis."

But they were out of there like a shot, holding hands like girls, running as fast as they could up the stairs and into the wild rose wall-papered bower of Julia's bedroom.

*B*éribée swirled the shaving brush around and around the soap in the chipped, pale blue soapdish on the lip of his sink in his room. The walls had once been cream. They were now grey, a paler version of the battleship-grey verandahs of the courtyard Béribée could see through the window. It was snowing, and the roof of the greystone across the courtyard was covered in a thick layer of white.

Béribée had to work fast now, the hot water was steaming up the mirror with the border of sand-blasted flowers. The water flowed, eddied around the rust stain near the drain. Lathering the left side of his face, Béribée imagined himself walking Odette down the aisle. He could almost see her proud neck underneath the white veil, he could almost feel the warmth of her slender arm, as he scraped soap and hair and flesh from the side of his face.

Odette was going to wear Julia's wedding dress. Julia had pronounced peau de soie as po de soy when they got married, and she was still pronouncing it po de soy now that Odette was getting married. He thought she'd learn French. But she'd learned very little, and what she did learn she pronounced like a vache espagnole.

Béribée rinsed the razor under the tap, looked at the neat trail of scraped flesh he'd just created on the left side of his face. It was getting hot in the bathroom, he could feel the hairs of his armpits getting clammy with sweat. Goddamn Julia had been at the thermostat again.

Odette, married. The same Odette who stole books from him. She gripped books so hard she broke their spines. He knew that she hid them under her bed, books like the Hemingway one where the earth moves, or the John O'Hara ones where women with chipped fingernails long for their husbands' best friends. And she bought and devoured photo-romans, too, piles of them. The actors looked I-talian. The women with pencilled eyebrows were always betraying men with skinny mustaches and swelling up with illegitimate children. Everybody looked aroused, even when they were cooking soup.

The left side was done now, fresh and clean, with a couple of nicks at the neck. He'd never been able to shave without cutting, without giving a little blood to begin the day.

But Odette never showed him that face, the face that read photo-romans, the face that flirted with that pipsqueak Roger Beaulieu. No, what Odette showed him was the face of an agneau saiglante. Innocent. Martyred. Just like Julia's face. Just like his mother's face to think of it, pious Maman who'd sent him to a pensionnat to make a priest out of him. Those goddamn priests had taught him a thing or two about their God; what they did to boys, you wouldn't do to a dog. Made them expose their backsides and strapped them with thick leather straps. Told them they had the devil between their legs.

It was so hot in the house, goddamn Julia and the thermostat, so hot as he began to lather the right side of his face. Julia was forever jacking up the thermostat when he wasn't looking, and the hot air parched his throat, not to mention what it did to the monthly bills. He punished her by pushing the thermostat down when she was not looking so that the house went hot and cold with their war.

His right side had the dark eye, the brown eye. It was the mark of his specialness to have been born with a brown eye and a blue eye. Béribée had always liked his brown eye best. It stood out in photographs. He used to cut a dashing figure, that's what everybody said when he was a kid, and it was on the strength of being dashing that he'd run away to la Californie when he was eighteen. He had to run. He would have died in that pensionnat smelling of custard and wax and humiliation. He learned English with the men in the boxcars travelling south. Before the Depression, it was. In the low twenties when everybody was supposed to be rich. He'd reached California and worked as a stuntman in Mack Sennett comedies, running on top of trains, jumping from car to car, falling from roofs like one of Lucifer's angels. Then, he'd done westerns, and that's where his career came to an abrupt end when a horse threw him onto a fake cactus. Lost the use of a kidney there in the desert by Santa Monica. That had slowed him down, brought him back to Montreal, to a car showroom on Sainte-Catherine Street, and that's where he was when Julia came in one day with her father to buy a family car. She was wearing a yellow cloche hat and driving gloves. She had a driver's licence, a diploma from Miss Grady's secretarial school, and blue eyes so alive they flashed like mirrors. He showed that girl the inside of a Ford like it was the inside of his heart.

That girl vanished the moment she had Odette.

There was a picture of him, taken when they lived in Halifax, that he always liked. He was standing in khaki pants by the boat yard, holding Odette by the hand. Julia must have taken the picture. Odette looked like she was standing on three feet of air. He looked dashing in his captain's hat, like the navy man he never got to play on account of his bad kidneys.

Julia and Odette had never thought about that, that was for sure. All they ever did was pray for him, just like his maudite catholique de mère did. The two of them with their rosaries kneeling around Cardinal Léger on the radio, Julia doing Hail Marys to the cardinal's Je Vous Salue Maries, Odette looking like she was in a church basement movie, with roses falling out of the skies for tubercular virgins. Praying for him, for chrissakes.

All his life stuck with a bunch of whiners and squealers. Feeling the blood pound behind the skin of his forehead. Béribée took a towel and wiped the leftover soap from his face, then brought the towel down to wipe his armpits. The towel would smell but he didn't care. He was too hot to care. His right hand gripped the razor.

Jaw clenched, skin tight and dry from the soap, Béribée put the razor away in the medicine cabinet behind him and slammed the cabinet door. So hot. "Julia," he yelled. "Ju-lia, for chrissakes, turn that goddamn thermostat down. Now. I said NOW. Do you HEAR me, Julia? Do you HEAR me? NOW!"

"*T*hat'll be your father about the thermostat," her mother said.

"Sometimes I could kill him," Odette said.

"Don't say that about your father."

"I can't wait."

"What?"

"Mum."

"Oh, what am I going to do without you?" Julia said while powdering Odette's face. Odette stared at herself in the three-way mirrored vanity. Her blue eyes looked scared, just like her mother's.

Béribée was still yelling like a bull in heat.

Julia left off the powdering and opened her bedroom door. "I-never-touched-the-thermostat!" she yelled. And came back in, and slammed the door, and took the powder puff, all beige from the powder, and started to work on Odette's face again.

"Mum." Odette could hardly breathe from the powder flying around her face. It settled in a fine dust on the mahogany vanity.

"I like a house warm, is there something wrong with that? I ask you, is there something wrong with that?"

"Mum."

"I do my best. Is there something wrong with that?"

"Mum, please don't."

"What does he want? I looked after him. I looked after you."

"That's too much powder, Mum." Odette was almost crying now, looking at her beige-creased face.

"You came first, all of you."

Odette took her mother's hand in her own, and said stop. None of it now, she wanted none of it, not the words, not the cold place inside her that said me, it was me who looked after you, it was me who got in between. She shook her head. She stopped her mouth, her beautiful mouth in the mirror, from saying I wanted, for once. She said Mum, please get dressed. And took a big wad of cold cream and spread it on her cheeks, and then took a kleenex and wiped all of the beige powdery mess off her face.

*B*éribée marched Odette down the aisle, there was no other word for it, one two, one two, while she strained backwards, wanting the train to flow behind her smooth as icing. It had been snowing heavy water-drenched flakes when they'd walked from the car to the church, and some had settled on Odette's eyelashes. She didn't dare dab the wet around her eyes, for fear her mascara would streak.

Dragged up the aisle by her father, Odette could see that it was still snowing. The sun would have shot rubies and blues and purples through the stained-glass windows; but they looked almost black in this weather, and the air smelled of chrysanthemums, a bitter fall smell. Her father had said arrête-moi ça, when Odette said she wanted lilies. "Lilies in February for chrissakes," he said. "I'm spending enough money as it is." And when she said that Roger could get them a deal, he'd scoffed. "C'est moi qui paye, okay? Pas ton p'tit nouveau riche."

It was all going too quickly. They were almost halfway up the aisle and the choir was just starting to sing "Ave Maria."

"Daddy," Odette whispered through clenched teeth, "Daddy, slow down." He looked straight ahead, neck full of razor nicks.

People were looking at her, from either side. Roger's people on her left, her people on her right. The O'Shea clan was crying already, her aunts in corsages with silver bells left over from Christmas time, her uncles holding felt hats over their crotches. Sometimes they could look so silly, those O'Shea men, grinning, full of laughs, the same laughs for every occasion, as if they spent their lives orbiting churches and church halls, spreading Irish cheer like God's own archangels.

Odette didn't want to be laughed at on her wedding day. But they were bound to do it, her Irish uncles, bound to say to her mother, managed to peel her off the mirror, did ya, Julia? or some such thing. And her mother would laugh and say it was a job, Frankie, but I was equal to it, as if Odette wasn't standing right there. They always did that, smashed things by teasing, as if she belonged to them because she'd been a child once. Their eyes said she was theirs to play with. Like her father's eyes. Her father's eyes made her feel like stone.

Walking up the aisle, his arm wrapped around her arm, Odette thought about the tightrope that figured in so many of her dreams. She walked high above the crowd, in love with her own agility and grace under the bright lights, but there was always a point where she could feel the crowd below willing her to fall. She could never fight it, the force of that crowd, could never fight their will. In the dreams, she always fell.

She wasn't falling, she was being dragged to the altar by her father, but her knees shook like they did in her dreams. She could feel herself wobbling a little on her peau de soie high heels. No, this wasn't like falling, but it wasn't what she'd imagined either. She'd imagined floating in white to the sound of "Ave Maria," gliding to a choral destiny, eyes like lights making her body shimmer.

The Beaulieu side of the church was a sea of black hair and dark faces. The women wore heavy sheared beaver coats and reddish minks, the men held on to sheared lamb hats. Monsieur Beaulieu looked annoyed, as usual. With anything concerning Roger, Monsieur Beaulieu put on a special face of disapproval, of I will not be caught hoping. His children called him Seraphim behind his back, after the miser in *Les Belles Histoires des Pays en Haut* who was so cheap that he had the legs of his dead, adored wife cut off so she could fit into a bargain coffin.

Odette gave Monsieur Beaulieu her pure profile, just before reaching the altar. It was meant to say I know what to give Roger. You know nothing about him.

The priest welcomed her, her father gave her away. There was no one to say don't do it. No one to say I object. No one to say your heart is not yours to give, yet. She was twenty. He was twenty-five.

Roger looked handsome, but his smile was forced. The smile was for the congregation, it said I'm a good boy, grinning and bearing it, but his eyes said something else: "Wait till we're out of here." It made Odette want to laugh. She wanted to say yes, we're going to dump them all behind, forget them, it's gonna be just you and me from now on. When he kissed her, he forgot where he was, and pushed his thigh between hers. She stepped back, embarrassed, but he caught her waist with one hand. "Mon p'tit chou," he said, eyes gleaming, "à notre brillant avenir."

*A*t the reception, in the pale cherrywood Voyageur Room of the Mount Royal Hotel, Béribée drank too much and got into a fight with his brother Jean, and the O'Shea men came around to watch. The fight was about Duplessis. When the O'Shea men came, Béribée switched to English. He was right in front of Odette, who was being told by Paulette, her maid of honor, to get ready to cut the cake. He said he'd read in the paper this morning that Duplessis had given a speech in Saint-Louis entreating people to remember the ancestral dictum je me souviens, "le faire notre et s'en inspirer." "Calice," Béribée boomed. "With his bédaine hanging out and his goddamn gaggle of goons. Je me souviens all right, M'sieur Duplessis. Swing la packaise dans l'fond d'la boîte à bois. Le maudit Christ shoved down your throat. Wearing lies like a hair shirt on your back, gagging on hosties, kicked in the balls by pretty speeches about la race. La race, là, M'sieur Duplessis, it's a bunch of losers kissing bishops' asses, that's what la race is. It's Monsieur-le-Prosecutor Jeannot cruising la Main for les guidounes, c'est ça la race, M'sieur Duplessis."

Red-faced and sputtering, Béribée downed the rest of his scotch and soda.

"Tu vas regretter ça," Jean said, suspenders heaving.

"Des belles guidounes avec des beaux beehives, c'est ça le payoff, hein Jean?"

"Ta yueule, Béribée."

The O'Shea men stepped in between the brothers. Julia swooped down with the beribboned cake knife. Jean walked out of the Voyageur Room. His wife, Pauline, went after him. Béribée turned on the O'Shea men. "And what are you looking at?" he said. "What the Christ are you looking at?"

Julia took his arm and tried to lead him away. "She's going to pray for me," he said to the O'Shea men. "That's what she does, she gets down on her knees with the Cardinal Léger on the radio, and she prays for me. Don't you, Julia?" But he let himself be dragged away like a boy, and Julia managed to calm him down. She talked to him and walked him around the room, one hand tucked under his arm, the other hand still carrying the beribboned cake knife.

Eventually, Odette got the cake knife back from Julia, and cut the cake. It was fruitcake. None of the Beaulieux ate a bit of it, fruitcake being one of the many mysteriously bitter things that the English put in their mouths to celebrate special occasions.

"Tu danses avec ton père?" Béribée said. He'd come up behind her. His breath smelled of scotch. He took her by the elbow, led her to the middle of the dance floor. She put her cold hand in his, and he twirled her and she was ashamed of her stiff dancing, feeling the old-fashioned grace in his limbs.

"J'étais que'que chose dans mon temps," he said. "Si tu savais, Odette, if you could have seen me." He smiled. She looked at the shoulder of his suit, felt her forehead drawn to it, but pulled back at the last minute.

"La musique," he said, "ça été inventé pour flotter au-dessus de nos peines. Laisse-toi flotter, Odette."

They honeymooned in New York City. But before they left, they threw their own party at a restaurant called Au Lutin Qui Bouffe.

There is a photograph of them that night at the Lutin, where the specialty was suckling pig, petit cochon-au-lait. In the photograph, Odette is wearing a black dress with a square décolletage. She leans back against a cushioned banquette. She is smiling with dark lips, her blond hair frames her face in soft waves. Her eyes are round and innocent and smiling. Her eyes have nothing to do with what her hands are doing.

Roger looks straight into the camera. His face says I will give you all I am, force it through the pores of my face. His face has nothing to do with what his hands are doing.

His hands grip a small suckling pig on a formally set table. The pig is pale, its eyes are little slits, it is still not quite fully in the world, this little baby pig, and like an infant it must have been startled by the flash bulb that turned blue after it popped.

Roger's hands are holding the pig in place on the white tablecloth, and Odette's hands are holding a small baby bottle, trying to get the little pig to suck on the rubber nipple.

This is the photograph. Their eyes smiling, their hands trying to feed what they are destined to eat.

One year later, almost to the day, Odette was lying on her bed fully clothed watching the ceiling. Baby Janine was sleeping in the next room, in a pale wood crib with a big bunny rabbit painted at the foot of it. The ceiling had little peaks made by sand mixed with paint. The peaks were dusty grey.

She was so tired all the time. In the last stages of her pregnancy she had done so much, made muslin curtains, hemmed flannel sheets, covered the top of an old changing table with plastic piqué, bought wooden wall figures, Mary and her lamb, Jack and Jill and their pail of water, and put them up on the walls of the baby's room.

She'd had to quit the job she had modelling in Eaton's fashion shows in the fourth month of her pregnancy, when she was beginning to show. And she'd been glad to be at home to prepare the baby's room. Roger said tu va être une bonne mère de famille, Odette. And that made her feel blessed and warm inside.

But now that she'd done it, brought life into the world, she was surprised by her moody tiredness; there was tenderness, yes, but it was mixed up with resentment and loneliness and a curious sensation of defeat.

They lived in a third-floor apartment on Côte-des-Neiges until the duplex in Montréal-Nord was ready. It was one of Monsieur Beaulieu's duplexes. He was going to let them have it for free on condition that Roger show the other duplexes and try to sell them. Roger was managing his father's flower shop until then. It was called Les Fleurs de Louisa, a name Roger had chosen to honor his mother.

The flower shop wasn't very far from the Côte-des-Neiges apartment, but Roger never came home for lunch. He was gone all day, and sometimes he was gone for a good part of the night, too. When he did come home, he smelled like a boozy funeral director, the scent of carnations and roses had gone right into his pores. He always said j'ai rencontré Jean, or j'ai rencontré André, juste comme ça, imagine, on est allé prendre un drink. Odette didn't imagine. She was too tired to imagine. At night, she refused to get up when the baby cried, so that he had to. She screwed up her eyes tight while he dragged himself barefoot into the kitchen and fixed formula and carried Janine until she fell asleep again.

"T'as pas de fun avec ton bébé," Roger said on weekends. And he smiled and he cooed and sang songs to Janine. "T'as pas le tour. Relax." Easy for him to say. She was too tired to have fun. She was too scared to have fun. She feared harm from every source. The wall that jutted out by the bathroom had once been perfectly innocuous. Now it raised spectres of cracked skulls. Odette was scared of the car exhaust at baby carriage height, of dropping Janine when she bathed her, scared of loud noises, of Janine's breath stopping, of her feet freezing when they went out in the February weather.

Worse, she feared the dangers she carried within her, the great swelling waves of anger, the moments when she slipped out of herself and would have done anything to keep Janine from crying. Nobody had said anything about that. Nobody said anything about the broken feeling inside. Her mother said it's the most natural thing in the world.

Now everybody looked right through her and said the baby is beautiful. And she, Odette, twenty-one years old, was not supposed to have any more life. All the people, they looked right through her as if she didn't exist any more, except as a mother, whom they could judge. Odette gone. Pouf. She disappear. Just like she did when she was five or six and her mother brought her from Halifax and left her in Montreal. A breaking feeling like that.

Time to get up now. Odette tore herself from the great softness of the bed with the pink satin coverlet and tiptoed into Janine's bedroom. She stood above the crib and watched her breathing, the little chest going up and down in a flannel nightie. Janine was not an easy baby. Odette found she loved her baby the most — her pudgy hands, her tiny fingernails, her soft cheeks — when she was fast asleep. "Oh, my beauty," she whispered, "my pumpkin, my angel, my sweet, sweet pea." To die for. To die for, she thought.

She should have been washing the diapers, which were soaking in ammonia in the pail in the bathroom, but she was so tired that she went back into her bedroom and lay down on the soft bed and started to think about her labor again. Three months later, and she was still trying to get over it.

Nothing had ever prepared her for what happened the night she gave birth at the Royal Victoria hospital, Roger gone missing somewhere in a bar, drinking and eating peanuts like a starved squirrel.

Remembering that long night, Odette's body stiffened on the bed. She felt weak, and thought she must be hungry, but there was nothing to eat in the house, just formula and some bread and milk. She was going to go shopping when Janine woke up. Watching the little peaks on the white ceiling, watching the grey mackerel light of the February sky through the window, she imagined a green island where men and women entwined like the roots of cedar trees. She had seen this picture once, in *National Geographic*, of a green island, and this other picture of cedars in a swamp, their roots braided together, and it reminded her of the way her limbs felt sometimes, wanting to curve around something safe and secure.

She could not see the ceiling in the hospital. There was too much light in her eyes. But she went up to the ceiling when she couldn't stand it any more. The pounding was like being hit from inside, over and over, with nobody to help her, nobody to protect her, just the doctor at her feet, her feet strapped down in the stirrups, the searing pain and blinding white light driving her out of her body.

From up on the ceiling she saw herself strapped and screaming no, no, no, don't touch me. She saw herself screaming but she wasn't screaming. She saw a man in white cutting the flesh between her legs with a small knife, pulling at her insides with gleaming pliers. The doctor said push, push, come on that's a good girl, hush now and push. The part of her that was on the ceiling thought he was right to say these things. She was a good girl. She wanted to be a good girl. But the body on the delivery table didn't want to be a good girl, that body wanted to scream. And then she did scream, and it was so loud and scary that the nurse brought a mask down on her face, and in the sharp intake of ether, the lights turned red and yellow and purple, spun in circles around the clearest picture of her father's face in a captain's hat like the one he wore in Halifax.

Then she heard voices from far away, the doctor talking to the nurse saying let's sew her up now, I'm going to give it an extra twist, make the husband happy. And he laughed, a long cackle reverberating in ether.

When she woke up in her room, there was no baby, just Roger holding on to a cigar, lighting it with the lighter she'd given him for his birthday. It was gold-colored, with a rhinestone star. "Une belle p'tite fille," he said, and kissed her on the lips. "Mon Dieu, que t'as l'air fatigué, ma pauvre Odette." He said that he had come and had heard the screaming from the delivery room, and he had to leave, he couldn't stand it. "Je suis trop sensible pour ça, Odette. Pis a part de ça, personne parle français au Royal Vic."

Then he asked her to close her eyes. And she did, and she heard him go out in the hall. He was laughing with somebody. The door banged open and he said okay, Odette, tu peux t'ouvrir les yeux. And she did, and there was André Laurendeau, one of her old boyfriends who was now a friend of Roger's, standing behind a stretcher covered with vases of flowers. There were lilies, and roses, and daisies and gladiolae that came, Roger said, all the way from la Floride. The room was filled with their scent, sweet and cloying in the radiator heat.

"Un instant, pitou," Roger said. "C'est pas fini." Odette tried to smooth her hair for André, she bit her lips to make them red.

Roger went and stood with André and they sang, "Auprès de ma blonde, qu'il fait bon, fait bon, fait bon." It was off-key, and they were so funny, the way they stood, pulling at their shirt cuffs to make themselves look show-biz. All the nurses came from their stations to see this and Odette had to laugh, it felt like she was in a gay heiress movie.

But afterwards, when all the flowers were positioned on the windowsill and on her bedside table and on her food tray and in the bathroom, she felt exhausted. The nurses kept saying Monsieur Beaulieu, c'est magnifique, and he loved it. She was embarrassed by his flirting and was glad when they left. She was even more relieved when André left after drinking half a bottle of champagne. "Aimes-tu mes arrangements?" Roger kept saying, going from one bouquet to another.

She said oui, oui, Roger, c'est beau. And he kissed her on the eyelids, on her cheeks, on her mouth. Then she asked for her baby and he said he would go and get the nurse, but the nurse walked in just at that moment with a menu. Odette said I want to see my baby. The nurse said you have to rest, dear, then you can see the baby. She's a beautiful, healthy baby girl. No need to fret. Odette could hardly keep her eyes open. She ticked off roast pork, applesauce, tapioca, a glass of milk for the calcium. The nurse said are you breast or bottle? Odette didn't know. She said she wanted to try breast.

And she did try for a while. Sitting on the hospital bed, smelling the sweet scalp of Janine, the winter sun through the venetian blinds throwing bars of light on her lap, she gave the baby her breasts. But it hurt too much. One of the girls who'd modelled with her at Eaton's had said, "Don't nurse, whatever you do. They suck everything out, and then you're left with these tiny, sagging sacks." So she had given it up. And the nurse came and wrapped her breasts in tight bandages, and something would leak sometimes out of her breasts when Janine cried, but it was too late by then, the nurse said you're almost dried up. With the formula, the doctor said, you could be sure that the baby got all the nutrients. And that made her feel better.

Now, clutching the pink satin coverlet of her bed, Odette thought, I did all right. I was all right.

Janine was crying. Sounded just like a kitten. Odette clung to the pink coverlet. Not yet. She couldn't get up just yet.

The doctor had said you'd better have another one soon, you've got a tipped uterus, you better give it another shot before the tip's permanent. She had beamed at him. "I'm so happy, yes, I want another baby, Doctor, desperately." But she was full of darkness inside.

Odette got up and walked into Janine's bedroom. Janine's face was red. She was hiccupping from crying so much.

"Oh, my poor little baby," Odette said, and set about changing her diaper. She took off the plastic pants and unpinned the soaking diaper, and put on a fresh one. Janine looked at her. Her eyes were still blue. She was quiet now, as Odette powdered her with Johnson's baby powder. Such a sweet smell. "Now baby, I'll get you a bottle," she said, and carried her back to the crib.

But when she got to the kitchen, she saw by the clock that it had been only two hours since the last bottle. Every four hours, the doctor said. Don't spoil her, her mother said. Odette was so hungry. She opened the fridge door. Thought of making some toast, went back into Janine's room and said it's not time yet.

And then, as if she were moving in a dream, she put on her sheared lamb coat and her black fur-lined rubber boots over her flat shoes. As she closed the apartment door, she could hear Janine crying, but there was nothing she could do. So she went to the épicerie around the corner and bought some Salada tea, lamb chops, a can of creamed corn and a copy of *Echo Vedette.* Then she stopped at the patisserie and picked up a mille-feuilles.

All the way there and back, she felt something in her belly stretching and breaking, like an elastic that had lost its bounce. Janine was quiet when she got back. She made herself some tea, squished down the glazed, marbleized top of the mille-feuilles with a fork and saw the custard pop out at the other end. Odette scooped up the custard, brought it to her lips. From an ad in *Echo Vedette,* she saw that Tino Rossi was singing at Le Grand Palais, and that the comedian Bourvil was held over at the Vendôme. Maybe if they got out like they used to. She could wear the blue-grey taffeta dress and pearls, put up her hair, show off her long neck, and have drinks afterwards at the Nuit Bleue. She imagined herself in that dress, and swallowed the flaky pastry that was melting in her mouth. By the time Janine started crying, she'd washed all the diapers and everything was good again.

Claudine July

THERE'S SOMEONE ELSE AGAIN. THE WAY COLIN'S EYES ALMOST pop out with fake innocence. The shiny look on his face, as if he'd just gotten away with something.

It's hot and humid and miserable and Colin's home before the bars have closed, looking happy. Something's up.

He's sitting at the round table by the windows of their place on Adelaide. Claudine, who's just filled a vase full of water and set it down on the table, watches him through the spear-like leaves and salmon blooms of the gladiolae she bought on her way home. She was so surprised to find him here. She's usually home first. Lately, she's been trying to outdo him, to stay out later than he does. But it's exhausting.

"How was your day," he says, feet up on the table, holding a beer.

"Fine. I couldn't get an editing suite until four this afternoon, though. Too many people making videos."

"That's too bad."

She can't tell how many beers he's had. You can't tell with him, until it's way too late. He can drink and drink and show no effect, and when it kicks in it can go in all directions, funny, angry, outrageous, even romantic where he mythologizes their relationship as if it were being written about twenty years down the line. And then he has what Claudine calls ancestral drunks, when he talks about being the last in a mad line playing crack-the-whip, blaming the force of his ancestors' denials for whipping him out into the darkness. The ancestral drunks embarrass Claudine even more than the romantic drunks. There's so much luxuriousness in his self-inflicted doom, especially considering the fact that he squandered the fortune his father made in luncheon meats. There is something in her, from a long time ago, that wants to spit on the idea that the rich English could ever be dignified by suffering.

"What's the matter?" he says. "You look funny."

"Nothing's the matter."

"I had an excellent day," he says.

"I'm hungry."

"There's nothing in the fridge. Have a beer."

"I know there's nothing in the fridge," she says, untying the laces of her running shoes and kicking them under the table. "If I don't shop there's nothing in the fridge."

He swigs his beer.

Maybe there's an egg. She can have egg and toast. No. Too much trouble. Looking at his feet on the table, she notices some white hairs all around the bottoms of his jeans. "Do you know someone with a dog?"

"No."

"Well," she says, "there are dog hairs on your cuffs."

"Pardon me, I'm not sure I heard this right. There are dog hairs on my cuffs? I didn't even know I had cuffs."

"You know what I mean. On your jeans, there."

"Show me."

She shows him.

"Gee," he says, eyes round and innocent. "You're right. There are dog hairs on my cuffs." He brushes the hairs with his hand. "Must have run up against a stray."

"Ha ha ha," she says, and picks up a cigarette. He slides his

Zippo lighter across the table as if it were a hockey puck. She catches it and lights her cigarette.

"You look beautiful tonight, honey. Really beautiful. You look so good when you're suspicious. You come alive."

"Oh yeah?"

"Here, come on, have a beer." He pours the rest of his beer in her empty glass. He's smiling now.

She looks away. In the dark windows, she can see the reflection of the gladiolae, the milky orange skin straining in the light that falls from the green porcelain shade above the table. And she can see her face below that, dark bangs and chin-length hair framing what she thinks of as her too-round face.

"At least I'm honest," she says.

"I don't like it when you buy flowers," he says. "You always start some sort of reform program when you buy flowers. Do you want to see what I did today? Look at this." The round table is full of his papers. He gets about five lines to a page in his big loopy writing. He gathers them up and says see, fifteen pages today.

"That's great." She walks over to the fridge in the kitchen island of the loft, opens the door. No eggs. She goes into the bedroom, takes off her damp jeans and puts on a long yellow T-shirt.

"Sure, you're honest," he says when she comes back into the room. He gives her a conspiratorial look.

"Well, I don't start it."

"You mean," he says, "I go tit, you go tat."

"That's disgusting," she says. She leans across the kitchen counter and rummages in the bread basket. There's only the heel of a whole-wheat loaf, mildewed around the edges. She pitches it in the garbage.

"So," he says, "is this an interview, because if it's an interview . . ."

"What?"

He takes a drag of his cigarette. "I'd like to know about the time I was in Saskatoon, doing a reading, hacking with walking pneumonia, and I called you all night long. Remember that? No answer, all night long. Tell me about that time. Please. I'd like to hear about it." He gives her a bright, false smile. "I'd like to hear about your honesty."

"It's the straining for equality makes me do these things," she says, and smiles back.

"Convenient as shit, if you ask me, this equality business."

"Whenever I ask you anything, you throw the Saskatoon thing around. I'm sick of it. It was just that one time. And I even told you about it. Not like you. You like to sneak."

His face goes blank. "Well, we could count the dog hairs. Would that make you feel any better?"

She doesn't answer. He's peeling the label off his bottle of Ex with serious eyes that say I am floating above your petty emotions, the petty woman stuff.

"Lighten up," he says, and walks over to her and puts his arms around her waist. He leads her back to the table, walking backwards. "Lighten up. That's better."

"I'm crazy, is that it? I'm hungry, I know that much."

"You like to make yourself crazy," he says.

Maybe he's right. Maybe she's imagining things. She sits down. They've had their little sword fight, a little stagey flurry in an otherwise predictable show and, as usual, she's left with everything in her belly. It's a gut instinct, or she's imagining things. If only he said yes and it's so and so. That would have cleared up the infection of her jealousy. But no. He never takes the hook out.

She takes a gulp of beer, sets her glass down.

The round table is his, as are the strained, flowered brocade chairs they sit in. Horsehair sticks out of the frayed arms of his armchair. In the long view, she thinks, none of this matters. In the long view, these horses, now stuffing this chair, galloped once on the fields of Upper Canada farms.

He gives her a look that says I tried, and reaches for *The Atlantic*, which has ended up on the floor.

Staring at his fingernails full of bunched-up gold from the Ex label, she starts to yawn. She wants to say let's start over, wants to find the button that erases what they do to each other. She watches him read, the heavy lids, the soft mouth, the long straight hair falling in his face.

"What matters, then?" she says.

He looks up from his magazine, pushes the hair back from his face with long, thin fingers. "You don't want to know."

"I do."

"I don't want another round."

"Please, I want to know."

"What matters," he says, impatient and professorial now, "is what we create in the moment. You. Me. The work. That's all that matters."

"The work?"

"It's what ends up on the page that matters."

He's serious. She wants to laugh. "This is not an interview, Colin, honestly."

"I'm telling you what I think."

"Did you get the car?"

"No. I'll do it tomorrow." He gives her a dark look. "You ask me what matters, is that what matters?"

"Well, yeah, you're the one who got the car towed. You should get it.

"That's bullshit. That's not what you're really on about."

"It's been a month," she says. "A month, Colin." He keeps on reading. "It's no use," she says, and sighs.

The simplest things, she wants to say. You wrap so much around the simplest things. If she pushes any more he'll get violently angry and go on an intense monologue that's bound to begin with Blake's sooner murder an infant in its cradle than nurse unacted desires and end up with Burroughs's accidental shooting of his wife. Testing the envelope, he calls it, and never mind about the space debris.

"Please, Claudine," he says. "I don't want this. This is the truth. One, I love you like crazy. Two, I'll get the car, I promise. And three, I'm not having an affair. Look at me. I am telling you the truth."

"All right. I'm sorry. I don't know what's gotten into me."

He looks so crestfallen now. She is too much to bear. She may even be crazy. He is so big in her mind sometimes, but when she holds him she feels how small he is, how scared he is. Fear comes off his skin, soaks the sheets at night. "What are you so afraid of?" she asked once. "That I'll be discovered," he said. "That they'll find out I'm a fake."

"You're not a fake," she said, with absolute uncertainty. It was like looking into a mirror.

It takes a great deal of effort, but she gets up from the table. "I'm going to talk to my plants," she says. At the sink she fills the red watering can. From where she stands she can look through the opening in the kitchen partition and see him reading in the yellow pool of light above the round table. She can tell by his serious face that he's conscious of her watching him.

She tries not to spill the water as she walks out the door and up the metal stairs to the black rooftop where she's asked her brother-in-law, Jim, to help her put up a small deck and a trellis.

From this height, you can see the lights along the Gardiner Expressway and sense the expanse of the lake beyond it. The black-tarred roof has retained the heat of the day, and the wind carries the warmth to her body, shaking the soft cotton of her T-shirt against her breasts. When she spills some of the water on the deck, it brings out the smell of white pine.

She waters her potted tomato plants, grazes them with her hands so she can smell the sharp mustiness of their leaves on her fingers. They're doing fine. Some of them have already gone from yellow flowers to tiny hard green tomatoes. The morning glories she's planted to cover the trellis and provide good cover when it gets too windy aren't doing so well. They're still seedlings.

She kneels down and pinches the heads of basil so they'll bush out. Such a green, pungent smell, with a hint of licorice. It never gets pitch dark in this part of the city; there's always light bouncing into the sky, light and noise. The hum of the city rises into the night sky as if piercing through the weave of a giant speaker.

Just as she's about to stand up, she hears the roof door opening and closing. Colin never comes up here. And there's nobody else in the building at this time of night. Most of the tenants are in the garment business, and there are a couple of furriers. They got the place from this guy who worked with glass and half-lived here.

She's almost too scared to turn around, but she does.

"It's me," Colin says. "Hey, it's nice up here. Your mother's on the phone."

"Now? Is she here?"

"No, she's in Jamaica. Hurry." His voice is flat. *The Atlantic* dangles from his arm.

"I hope there's nothing wrong," she says and gets up.

"She sounded fine."

She runs down the two flights of metal stairs in her bare feet. Her heart is pounding by the time she grabs the phone.

"Maman?" she says. "Mum, are you there? Maman?" She hears

something faint and realizes it's her own voice, delayed and thrown back over the line. Then the phone goes dead. "Operator," she says. "Operator."

Colin is looking at her from the front door. He shoves his hands in his pockets. "So," he says.

"We've been disconnected. Did you tell her I was on the roof?"

"Yeah. She said she wanted to wait."

"Oh well, she'll call back. Or maybe she'll call Janine. She always calls her when she can't get me."

She rinses her hands at the kitchen sink. "By the way, we're supposed to go there tomorrow night for dinner. Remind me, okay?"

"To your sister's?"

"Yeah. Please remind me."

"Okay."

"I wonder what she wants."

"Your sister?"

"My mother. She hasn't called in so long. Anything interesting in there?"

He hands her the magazine.

"Colin?"

"Yeah?"

She takes a step closer.

He turns away from her, unzips his jeans, takes them off with his underwear, steps out of both, leaves them on the floor and walks behind the bedroom partition.

Harnesses
1950s

THE HARNESSES WERE MADE OF LEATHER, CARAMEL-COLORED with beige stitching, and the leather was lined with grey felt cut with pinking shears. In the bright afternoon sun, in the back yard of the duplex they'd been living in for three years, Odette was fastening the harnesses to ropes dangling from the clothesline.

Baby Claudine, who was now three, was harnessed to one rope, Janine, who was four and a half, was pulling on the other. Above the clothesline, the sky was a sheet of blue light with thin clouds stretching and breaking apart in the wind. After securing the children, Odette walked towards Monsieur Perrault's yard, and sat down in the chaise-longue she'd positioned away from the clothesline. Red-winged blackbirds hopped and trilled in the bushes of the field behind the suburban yard. To the girls, Odette's shadow as she walked away was like a stain spreading in the grass.

The girls watched their mother, eyeless behind sunglasses, sprawl on the chaise-longue in a red and white bathing suit that felt spongy to the touch. The bathing suit looked the same whether it was on Maman's body or not. Sometimes the girls couldn't resist poking their fingers in the stiff cups to see them bounce back into their cone-like shape.

The cups were one of the mysteries of Maman's presence in the world, as mysterious as the way she squeezed her bum into a flesh-colored rubber tube before she went out, or her legs into nylons that turned her legs dark brown. The feet of the nylons smelled like popcorn.

Now Odette was trying to turn her legs brown with the help of the sun. The girls were getting used to the picture of Maman lying in the sun. Today she said she needed un peu de couleur pour un party ce soir chez les Dupré. They watched as she rubbed oil on her legs and arms and chest, oil that she made herself from baby oil and iodine and something she called le Coppertone. Le Coppertone smelled sweet, like the coconut on the little Vachon cakes that the bread man brought to the door sometimes. After oiling herself, Maman unwrapped a silver sun reflector and stuck it under her chin. One moment her face was there, the next moment it disappeared in a flash of white aluminum light.

The ground was alive with the humming of crickets, with jumping grasshoppers as the sun's heat beat on the girls' moist white temples. The harnesses gripped their backs as they moved back and forth, testing the ropes that fastened them to the clothesline. They waited for Maman's face to reappear from the shield of white light. After a while their eyes hurt from looking into the sun. After a while they gave up. In the giving up, the world lost some of its color.

Claudine was glad to be outside, the smell of cut grass was so strong that it felt as if it were staining her face green. It was so much better than being inside the duplex with the canary carpeting and the silver-flecked green couch and the black panther lamps with zebra-striped shades. From the front window of the living room you could see other duplexes with tiny trees in front of them, tiny trees held together with wires and bandages.

The backyard was better. It had a forest behind it. Bending down now, and kneeling, Claudine ripped the milky stem of a dandelion, and then licked the milk from her fingers. The bitter taste sent waves of aching to the back of her mouth. She was spitting and licking her forearm to get the taste out, but it was like a wave this ache, up and down her palate. Spying the drooping heads of pale pink peonies in the flowerbed, she imagined that these petals would soothe the bitter ache in her mouth. Stretching the clothesline behind her, Claudine headed towards the flowerbed. The line screeched in the hot sun, just like the aching in her mouth.

Janine, who was sitting in the grass and rocking on her bum, watched her walk towards the flowerbed. Janine's stomach was growling. She sniffed her arm while holding a strand of her hair between her fingers. She stroked her hair and flipped it up while sniffing her arm. She could do this for hours, sniff and flip; it was soothing to smell her own skin and stroke the cool of her hair between her fingers. She wanted to block out the screeching sound of the clothesline from Claudine's pull. It hurt her ears. Claudine was always pulling and pushing and taking things from her hands. They liked her better. They made excuses for her all the time.

Now the sky was cloudless, the wind had taken the clouds away. In the infinite blue, Janine sniffed her arm, Claudine sniffed the peonies, Maman burned in her chair.

*T*he peonies were like balls of shredded fluff, pale pink petals having fallen all around the glossy leaves. Claudine wanted to eat the petals if there were no ants in them; sometimes there were ants in the blossoms, black spots crawling in the pale pink. She walked as far as the rope would let her, but the rope was not long enough, the harness gripped her body and bounced her back.

Janine started to cry because she wanted to walk to Maman's chair, but Claudine had stretched the clothesline in the opposite direction. As Janine strained towards her mother and Claudine strained towards the peonies, the clothesline stretched and screeched in the hot sun.

Janine stopped sniffing her arm. She walked over to Claudine's line and gave it a sharp yank, like she'd seen people do with dogs to make them sit and go still. The jerk of the line tripped Claudine, and she fell, face crashing down into the grass with a shock of white bright pain in her nose. She howled. Janine howled to drown out Claudine's crying.

Odette opened her eyes, folded her sun reflector, got up like an oily giant in the sun. Her teeth were clenched. Her hand was out. "J'ai jamais de paix!" she yelled. And now it was as if the shadow that followed her on the ground was around her body, a black cloud billowing. She took down Janine's plastic pants and spanked her. Janine screamed. "J'ai rien fait, j'ai rien fait!" she screamed. "C'est pas moi, Maman!" Then Odette walked over to Claudine, picked her up, wiped her nose with the back of her hand, and spanked her on her shorts. The spank brought the white hot pain on the nose down to Claudine's bottom.

Odette screamed arrêtez de pleurer. The girls had trouble breathing now. They were shaking and hiccupping. Their chests heaved up and down together. Heaving and crying, tears like hot water washing their faces, heaving and crying, harnessed to the clothesline.

*A*lthough the girls were a year and a half apart, Odette dressed them exactly the same. In those early years, when she was beginning to model on the runways of department stores and for advertisements in the color weekend magazines, she preferred le style anglais for children. She noticed what Princess Anne and Prince Charles were wearing and bought plaid skirts and leather leggings at Ogilvy's. Because Ogilvy's was so expensive, Roger wanted to know why Dupuis Frères in the east end of Montreal wasn't good enough. Odette couldn't explain it. "Ça l'air Dupuis Frères," she'd say with disdain about another woman's dress, Dupuis Frères meaning cheap and gaudy to hide bad seams and sloppy cutting, Dupuis Frères meaning habitant. Roger understood that, gave up the fight and let his children go about looking like English royalty.

Roger liked everything moderne. In the hall of the duplex where the girls hung on to their parents' legs when they left the house, there was a light fixture that Roger called the sputnik. It gleamed, a gold ball with spokes sticking out of it. Roger was proud of it. He always said on est moderne, on est pas comme les autres. And he liked to pick up the girls and fling them high to the ceiling, their feet almost touching the sputnik. The girls imagined walking on the ceiling, stepping over light fixtures, while couches and tables floated below them.

When Odette started to work in earnest because Roger was bungling things at the flower shop and drinking away much of the money he did make, she hired a seventeen-year-old girl to look after the children. Louise Gallipeau was an orpheline who'd run away from her adopted home. Louise spent a lot of time looking for her real parents in the phone book, phoning every Gallipeau on the island of Montreal. The girls watched her make the phone calls, and listened to her crying. Sensing the seriousness of her quest, they would lie on the carpet by her feet, and play with her toes while she dialled and dialled. "Allo, je m'appelle Louise Gallipeau," she'd say and quickly hang up.

The best time for the girls to catch Maman's attention after Louise came was when Odette was making herself up in front of her mirrored vanity. The girls watched as Odette tried different faces in the mirror. She tried to smile without showing teeth, tried to make her blue eyes twinkle without smiling. She was so beautiful, the skin on her cheeks soft and cool, her eyes full of bright light. Sometimes when they stood by the vanity the girls tried to catch her eyes in the big flash of the mirror. Odette looked at herself and then at their eyes looking at her in the mirror. Sometimes she smiled with a large, generous mouth, a smile of such grand conspiracy that it took their breath away.

They pawed at her cool arms, tried to get so close to her they could sneak onto her lap, but this she refused, by saying mon make-up, mon make-up.

The moderne bedroom with the black drapes, black bedspread and blond furniture smelled of cigarettes and lipstick left too long in purses. Above the bed hung a huge color studio photograph of Odette in a black décolleté with pearls. In the photograph, Odette's face was so smooth and brown it was like she had a nylon stocking over her head.

Odette confided in them while applying what she called pancake make-up to her face. "Vous aimez mes cheveux comme ça, mes darlings?" she'd say. And they'd say, "Oui, Maman, c'est beau." And then she'd put a scarf over her face so the make-up wouldn't go on her dress when she pulled it through the hole of the neck.

When it was over, she couldn't be touched. When she left, their insides felt pulled down, like water draining from the bathtub.

Louise always ended up putting them in opposite corners of their bedroom because they fought and bit and hit their way through their sadness. "Dans le coin" was the punishment. They had to watch two walls meeting, and not move. Afterwards, they napped together on one of their single beds, spooning and holding hands and calling each other mon p'tit bébé.

The days were always better than the nights. In the day, they could make up games, call each other by different names, make up songs with all the bad words in them, pipi, caca, crisse, tabarnack, duplessis, diefenbaker, fesses, tetons, they could play what they called allo, je m'appelle Louise Gallipeau, a game where they pretended to be orphans looking for their real parents. The parents would have the beige faces of the colored ads in Maman's magazines, the mother would wear an apron, the father would smoke a pipe, and they would all sit down to roast chicken with gay paper rosettes stuck onto the drumsticks.

But at night they got scared sometimes when the whole duplex heaved with their parents' voices. It was like toy guns going off, a bitter smell, the red of the pétard turning black and smoky.

Janine said she thought she had cauliflower ears because she always woke up first, and her ears felt like they were growing to understand what was going on in their parents' bedroom. The first signs of danger could be anything, it could be the sound of wooden hangers being pushed aside with a jerk in the closet that adjoined their bedroom, or it could be in the tone of their voices, like tires squealing.

"Je t'ai vu, Roger, toute la soirée tu lui regarde les seins."

"Ben voyons donc, Odette."

"T'es chaud comme d'habitude. Tu sais même pas ce que tu fais."

Chaud was hot, but it also meant Papa drunk.

Sometimes the fighting stopped as mysteriously as it had begun. Sometimes the furniture moved, scraping floors, falling over. When it reached the point where they threatened to kill each other, the girls got out of bed and watched their mother cry, and their father scream, until one of them would accuse the other of disturbing the children's sleep. The girls knew what they had to do. Janine wailed and sobbed until Odette snapped out of her sobbing to comfort her. And Claudine played the clown, tried to make them laugh, until Roger turned to her and picked her up, and fixed her a bowl of Trix in the kitchen with the dark, sweaty windowpanes.

Janine
July

JANINE WILL, WELL SHE DOESN'T EXACTLY KNOW WHAT SHE'LL do, but she'll do something awful if Claudine and Colin don't show up tonight. Sometimes they say they're coming, but they don't and call from a phone booth, giggling, pissed to the gills.

The thought of it makes Janine furious. And the weather's too hot for fury.

It is the driest summer on record. The sky refuses to rain, lawns are yellowed, the cement back yard of her Portuguese neighbors is so hot that Janine sees waves of heat rising in the air. Orange poppies droop in the cracked flowerbed where her daughter sits with a yellow plastic watering can. Although she is three, Marie-Ange wears a baby bonnet, a pale pink thing that makes her look like a miniature Mennonite.

Janine stands in her kitchen with a piece of frozen arctic char in her hands, watching Marie-Ange through the open French doors. There are no steps down into the yard, just two cement blocks propped against the foundation. Jim hasn't gotten around to building the back deck that's supposed to spread out from the French doors.

Janine puts the fish down on the counter and gathers her long hair on top of her head. She sees a pencil on the floor, picks it up and sticks it through the twisted bun she's made of her hair. The sweat on her neck cools, sending a shiver of pleasure down her spine. She picks up the plastic-wrapped char and puts it on her forehead.

Last night it was so hot that she asked Jim to take them down to the beach in their pick-up truck. She had to get away from the city, she thought she was going to die of heat-stroke. So they sat, the three of them, gasping for air by the wooden lifeguard chairs of unswimmable Lake Ontario. Dead alewives with silver bellies ringed the shore. From far away they looked like bits of aluminum foil. The air was no different at the beach. The only relief to be had was in watching the expanse of water stretch to a blank horizon, the pink-tinged clouds floating above the yellow haze of the city.

Today, the house, which she cleans sporadically, feels as if it is melting into one large sticky stain of orange juice and peanut butter and city dust. Janine wants time to stop, to stop feeling time as something that drowns her in bottomless tasks. She does nothing all day long but push objects here and there, picking up stuff and putting it down, each small task interrupted a million times by providing bearings for Marie-Ange's mysterious encounters with the new world.

Nothing ever feels done. She would like to accomplish one thing that would get her out of the gravity of being a thirty-three-year-old mommy. Ever since Marie-Ange was born she has felt herself unravelling like a wool sweater in somebody's hands. Without her consent, the hands pulling on the yarn are making another garment out of what she once was.

Jim's fault, all of it. As if it were possible to do this without making a mess of some kind. No, that's not fair. He tries. It's just that his trying is so deliberate, so perfectly calculated, so good, that's what it is, he's so good and patient all the time. That's what she'd wanted, to coast on his safe seriousness, to be with a man who measured things and cut things, who kept his tools in order, who *had* tools for heaven's sake. So why is it a flaw all of a sudden? It isn't, she thinks. It just makes her feel flawed.

Janine spots a bag of cheesies by the fridge. She puts down the char and snatches the bag. She grabs one cheesie, and then two, and then three, eats them all, automatically, one after another, watching Marie-Ange play in the yard.

"Mummy," Marie-Ange yells. "Mummy, I want hose. I want hose. I want hose now."

Eyes glazed, fingers orange, Janine walks towards the French doors and steps down the concrete step into the yard. In a trance she thinks, I have a child. I am making dinner for my sister Claudine and her boyfriend Colin, my husband Jim is tiling a roof somewhere in this heat. And this is what I'm doing. Turning on a hose. Other women don't do this. Don't care the way I do. Selfish women. This is the most important job in the world. I never had this. I never, never, never had this.

Jim doesn't understand what she means. When he comes home and she complains about her day, he says it doesn't seem so bad to me. He sits there, looking at his calloused hands, saying well, do you think I want to do this? It doesn't seem so bad, his world. At least he's with adults. Two-by-fours rising clean in cathedral-ceilinged additions, A.M. radio blasting, reno boys bonding, holsters full of hammers.

She can tell he's angry about the way she keeps the house, but he doesn't say it. It's in his body, his face, it's in the way he breathes and moves his legs and arms in Tai Chi positions when she talks to him, as if the joints of his body were infinitely more interesting than anything she could ever say.

Janine stoops to the garden tap and turns on the hose. She sees the patch of bright green grass growing under the leaky faucet. The soft grass fills her eyes with light. That's all it takes, she thinks, a constant drip of water, for the greenest of greens to shoot out of the earth. She runs her fingers through the soft grass as if it were a head of hair.

The water spurts from the hose, throwing Marie-Ange back on her heels. Marie-Ange squeezes the nozzle, and a rainbow arc of droplets appears in the sun.

Janine walks over to Marie-Ange, who is laughing and spraying the heads of tiger lilies. Overcome, Janine bends down and kisses Marie-Ange's face. "Oh baby, baby, baby," she says, burying her face in the soft flesh. "Mummy, you're hurting," Marie-Ange says. But Janine can't stop kissing her daughter's cheeks. Marie-Ange pushes her away. Janine opens her eyes, as if awaking from a dream. There are orange cheesie streaks on Marie-Ange's cheeks. "I'm sorry," she says. "I love you so much."

*J*anine had made it through all the hard times in her life by getting sick. Every job she'd ever had always came to a point where she stayed in bed for a week, called in sick for the first few days, then invented tests and hospitalizations and, finally, stopped calling. Stayed in bed, whispering leave me alone, leave me alone, for days and days. Drinking ginger ale. Eating chocolate-covered marshmallows. Having amazing dreams about bears, mad dogs, about houses with walls that cried, about losing babies like sets of keys, about drowning, dreams so vivid they turned the daytime into watery tea.

They usually fired her. All the fuck-faces with the sour lips of control, walking behind her, straightening up the displays she'd already straightened, the fuck-faces fired her. She abandoned them and they fired her.

And she had to start over again, yelling Emergency at all the people she knew. Emergency. Emergency. And money would come. Two hundred dollars from here or there. And eventually she would start over, get another job. Forget where she had been.

Move to a new apartment, get a new job. Be happy falling in love with men who didn't matter to her. For the exercise.

She worked as a receptionist for Domtar, as a researcher for an encyclopedia company, as a substitute teacher, as a telephone researcher of the shopping habits of males over thirty, as a photographer's assistant, as a salesperson in a fancy kitchenware store on St. Clair, as a salesperson in a fancy custom leather clothes-shop in Yorkville. Life was always about to happen, around the corner. There were movie deals for unwritten books, acceptance speeches for imaginary performances, humanitarian awards for work in Africa. It was all possible, tomorrow, after she got enough money from the shitty job.

Until a persistent ache in a leg, a possible embolism, or an incipient brain tumor would send her to Emergency in the middle of the night, three 222s in her belly, eyes so round they felt ringed. She had cards for every hospital in Montreal, and then for every hospital in Toronto, where she moved in the mid-seventies, sick of the sick feeling of her hometown. She got dye tests for her kidneys, cardiograms, barium in the intestines, brain scans. The pain never settled anywhere for long. It was like a star, a shooting star moving over the expanse of her body. She'd starve it or feed it, depending on what she felt was her hold on the world. Sometimes she needed anchoring, and so she ate anything and everything and grounded herself through weight. The puffing of her body kept other bodies at bay. The pain was insulated. And sometimes she needed to purify herself, so she starved herself, and the pain became like a hard pea she imagined sleeping on.

"Tell me," she'd say to wall-eyed interns, "I'm not going to die, am I?" And she asked Claudine the same thing before Jim took over the job of Emergency companion. "J'vas pas mourir, Claudine, hein, dis-moi que j'vas pas mourir." And Claudine would look at her with serious eyes and say, "Non, Janine, tu vas pas mourir." Janine could feel the impatience in her voice. Afterwards, when Janine was wrapped up like a little girl in her own bed, beaming with the medical knowledge of her essential well-being, Claudine would say, "T'es ben que trop dramatique."

That's what they always said. Maman Odette. Papa Roger. Claudine. And then later, stepmother Jeanne. "T'es ben que trop dramatique." Later still, stepfather Walter added hysteria to the drama. "You're making yourself hysterical," he said, and fed her Gravol throughout her adolescence. It calmed her down.

After she met and married Jim on the edge of thirty, slipped into him, cooked fish with ginger like he did, put anise in her tea like he did, covered herself in the third world fabrics he liked, after all that, she stopped asking for anything. She became the stable one. Presto. A kind of magic. The wife and mother. It was Claudine's turn to be on the loop. Claudine didn't ask j'vas tu mourir? Everything Claudine did these days was je veux mourir. She was drinking, and snorting coke, and smoking dope. She had horrible fights with Colin. One time she showed up with a black eye. She'd stayed over, but spent half the night with Colin on the phone.

When Claudine was fifteen, after Odette remarried and they were all expected to turn English, as easy as being flipped in a pan, Claudine said I'm not going to be a lady, I'm not going to cross my legs and hope to die. So. So, she'd uncrossed her legs and hoped to die. Big deal difference.

Claudine has always had this look in her eyes. As long as Janine can remember, Claudine's had this look of I'm going to win in her eyes. At fourteen, feeling the ache of new breasts, wanting to brush their tenderness against boys smelling of Jade East, of Canoe, Janine watched the boys turning away from her when Claudine walked into the room, Claudine whose eyes said I am just as hungry as you are, and don't you forget it. It was so embarrassing the way she pushed so hard.

She's still embarrassing, now she makes shocking documentaries of people in trouble, she calls everything that doesn't hurt, or threaten, or spit, lies. Lately, she makes Janine feel small, weak. Now that she is a mother, she feels consigned to the heap of the disorganized, the dishevelled, the used-up.

It wasn't always like that. "Loosen up," Claudine says. "You're getting so uptight." As if it was a choice. Being a mother is like being a filter, a filter so bad things don't get into Marie-Ange. The filter gets disorganized and used up and uptight so the child won't. But Claudine doesn't buy it. "You're making her uptight by being so uptight. Just relax," she says, and takes a long drag on her cigarette.

The drugs keep her loose, she says. She gets all that stuff from Colin who's about the most uptight guy Janine has ever met. His face wobbles when he talks, his hands fly around, his elbows resting on a table make the whole table shake.

"I don't know about Colin," Janine said to Claudine when they met. "I think he's bad news." Claudine looked at her and said, "Don't say that, this is the best, ever."

"I just care about you, okay?" Janine said. "You're my little sister." Janine's heart felt huge when she said that, but Claudine looked stunned.

"Sorry, honey." Janine wipes the orange streaks from Marie-Ange's face and walks away. Marie-Ange goes back to playing with the hose. Janine's knees are weak from something, her belly hurts. Marie-Ange turns the hose on her, and the cold spray shoots through her body like an electric shock. "Don't," Janine yells, running to the cement block and climbing inside the house. The water follows her, spraying windows and doors. The sound of it is like hard rain on a tin roof.

But now the cold water feels lovely on her body. And Janine

can't help laughing while fanning out her skirt to see how wet it is. There are dark splashes on what she calls her aquamarine skirt. Marie-Ange sprays in her direction one more time and then brings the hose to her mouth and drinks. Water drips from her pink bonnet and gleams on her face, like a coating of light. From the threshold of the French doors, Janine watches the grace of her daughter as she gambols about in the yard. "Have fun, sweetie," she says.

At the butcher block counter she takes out a knife and starts chopping ginger and scallions. The light is very pink in the kitchen, from the sun hitting the walls Jim painted salmon. Cutting and cutting, she keeps hearing Jim's voice, the ginger's got to be finely cut, tiny tiny pieces, Jan.

It makes her furious when they don't come, Colin and Claudine, but it makes her so nervous when they *do* come. They drink too much and that reminds her of too many things. At least Janine remembers. Claudine remembers nothing. Just pictures of objects, the yellow tiles of a bathroom, the rust color of a coat of their mother's, their father making a snowman in the bath that time because he'd promised and come home too late to do it outside. Claudine remembers stupid, weird details without the warp of terror.

One time she said do you remember the boarder we had in the basement? He had a black cape, a black mustache, and he played the violin?

What was she talking about? There was no such thing. Janine said you must have dreamed that, and was surprised by the look on Claudine's face then. Claudine looked stunned, as if she'd been slapped with a wet towel.

"J'ai inventé ça?"

"Ben oui," Janine said. "T'as inventé ça."

Janine puts the clay pot full of char and ginger into the

refrigerator to marinate. She sits at the kitchen table, lights a king-size du Maurier. Her upper lip is wet with sweat, her skirt is full of water splotches, like dark clouds on the thin blue material. She picks up her Danielle Steel book, opens it, finds her place, and takes a deep drag.

Outside, Marie-Ange watches a ladybug walk on a tulip bulb she's just dug up with a tarnished serving spoon that once rested in a satin-lined Birks box. Odette had picked the pattern, a cluster of flowers, because of its name, Eternally Yours.

Claudine July

DRIVING OVER TO THE EDITING ROOM, CLAUDINE TURNS the corner onto Spadina, and there, looming above the Front Street bridge that spans the railway yards, is the biggest moon she's ever seen. It is as big, as flat, as white as a satellite dish.

Claudine drives towards the moon, and her heart surprises her by opening for a moment. She thinks of how deliberately she goes against the grain of herself. What she has forgotten is awe. What she has forgotten is the bigger picture.

He'd collected the car, as promised. He went to a pound on the outskirts of the city and came back sweating and panting with the ecstasy of having wrestled with what he called the real world. You would have thought he'd stumbled into the middle pages of a Norse epic. There had been dogs at the gate, fat men withholding keys until he paid and signed, sleek crows alighting on rusted fenders.

He handed her the keys with a flourish, and then hung his head and said it cost him half his B-Grant. Come on, she said. He wanted so much gratitude. She said thanks, as simply as she could. And then he shrugged his shoulders and closed down because this was confirmation that she could never be satisfied.

Making a left on Front Street, Claudine leaves the moon behind, tucks it away somewhere, and thinks, he's trying. It's hard for him to do the simplest things, but he's trying. She should have been nicer, been more positive. It's not his fault that his love makes her uncomfortable. Besides, she knows that if it were comfortable, she would leave him. That's what she's always done before. She's never been able to bear the boredom of comfort.

The moon is a retinal memory. Claudine parks in the lot behind the white wedding-cake building on Queen Street and steps out into the muggy July air. Her jean skirt feels heavy on her hips. Her black T-shirt is soaked through. She is stunned to think that she doesn't remember driving here, doesn't remember one minute of the drive after seeing the moon and turning onto Front Street.

She swings through the brass revolving doors at top speed and steps into the ancient elevator with the accordion door.

The editing suite is on the third floor. The equipment was purchased by a loose cooperative of video artists and independent art film-makers with the help of government funds. Because of her background in TV news, and because she steadfastly refuses to investigate the ideological biases of the documentary form, Claudine is considered mainstream by the cooperative; most of the artists tolerate her by exercising their considerable powers of condescension.

Claudine doesn't really mind. For a while she berated herself for wanting to be accessible, but then she forgot about it and went back to her old ways. She learns a lot from them, has learned about using video as a stylistic thing, bits of which she transfers to film. It adds a texture that people recognize as more real than film, somehow. And it's easier to use in tight interview situations. She used to miss so much because of the long set-up time.

The hall is deserted, fluorescent light bounces off the black and white tiles of the floor, paints the speckled glass of office doors grey and milky. The doors are right out of an old Raymond

Chandler movie, but the names on the doors belong to her time, CompuGraphics, Industrial Age, Total Look, Tangredi Designs. Behind those closed doors, frantic searches for the authentic are taking place, menus and letterheads are being redesigned, spaces are being gutted and clad in industrial-strength materials, houses are being hammered into simulated nineteenth-century factories. Bits of funk from the once-rejected past are being recycled with a conscious edge.

Claudine unlocks the door of the co-op, turns on the overhead lights, checks for mail in her cubby behind the reception desk, and turns in to the first editing suite. It's stuffy, it smells of hash, with a hint of camel dung. There's a little bit of burned hash left on the head of a pin of a button, beside a glass. She turns the button over. It says Union Carbide: Corporate Murderers. Andy must have been here, he's the only guy who smokes hash in the co-op. Andy does videos of his friends talking while jerking off. In catalogues, his work is described as "extending the boundaries of the utterable."

Claudine props the window open with a brick. Streetcars screech along Queen. There's a siren somewhere by the lake. The sky is navy blue. So hot. Such a hot, muggy, airless July, everything singed and drooping. She sweeps the table with her hand, wipes her hand full of ashes on her jean skirt, finds the field tape on the shelf above the suite, and sticks it in. It's the manslaughter tape. She's yet to look at the footage of Cindy at the correctional institute. In fact, ever since doing that interview, she's been avoiding her work. It's not a good state to be in. When she's avoiding her work, she concentrates on Colin. He becomes the tape she wants to edit.

Claudine pushes the play button, and then the pause button so she can contemplate the freeze-frame picture of Patsy Duncan, a moon of a face, condemned to life imprisonment for manslaughter. Lines bracket Patsy's mouth, her eyebrows are pencilled in, her scalp looks sore from dyeing her hair ash blond. Her eyes are sad, beseeching. It's a strong image.

But Claudine already has too much material. Patsy Duncan will probably have to go. She pushes the play button.

"I was asking him something," Patsy says in her flat voice, "and he was watching hockey, just breathing heavy watching hockey. I said, I asked you a question. He didn't answer. He had one of those big padded chairs, and it took up a lot of room in the apartment. I remember I wanted to push that chair right outta there, I wanted to push him out. That's what I kept feeling, his weight in that chair. Like he was a ton. I wanted to push that chair out. Everything that bugged me was in that chair."

Patsy Duncan looks sideways and says, "Am I doing okay?" And Claudine hears herself, very concerned, saying, "You're doing just fine."

Patsy Duncan closes her eyes. "You're just like my daughter, eh, the way you talk to me. She always said, Jenny did, what are you puttin' up with this for. It's hard to say. It's like I was crazy then. I'd raised the kids on my own, and I was gettin' on and Rusty was a good talker. It filled up the place, the big talk, the drinking, the getting pissed off. Filled it up. But that time, there was nothing. He wouldn't answer me. It was like I was invisible or something. I kept saying answer the question, answer the question. And he just stared, you know, and the sound of cheering on the TV was going on and I was screaming answer the fucking question. Answer the fucking question."

Patsy Duncan's hand is gripping her knee, and then it's just as if somebody had pulled a string, her whole body relaxes, the life drains out of her. After that she talks about her daughter visiting, and her granddaughter's popsicle-stick house, in a sing-song voice.

Claudine lights a cigarette, pushes the pause button, watches Patsy Duncan's face through the blue smoke. Patsy Duncan stabbed Rusty to death because he wouldn't answer her, because he hit her, because he told her daughter she couldn't wear make-up, because he wouldn't answer the fucking question.

Her rage makes complete sense to Claudine. But something has gone limp in her, too, there in the editing suite on this hot, muggy July night. She presses the rewind button, watches as Patsy Duncan's face reverses itself at top speed. Stops, presses play, hears herself saying "You're doing just fine" in a kind, soft, reassuring voice. Something about her voice is so familiar. It is not her voice at all, it's the syrupy actress voice of her mother.

Claudine puts her head back on the padded swivel chair and starts picking at her nails.

Everything is in pieces, she can't find the glue to put this thing together. She's stuck. She's stuck in the dead place before something kicks over and insists on being born, before the joy of making takes over. It makes her dizzy. She feels like she's going to faint. She hears her mother's voice saying put your head between your legs.

She doesn't put her head between her legs. She rewinds some more and erases Patsy Duncan.

Ascension
1950s

ODETTE AT TWENTY-SIX SAT IN A MAKESHIFT DRESSING room on a wing-back orange cloth chair. She was wearing a blue dress with raised white polka dots. She kept smoothing the dress down over her knees, feeling the polka dots like grains of sugar on her fingertips. She licked her lips. Her lips looked better wet and glossy, and she hated the way the lipstick dried them out. While licking and tasting the red-perfumed taste of the lipstick, she checked for smudges on her teeth in the mirror of her compact.

That morning Claudine, who was now four, had told her mother that her teeth looked like corn on the cob, and Odette debated again whether to have them capped by Docteur Joly, who did all the girls' teeth at Audrey's agency. It would cost a fortune. Odette still used baking soda every day to bleach them. The taste of Arm & Hammer in her mouth, just before she left the house, always made her feel weak because that's what her mother had given her when she was sick.

Odette enjoyed leaving the house, all dressed up, carrying her beige make-up valise edged with dark brown crocodile skin. In the valise, there was order, there was purpose. The brushes, the pencils, the pancake make-up sticks were all tucked away in little satin pockets with elasticized trim, and the lipsticks had their own little elasticized loops, where they could stand like soldiers, ready for action at a moment's notice.

Sometimes the make-up valise got messy, and then everything had to wait until she lined up her lipsticks and her powders and her make-up sticks. And there was the pleasure of getting cheques, fat ones, Roger called them, adding up in her bankbook with the liver-colored cover and a cut-out window for her account number. Odette never tired of opening it and looking at the deposits. My money, she said to herself. Mine. Roger couldn't be counted on to make any. He'd defrauded his father at the flower shop, borrowed against something he didn't even own. At least that's what Odette thought had happened. Roger just cursed his father and stopped going to the flower shop. Monsieur Beaulieu called Odette and said, "Le vaurien a des dettes dans tous les bars d'la ville, pis moi, là, je paye pus rien. I pay nutting, no more." And the bills piled up. And the collectors kept coming to the door. Odette felt such shame, and nobody lifted a finger to help her.

It was February. Not the time to wear a blue puffy-sleeved dress with polka dots, but that's what the producers had wanted. All morning and afternoon soft snow had been blowing around the city, blinding pedestrians and drivers. Looking through the window of the high-school locker-room that served as backstage, Odette could see fine powdery snow falling as if sifted from above. Fine snow, like thin hair, but lots of it. Odette always regretted the flat plane of her head at the back that needed to be corrected with a teased nest of hair.

The producer of "Les Jérémies," the comedy TV show she was doing the commercial for, had to go down to neighboring businesses and see if he could pay employees for an hour or two so he could get an audience for the live show. You would have thought nobody in their right mind would come out in this kind of weather, but they did, they came and shook the snow from their woollen overcoats and beat their hats against their hands and sat down in the Jarry auditorium as if they'd been sprung from jail.

From the skit she was hearing, Odette could tell that she had about four minutes before walking out in front of the television cameras and all those people to do the live commercial of the Plymouth. She imagined her walk, over and over again, heart beating, armpits sweating, hands clammy, saw the polka dots blowing against her thighs like a snowy dream.

The three men who made up the comedy troupe called Les Jérémies were doing the skit about Edith Piaf. Odette had seen it in rehearsals that morning. Gérard Pelletier was on his knees, singing, "Non, rien de rien, non, je ne regrette rien" in a whiny, nasal voice while the other guys did terrible things to him. They threw flour over his suit, smashed a presmashed tennis racket over his head, tied a noose around his neck, pretended to kick him in the crotch. "Non, je ne regrette rien, ni le bien, ni le mal qu'on m'a fait, tout ça m'est bien égal." Bash. Kick. Odette could hear the audience laughing. But when she saw it in rehearsals, a little space opened up inside her, very still, very bright.

Two more minutes of sitting on the cloth chair backstage in an old locker-room with chipped stone floors, waiting for Victor the stage manager to say "Madame Beaulieu, s'il vous plaît."

She wanted to swear, to let out the steam that was building in her. Maudite cochonne de vie. What I have to do. Ce que je dois faire. Maudit Crisse. She was muttering. She didn't know where the voice came from.

In the last commercial six ten-year-olds had gathered to sing a song about Mapo Spread, the maple syrup butter that tasted like the metal of the can it came in. Some of the children were off-key, one of them had spent a good deal of the song trying to straighten out his underwear, poking out his bum, fishing cotton out of his crack. The boys wore blue pants and red bow ties, the girls wore blue dresses with red bows. Janine and Claudine could have done that, sung "Mapo Spread, c'est délicieux," all together, wearing the same kind of dress, the mother and her two daughters, holding hands in front of the cameras, and people would think how amazing, so young that Odette to have such big girls, so beautiful, just like their mother. But the fantasy collapsed with a vision of Claudine biting Janine's arm on stage, the way she'd been doing lately, while Janine yelled je vas être malade, Maman, je vas être malade, and described, like she did last night, how her heart felt like it was going to come out with the throw-up and land in the toilet. There was nothing Odette could do to reassure her. And Roger, who had come in late and half-cut as usual, was pouring himself a scotch, and then he put Tommy Dorsey on the hi-fi and said les girls, on pratique notre jitterbug. He got them all wound up, and by the end of it Janine was white and hiccupping because Roger was paying more attention to Claudine. He always paid more attention to Claudine because she was dark like the Beaulieux, and Janine was blond and delicate like Odette. It wasn't fair. But there was nothing Odette could do about it. Claudine was fearless; Janine was scared of her own shadow. When it came time to throw someone from jitterbugging hip to jitterbugging hip, Claudine was right there, screaming with laughter, making faces that made everybody laugh. Even Odette was drawn to her high spirits. And Janine fought back with sickliness and hysterics.

Here was Victor now, Victor with the thick brown eyelashes she could kill for. "Wasted on you," she said to all the men with good eyelashes. She had to curl hers, and spit on dark mascara powder and apply coats and coats of the stuff to look like she had eyelashes at all.

"J'ai tellement froid," Odette said. "Victor, si tu savais comme j'ai froid." Victor said pauvre madame, and started the countdown. From the wings, Odette could smell the damp coats of the audience, the scent of old mothballs coming to life now like roses blooming in water, the dry heat of silver radiators drawing out the smell of soup and cigarette smoke and fast-order grills from people's clothes. She had to start walking now, in a straight line, without making too much noise in her metal-tipped high heels, straight to the gleaming convertible with the red vinyl inside as if this were the most natural thing in the world for her to do.

*F*rom her coldness, there was great stillness. A hush. She walked right by Les Jérémies, who were standing in front of microphones that reminded her of golf clubs. Odette was afraid that they'd make fun of her behind her back, that they'd raise their eyebrows, mime va-va-voom with their lips. She could feel the bright lights on her, on her blond hair, on her pearls; Audrey at the agency always said get a trademark, it doesn't matter what it is, and Odette had chosen pearls. Classy, Audrey said. Like Grace Kelly.

Now one of the Jérémies started to read the advertising copy. And she wasn't even standing by the car yet. She rushed a bit to make the sweeping gesture, elegant, fluid, that said consider the whole car. Then she saw her hand, so pale in the lights, with the red nails gleaming, coming down to caress the red vinyl seats. She caressed where the shoulders would rest, then she had to turn towards the camera and smile, showing teeth and openness. She had to stop herself from licking her lips even though she could feel them drying. And then in a swirl that made her dress lift a bit to show knee she walked towards the trunk of the car, pressed a button and opened it. She had to do this quickly, suggesting roominess and plushness because there was no camera behind her. The pleasure in her face had to be the camera.

She could feel the eyes of the audience on her, could feel the rhythm of their breathing. Sometimes she thought she could slip into those eyes, that breath, as if it were a warm blanket. She was coming to the end of the routine now, her mouth was dry, sweat was pouring into her dress in spite of antiperspirant and the white shields tucked like inverted wings under her arms. Thank god it was almost over. She was coming to the part where she always felt herself ascend like an angel to the grid of lights on the ceiling. At some point in her routines, she tried to give herself over to whatever force had brought her to expose herself, floating in the eyes of the people beyond the bright lights, on their breathing in and out like one giant creature focussed on her alone.

In front of the car, she had to make the sweeping gesture of this is my body, this is my blood, and, finally, project the thrill of buying the car by opening the door. She got in. Touching the steering wheel lightly, she pretended to turn the key in the ignition.

Her back stuck to the vinyl as she got out. Leading with her legs, she straightened up with grace. Closed the door. Turned with elegance to walk back into the shadows from which she came, but was suddenly brought up short by a terrible wrenching. Her skirt had caught in the door.

Opening the door quickly now, slamming it, that would cost her another car job, that slam, she started to walk away. She could hear their laughing. God damn this. She had broken the heel of her shoe in the wrenching pivot.

From backstage she heard Gérard Pelletier singing "Non, rien de rien, non, je ne regrette rien." The audience roared. It sounded like someone had opened a furnace door.

*A*ll that time, she had to ignore Roger, pretend he didn't exist. She ignored him, the humiliation of the work, did anything that came her way, Noxzema commercials, where she went ouch while exposing the white skin under the shoulder strap of her bathing suit, bridal layouts in advertising supplements, catalogue work for Eaton's and Simpson's, runway modelling for the big department stores and for the French couturier houses on Crescent Street, she impersonated women who golfed, who cooked, who water-skied, who sat by blazing fires in après-ski clothes, who skated, who had romantic thoughts in demure lingerie, who squirted mounds of Reddi Wip over Jell-O, who changed their hair color without anyone knowing, who would bake cakes only with Monarch flour. And from the money she made, she got them out of the Beaulieu duplex and into a house she bought in Notre-Dame-de-Grâce.

She had to ignore Roger, and not wait for him to make money. The moment she counted on him, or egged him on, or prodded him, or shouted at him, she would get bags under her eyes and lose jobs she would have landed otherwise. He got a job at a respectable firm selling bonds and securities, but he hated to speak English and retreated to bars as soon as the Stock Exchange closed. It wasn't too long before his wages were garnisheed for tabs he'd run up all over town.

She had to ignore that, ignore his drinking and his cochonneries like the time he was so drunk he walked into the maid's room and got into bed with her.

She had the Notre-Dame-de-Grâce house painted a pristine white and painted old furniture she bought at auctions white and antiquey gold. By then, they were abandoning the moderne style and moving into antique. It was her idea. Everything, her idea. Even doing up the bathroom with little gold and white ceramic tiles that Roger and one of his drinking buddies had stuck in grout. They'd gotten so drunk that the little tiles departed on paths on their own, making curving lines around the sink. Every morning she was forced to look at it, the curved line of Roger's incompetence.

When he screamed now, it was that he was dying, that she was killing him with her contempt. Sometimes he made her call the priest to give him extreme unction. The girls watched from the foot of the bed, while the priest tried to convince him that he was not moving to the other world.

Afterwards he would cry. He would open up her closet and look at all her clothes and say. "Et puis moi, j'ai rien. Rien."

"Tu fais rien, Roger," she said, and slammed the closet doors.

Tango July

THE LIGHT ON THE PHONE IS FLASHING ON AND OFF. CLAUDINE notices it out of the corner of her eye. She is staring at herself bent over a tiny little piece of mirror with two coke lines drifting off like snow tracks. A rolled-up five-dollar bill is sticking out of one of her nostrils. She pinches her other nostril and snorts the coke back, taps the rolled-up bill on the corner of the mirror and picks up the phone, sniffling.

"Allo, um, hello. Video co-op."

"Claudine?" It's Janine, with punishment in her voice.

"Hi," Claudine says, feeling unbalanced but cool with coke.

"You-were-supposed-to-be-here," Janine says.

"What?"

"Dinner, Thursday night, remember?"

"Oh. Oh, I forgot, oh, I'm so sorry. I can't believe this, I forgot." Guilt like worms in the belly. "Can you hang on for a second. Jan, hang on." Claudine puts the phone on hold, tightens the five-dollar-bill roll, and does the other line. She rubs her nostrils, inhales deeply, feels the frozen buzz, the tightening of her jaw, the metallic taste. She is floating now.

"I didn't say it was all right, putting me on hold," Janine says.

"I'm sorry. There was someone on the other line."

"I phoned everywhere. I got hold of Colin. He said you never even told him about it."

"I did. Really I did. I just, I needed to do some editing, and I came here, and I forgot. I'm really sorry. Please don't be mad at me. Please."

"You sound awful. You sound like . . . Mum. All thick-tongued."

"Please don't say that."

"I'm worried about you."

"I'm fine, really." The spiral is coming to take Claudine away, down down into the little sister who can't take care of herself, such a sham, she's the one who's always done the taking care of. Always. Of Odette. Of Janine. Even of Roger.

Claudine taps the rolled-up bill on the edge of the desk. "Did you get a job yet, Jan?"

"Taking care of Marie-Ange is a job," Janine spits out.

"Don't be mad," Claudine says, "I'm just asking. Hey, did you know I was nominated for an award at this small festival out west?"

"That's great."

"I'm really sorry about tonight. I'm so sorry. Can we make it tomorrow night?"

"I made this big meal. Jim drank all the wine." Silence again. They listen to each other breathing.

Claudine feels so powerful, she imagines saying bring all the world's problems right here, line them up, I will solve them one by one, rub my hands in between the tasks.

"I miss you," Janine says. "Marie-Ange misses you."

"I miss you, too, I miss her." Claudine remembers the warm feel of Marie-Ange on her lap, the way her eyes look into hers; it's as if they have always known each other, as if they were variations on a theme. "How is she, the sweetie?"

"Okay."

"I'll be better when I finish this thing."

"You always say that."

They've come to the moment when they have to cut off. And both of them are juggling with who's going to hang up first.

"I'll bring Chinese food. We'll come tomorrow. Okay?"

"Okay. Jim hates Chinese food."

"Okay, bye."

"Manges tes carottes," Janine says.

"Toi aussi."

They laugh. It's their code from when they were little girls. The idea was that they'd send this "manges tes carottes" message to each other if they were ever kidnapped. It would mean I'm all right but call the police.

Claudine hangs up and rubs her hands together. They are always cold, even in this heat. The coke racing through her bloodstream makes cleaning up a breeze. She puts away the tape, shelves her guilt towards Janine, too.

She'll go home now.

She's going to drive through the dark night, her body like a moist print on the car seat, inhaling the rot of summer in the city, feeling the sand in the concrete of monolithic buildings shifting a little in the heat. It is not the kind of city where you can climb in a lighted fountain and feel the wash of water soak your summer dress through, not the kind of city where abandon is welcome. Someone is always watching, judging, bracketing. It is easier, here, to snort abandon in small rooms, face down into a mirror, guessing at the old face hiding in the slack of the young one. Easier to implode, and leave the explosions to the ones who come from elsewhere, shifting and twisting in the vacuum of well-guarded indifference they find here.

Claudine turns off the lights.

Three years ago, she thought Colin had a key to another

Toronto, the hidden one, the one where people laughed and showed each other themselves in bright circles. She had wanted some of that, a sense of belonging. Colin had many friends, artists, writers, musicians, actors, whom he dominated with equal doses of flattery and sharp truth-telling, the kind that digs in like splinters; you have to keep going back to the source in the hope that it will be removed. He was always available, that was his main attraction, available for drinking and anyone's breakdown. When his friends were low, they went to him because you couldn't get lower than Colin, somehow, and that was deeply reassuring.

When she saw him read his work, she could see who he attracted, young men in leather jackets, hoping for a beat revival, for anything that would sweep the feminist fact under the carpet and restore them to their rightful place; and young women who wanted to be bad; and slightly older women who wanted something wrong to right.

Closing the door of the co-op now, Claudine thinks, I'm different. What I want, more than anything, is to prove he's wrong about everything.

"***I*** can't believe she said that." Janine is holding the receiver in her hands.

"What? What did she say?" Jim is lying on the bed, naked with a book of listings draped over his thigh. He wants to branch out now, from renovating to actually buying, then renovating and reselling. If he can scare up one down payment. Somebody told him he could use his house as collateral. There's people out there turning houses over and making a hundred grand pure profit. "Well," he says, eyes sizing up a semi with brick front, "what did she say?"

"She said I should get a job, that it wasn't fair to you."

"Yeah?"

"This is a job, this is a fucking job. What does she know about it?"

Jim stares at the semi, admires the ceiling fan he installed in their cathedral-ceiling bedroom, the way it cuts the air, spins shadows on the mauve walls.

"Marie-Ange looks pale," he says. "You should make her eat more."

"She doesn't like anything but macaroni and cheese."

"You've got to trick her," Jim says, getting excited now. "Make the food into trucks going into a garage door. Or something. I can always get her to eat. When you're not here, she eats everything."

"Yeah, everybody's better than me. You're so superior to me, I don't know how you can stand being around me."

"I didn't say that, Jan. Come on, we're just talking."

"All of you. So much better than me, hey. Well, you do it, then. I'll get a job and you stay home and do it if you're so goddamn good at it. See how you do. I don't give a shit any more."

Janine stomps out of the bedroom, tying the sash of her bathrobe. Her whole body is shaking. She wants to scream. She slams the bathroom door behind her, picks up her Danielle Steel book from the top of the toilet tank, opens it. The letters are ringed in red, her hands are shaking so hard she can't keep the book still.

Breathe now. She tries to do labor breathing, panting in short hot breaths as if she was pushing. She needs to float away now, to reach for the high notes of the day, but all she can see is Jim's drawn face, the way he was in the labor room, holding up a card of the yin and yang sign and saying focus, breathe, focus. And how she wanted to scream fuck off, fuck off, fuck off, in front of the nurses, Marie-Ange's dark head crowning between her legs.

"Oh my baby," she says aloud now, holding the book against her forehead.

She really needs to float away, to reach for the high notes of the day, to reach for what Colin said on the phone, what he said when she called to find out where they were, dinner steaming on the table, the burning of waiting for them in her chest. He said gorgeous, you sound gorgeous. So sorry about this, you know your sister. She forgets, and how are you, he said, in this voice that knows her. That last time they were all together, he had said it then, too, had said she was gorgeous, when they found themselves alone in the kitchen.

He had even touched her. "Gorgeous," he said, and touched her hand. He can look quite gorgeous himself with his scruffy long hair and his black leather jacket. Janine flies away now, repeating the scene in the kitchen while Claudine was talking to Jim in the dining room, her secret, her warm secret, and it melts her rigid body to float up and up into that dreamy, blissful place where his eyes met hers, lighting her up as if she were a singular, unique, beautiful being on an empty stage, warmed in the light of a thousand eyes, rocked by the breath of a thousand mouths.

It was like growing wings, this, this small dreaming on the cold porcelain edge of the tub, willing the scene back to life.

Wings. Janine needs wings. Has always needed wings.

"*Jan*, open the door. Open the door, would you just open the door?"

"What?" Janine says, in a small voice, staring at the black and white tiles of the bathroom floor.

"Angie's calling for you."

"I can't move."

But she does move, seeing her pale face rise in the mirror as she gets up from the edge of the tub, looks at her new blond streaks, at the full mouth her mother always said was like Ingrid

Bergman's. She wipes her wet face with the back of her hand, blows her nose in a piece of yellow toilet paper.

"What?" Jim says from the other side of the door. "What did you say?"

"Nothing," she says, opening the door. She walks right past him and into Marie-Ange's bedroom.

"Oh baby," she says, scooping Marie-Ange into her arms, burying her face in her daughter's sleepy warmth.

"Mummy," Marie-Ange says, "I had a bad dream. I dream you die."

"I'm not going to die, Sweetie. Don't worry about that." Marie-Ange wraps her sleepy-warm arms around Janine's neck and settles half-asleep on her lap. "I love you," Janine says, "I love you so much."

"All right, that's enough," Jim says and takes Marie-Ange from her mother's arms, and carries her back to her bedroom, and lies down with her until she goes back to sleep.

When he comes back into their bedroom, his eyes are puffy, half-asleep. Janine is feeling guilty. Her shouting must have been the thing that woke up Marie-Ange. Jim takes off his bathrobe and hangs it on the hook behind the door. His body is long and lean, his arms strong and brown.

Janine takes some moisturizer and spreads it on her legs. The cool cream feels good, smells of tea roses.

"That smells good," Jim says, and crawls in beside her.

Janine feels her throat tightening. She wants to really talk to him, to feel that he's listening, but she's afraid.

"I'm sorry," she says. "I don't know what go into me."

"It's okay."

"Do you get scared sometimes?" she says.

"What are you scared of?" His face is serious, purposeful.

"I have terrible pictures."

"Pictures?"

"When we're in the park? And Marie-Ange climbs to the top of the big slide? I see her falling, sometimes, see her hit the back of her head. It's — "

"Stop it."

"Why do I have these pictures?"

"Everybody has pictures. They don't mean anything. Go to sleep."

"Please," she says. "Talk to me."

"I am talking to you."

"Please don't be mad."

"I'm not mad."

"Yes you are."

"No I'm not. You get yourself all wound up over nothing and then you turn it back on me. And then you say I'm mad." He's turned away now. "Please," he says, "go to sleep. I've got to get up early. I've got to plan my day."

A good carpenter is a prepared carpenter, that's what he used to say when they first met. She had been awed by this step-by-step approach to life. She was so used to the chaos of winging it. Her father. Her father couldn't even mow the lawn. In the last house they'd lived in, the Notre-Dame-de-Grâce, he'd had two tons of sand poured into the back yard so he wouldn't have to mow the lawn. "On est à la plage," he said. "C'est comme Old Orchard." And Odette rolled her eyes.

Janine stares at the white ceiling fan whirring above them. Her hair lifts in the breeze. She bunches a pillow against her chest, lies down facing Jim's back. The slope of his rib cage rises and falls with his deep breath. She is so close to him she can smell the sun and salt on his skin.

She closes her eyes and sees Colin, his long hair falling in his face. Gorgeous, he says. She touches her hair, feels the gold streaks radiating from her head on the pillowcase she bought in Chinatown. It has embroidered flowers, she can feel the silky bumps of roses rising under her fingertips.

"I love you," she says.

"I love you, too," Jim says in a groggy voice.

Claudine July

CLAUDINE COULDN'T DRIVE. SHE HAD CLIMBED INTO THE CAR, felt her head snapping and crackling with coke as she put the key in her ignition, and thought no, I don't want to do this. She was afraid of the shakes and the great white spaces in her mind, of where she could vault to behind the wheel of a car.

So she followed in the wake of other people walking on Queen Street, catching the life of other lives while thinking of Walter, whom their mother insisted they call Daddy when she married him almost twenty years ago. What would Walter make of all this? He always called throngs of people "the great unwashed." He always said, looking down from the height of his wealth at men and women walking the streets of Montreal, "Look at that. That has the vote."

The air is close, the clouds low. It's going to storm. Walking past The Parrot restaurant with its neon parrot sticking out in yellows and reds, Claudine can't shake the picture of huge Walter walking on Sainte-Catherine Street, his nose crinkling with disdain. Walter had entered their lives with the swiftness of a character in a fairy tale. Maman and Walter were going to get married. She had been to Belmont Park with him, and he had won a huge stuffed monkey. That was the offering. The monkey had a plush suit that covered up the pale plastic flesh of what could have been a thickset doll. Its face was stuck in a permanent grin, and it had tiny low pink ears. Claudine remembers holding the monkey on her bed, and feeling the snap behind its neck, and being repulsed by the plastic smell. She was thirteen, Janine was fourteen. They had outgrown stuffed animals years ago, were now smearing Beatles posters with peppermint lipstick lips. But this monkey was so big that it had a kind of glamor, the glamor of the oversized.

"We're going to knit two families together," Walter said. And Janine said to Walter, "What will we call you?" in her brave, broken English. And Odette said, "You can call him Daddy."

Daddy. A different word than Papa. But a betrayal nevertheless. And Odette beamed like a schoolgirl who'd won the first prize. Her lipstick was smudged, she smelled of Fleurs de Rocailles.

They had sat there, on their twin beds that were pushed together, the bedroom in the new apartment being much smaller than their room in Notre-Dame-de-Grâce, and felt the promise of something richer than they had been fed on. They watched their mother's newest performance and thought this one might take them where they'd never been taken before.

And it did. In time, they moved from the small apartment to Walter's house in Westmount. All of their furniture, dishes, linens, all that had covered them, held them, all of the objects they had poured their fears into, were packed away and moved into the high-beamed attic of Walter's house. Odette covered their old lives with sheets, and set about redecorating the new.

Janine and Claudine ended up calling it Cinderella time. That's what Walter's boys, who'd lost their mother to a stroke just a while back, called them. "Cinderella," they'd shout out from large rooms with overstuffed chairs, laughing at having their very own stepsisters to endure and torture. The boys, John and George, called the girls frogs, and Pepsi-maywests. The frogs never did turn into princesses; they just lost their tongues there in the castle, lost their tongues, and their culture and their sense of belonging anywhere at all. Imperceptibly, and slowly, they grew to hate what they had been, to feel shame in the shadow that wealth and Anglo certainty threw on their frittered history. In that world, they met the most perfect disdain money could buy. It hit them just at the point when their bodies were blazing with hormonal needs to belong.

"Isn't it time," one of the stepbrothers would say, "the girls got their teeth pulled out, Dad? Isn't that what happens with French-Canadians, they get them all pulled out, and get false teeth about this time?"

"That's enough," Walter would say, and send them to their room. He would wink at Odette, and Odette would smile. "We would never let that happen," he said.

Walter was as good as his word. He sent them to dentists and optometrists and remedial reading, took hold of their maintenance and paid for what had gone wrong in years of neglect. He sent them to private English schools, the shock of it, moving from the pace of nuns and cynical girls who wore white lipstick and read Jacques Prévert, to the healthy bustle of women teachers who fancied themselves bluestockings, and to the freckled faces of girls with braces who played muscular basketball in green pleated shorts.

They were the only French-Canadians to ever have gone to this school, and they played the only card they had, their exoticism, Janine making friends easily by offering effusive "Latin" affection, Claudine cultivating bohemian traits to stand apart. An old Parisian woman taught French, and she took every opportunity to humiliate them by correcting their pronunciation. "Je ne comprends pas, Mademoiselle Beaulieu. Répétez, s'il vous plaît." Claudine refused and collected new things called demerits, which, much to her surprise, enhanced her standing among the English girls who had a literary and artistic bent. And it was there that she found her niche, reading Leonard Cohen, Hugh MacLennan, astounded that writers actually existed who wrote about Montreal. The literature the nuns taught had all been from France, impossibly remote stuff redolent with virtue and arcane words that the girls all pronounced as if they were holding lace handkerchiefs away from limp wrists. There were so many different kinds of French then, the French most people spoke, the tense, learned French on Radio-Canada, and the French-French spoken by Parisians, who were called poufs or tapettes by the men.

Reading English that sounded just like the English she heard spoken, and seeing herself as a romantic figure in her own city, had been the bright vein in an adolescence otherwise defined by fighting Walter's authoritarian regime. She learned English like a guerrilla fighter learns to recognize mines. It felt like her life depended on it.

With Odette and Roger, they'd mostly been abandoned to their own devices; Walter was another story. Odette took a backseat, said ask Daddy to everything.

Walter would correct Claudine when she began a sentence with I feel. "You do not feel, Claudine," he'd say, "you think." He grilled her, and grounded her and suspected her of all the right sins.

He'd stand at the dining-room table with an electric carving knife, sawing a thirty-dollar prime rib roast, and talk about the country falling apart under that pipsqueak Trudeau. Trudeau, who gladdened the hearts of the girls by making their trying bilingual fate official, was nothing but a poufster. He had no respect for what had made this country, he was letting the rabble in, he was letting the rabble rule. The mahogany table shone in the reflection of the crystal chandelier, the silver salt cellar had a blue glass lining, the silverware sparkled, flowers from the greenhouse grazed the centre of the table. "In the old days," he'd say, "the darkies never walked on Saint-Catherine Street. And they never walked on Sherbrooke. They walked on Dorchester, they knew their place." Fires raged down south around this time, fires of rage at people just like Walter.

Claudine couldn't hear that and hold her tongue like Odette, who pretended she'd always lived with that kind of contempt, who said oh Walter, as if he were a boy going too far. It was almost as if Odette put her head on the block to show them what a good sport she was. Why was she so embarrassed by them? Why couldn't she fight for them? After leaving Roger, Odette had had moments of being direct and firm and understanding. But it had all slipped away, the moment she'd stepped into that house she disappeared. She had to pay attention to the boys, who were rigid with grief over their mother.

Claudine could see that Walter liked to argue, that something quickened in him when she accused him of bigotry, that he liked her fighting spirit. And she wanted his love. That was the hardest thing. Underneath it all, what she most wanted was for him to love her.

*H*er head is aching now, as she walks past the red-painted barbershop that was below the after-hours club where she met Colin three years ago. It is gone now, the club, and the barber-shop has closed down to make way for a dress shop displaying gaunt silver manikins with hunched shoulders, stumps for hands and feet. A white van parks just ahead of her. An ambulance wails somewhere on Spadina. There are patios now, along Queen Street, where people sit and drink while men and women with plastic bags huddle in condemned doorways. She thinks of calling Colin to say meet me at the Rivoli, but she knows he won't be home. She knows she'll stand there, in a phone booth, listening to the rings over and over again, and the bottom will drop out of her, as it always does.

It's so hot and muggy, the air is like a suffocating blanket. She stops by the guardrail of the terrace of the Rivoli, looks inside out of habit, always thinking she will catch Colin out in a corner with a blond waitress. Did she dream this, or did something really happen with a blond waitress? The image is so vivid, Colin reaching over to grab the waitress's black money belt, and the cool waitress with blond hair and a tight black skirt swatting his hand like a fly, and laughing, and then extending a finger to touch his finger like in the painting of Creation. Must have dreamed it. She thinks of a cool beer, of the feel of it going down her numb throat, and it is so real that she figures she's already had it and moves on.

To the next bar. Is that what she's doing, looking for him? Is that why she didn't want to drive, so she could hop down this stretch of road and catch him out with the woman with the dog? Is that who she is, now? A dog-catcher? The cool detective going for dirty pictures, looking for the final proof she carries inside her anyway. She feels ridiculous. She will have that beer after all. She will sit in a corner and drink and feel for eyes looking for her eyes, and catch a pair, and feel other possibilities for herself.

She walks back to the Rivoli. There is an empty black table inside. She orders a draft. It comes with cool frost on the glass. The perfect coke-agitation antidote. She drinks it down quickly, and orders another.

The light is dim with pale orange streaks coming from rounded deco wall fixtures. Her glass of beer leaves a ring on the black Formica. Claudine draws spokes like sun beams from its watery circle. A man with short hair and a pale blue short-sleeved shirt comes by with a deaf-mute card, and she gives him two dollars. He smiles and tips the card to his head, saluting her. His gesture is framed by the huge lithograph behind him, where native men walk on the high steel beams of skyscrapers. It is a picture. The pale blue shirt, the black girders like a web behind him, the pale orange of the light hitting his forearm.

Claudine looks down at the hand signals on the card. Perfect hands that appear stamped, crooked fingers for listening, fists opening and closing for heart. She thinks of Janine on the phone saying I miss you, and washes the thought away with a gulp of beer.

So much of that time, the time of the tyranny of Walter and his boys, seems locked in glass, seems to have nothing whatever to do with her life now. But Janine died there. And Claudine had something to do with that.

She knows it, has always known it.

Claudine grabbed the language of their new house, said terribly, oddly enough, quite, of course, however, ate it all up. The English language held possibilities of salvation out of the desert, she bit into it and wrestled it into the muscles of her mouth. A way out. It was a way out of the misery, chaos, emptiness. A way of controlling what she had no hope of controlling. A language that killed the past, buried it, where you could dance on graves with your nose up in the air. A steamroller of a language, flattening out old pains, covering up shame forever. Newborn. However, quite, I should say, nevertheless, of course, mysteries of qualifying the world until it came out pale and controllable. No memories. No detonations. The language in that house was the language of power, of the powerful, of reality, of how it was, of how it would always be, of refusal, of no to all the sadness that crept and seeped into the cracks of French. A language of slaps, of cuts, of chiselling, of blocks, of building, of rising above the petty, petty world of feeling, the language of abstraction, history, commerce, of art that hid and hid, and turned seekers into spectators.

She had been so ripe for it. All that had been previously problematic — her bookishness, her determination to slice the world and herself into manageable parts, her anger — were perfectly appropriate in the old wood and ticking clocks of Walter's Westmount house, where suffering was an embarrassment, love a parsimonious event to be hidden in the creases of private lives, where joy, such as it was, could be crushed by superior wit.

Janine died there. She could not make the switch. She died a thousand deaths and Claudine witnessed it, and saved herself, and let her drown. Janine was emblazoned in feeling, could feel the sap moving in trees, her throat moved in liquid sympathy with the warble of birds, her toes in the thick Oriental carpet could send her into inarticulate rhapsodies. Janine could not survive the contempt, for her being, her body, herself.

And Claudine moved over to the boys. And let her fail, and let her drown. At night, in the room they still shared even though there were enough rooms in the house for them to have two rooms apiece, Janine said je t'aime, Claudine. And in the new language they practised with each other, "You are the most important ting in my life." Claudine looked away. She said, "You have Nivea on your face. Wipe it off, it bugs me. And you should work on your th's."

Claudine finishes her beer, holding on to the last sip now warm against her palate before swallowing. Low rumbles from the dark sky shoot fear into her belly. She should get going. She pays for her beer. The waiter has a pony tail, a diamond stud in his left ear and a paperback copy of *Don't Shoot, It's Only Me, Bob Hope* in his back pocket. He gives her a flash of hazel eyes before pirouetting away with her money.

The beers buoy her until the downpour comes, right at the

corner of Spadina and Queen, rain like a bucket of water soaking her hair, her face, her clothes. Within a few minutes, dark puddles of oil-slicked rain gather in every depression of Spadina. Streetcar tracks are overflowing, water flows down with the sound of sea-pools into the dark holes of sewers.

The sky flashes electric white every few seconds, obliterating the image of the rain slanting against the halo of streetlights. The surprise of it, the cool violence of the storm rattles Claudine. Her first instinct is for shelter, but she pushes that away, wants to give in to what is coming down, to give her body up to the water. So she walks, tries to walk as if the rain and the lightning weren't things to fear. She walks across Spadina, tries not to run, like she's in a movie where she has to keep on walking through rain until the scene is over. She could huddle beneath the awning of the doughnut shop at the corner, but she doesn't, she keeps walking, water streaming down her face, inside the collar of her T-shirt, soaking her thighs, her sandals. She ploughs right through puddles, squishing soaked leather between her toes; she welcomes the rain cascading in sheets from green awnings.

And then, just as she is beginning to enjoy her body's embrace of the rain, she sees what she's been looking for. The fluorescent light of the Kentucky Fried franchise on the corner of Augusta bounces off the wet street like a white arrow to the yellow fire hydrant by the Duke. And there, tethered, is a dog. A soaked, yelping collie.

The dog is lying down, must have lain its soft body down on the sidewalk to keep a bit of ground dry. Claudine kneels down. The dog smells of wet dust and warm flesh. Its paws are crossed under its muzzle, and it is whimpering while licking its nose.

Lightning flashes across the sky. The dog and Claudine look at each other. Her heart swells for a moment. "Pooch," she says, "are you scared? Don't be scared. There's nothing to be scared of." The dog licks her hand, over and over, the rough tongue furls along her palm as if he is drinking the rain from her hand. The pressure of the dog's warm tongue is almost unbearable. Claudine forgets where she is, pats the dog's head with her other hand. "Okay, okay," she says. "You're going to be okay."

Opening the poster-covered door of the Duke, she is hit by the smell of yeasty beer and urine.

She doesn't like the Duke much. So many nights she's sat at the bar while Colin talked to Dan, the bartender. She watched Colin probing Dan's life, listening to his language changing to accommodate Dan's inexhaustible stories about his liver, about his kids, who were always in various states of arrest, detention, probation. At first, she'd admired Colin's ease, his compassion. But then she saw that Colin was only interested in using Dan's life, a life wound up, like so many others, by a bad start, as a template from which to reject the sufferings of those who were more privileged — especially women. In Colin's worldview, all women, no matter their origins, were middle-class. That was his ace, the most important card in his seduction deck. He could pull the ground from under any woman's feet by saying middle-class. They all crumpled at that.

Soaking wet, water pouring into her eyes, hand tingling from the dog's tongue, Claudine pushes back the wet hair from her face and looks around.

It's the laugh she recognizes first. There is a flash of blond hair by the laugh's side.

Colin is sitting at the bar. He's commandeered the clicker for the TV above the bar, and he's clicking channels. The blonde is trying to get the clicker away from him, and every time her hand gets near it, Colin shoots his hand above her head and changes a channel. "Uh-uh," he laughs. "No way. It's mine. You can't have it."

"Okay," she says. And pretends glazed boredom, and takes a mouthful of her beer. Then she reaches over and strokes the small of his back with her hand. He turns to her. "Oh," he says. "Oh," she says, and slips her fingers under the waistband of his jeans. "No fair," he says.

It's as if Claudine is watching a pantomime from very far away. The sound of pinball machines from the dark, smoky back of the bar is muffled now, and the lights around the bar are surreally bright.

She has to do something before she's seen.

She wants to run away, but she is moving forward, one step forward, in her squishy sandals, dark hair dripping on her shoulders, black T-shirt pasted to her breasts.

Dan sees her, and waves, and looks at Colin.

She climbs onto the stool beside Colin. "I'm thirsty," she says to Dan.

Colin's got the clicker up above his head. He turns slowly, brings it down.

"Will you just look at what the cat dragged in," he says. He's very drunk. He points the clicker at her and pretends to change the channel, and then laughs.

"It's really wet out there," Claudine says, ignoring his gesture. "Dan, can you bring me a draft?"

"Oops," Colin says, "sorry, I don't know why I did that," and puts the clicker down on the bar, and turns toward Claudine, blocking her view of the blond woman. Claudine would like to go to the bathroom and do a line, sharpen the bright steel of her mind, but she doesn't want to leave them alone.

"Aren't you going to introduce me?" she says.

"Certainly." Colin pulls away from the bar. "Claudine, Sally. Sally, Claudine." Sally smiles. She looks all of twenty-three, blond hair cut blunt with bangs. She has silver arrow earrings, wears a pale blue sweatshirt with cut-off sleeves and letters that say Wommyn's Sound Festival, Tanglewood. She has beautiful, strong arms.

"Sally's a brilliant actress," Colin says.

"Hi."

"Hi," Claudine says. "I saw you in something."

"I was in the Restoration take-off, at the Theatre Centre?"

Claudine has a vague memory of breasts, milky white and slightly marbleized with veins, pushed up in a satiny dress, and a shepherdess's bonnet.

"And I played Nina in André Traverse's *Seagull.*"

"Barely out of theatre school," Colin says, "and she's getting all these wonderful parts."

"That's great." Claudine gulps down half her beer.

"Janine called," Colin says.

"Oh yeah?"

"She said we were supposed to be there for dinner. You didn't even tell me."

"I did tell you."

"When?"

"Last night."

"Anyway, she was mad."

"I know. She got hold of me at the co-op."

Sally's watching the TV now, vacant and demure.

"They're really tight," Colin says to Sally. "Claudine and her sister."

Sally smiles, a broad smile like a woman who is used to being watched, who doesn't mind eyes moving across her wide face and full lips. Claudine notices parsley stuck between her eyetooth and her front tooth. It's a small thrill. They can't be that intimate if he hasn't told her about it.

"I haven't seen you here before," Claudine says.

"This is her first time at the Duke," Colin says. "She likes it, don't you, Sally? She's doing a Walmsley piece next. She's researching."

"Really?"

"I saw your film about prostitutes," Sally says. "They showed it at theatre school. We were rehearsing Genet's *The Maids*? It was sad."

"Sad?"

"Yeah, like all that waste."

"Sorry, I can't hear you." Somebody's put money in the jukebox, and Patsy Cline's "Back in My Baby's Arms" is so loud it's distorting the speaker.

"All that waste," Sally shouts. "Waste of talent."

"Whose?"

"I mean they could act, those women. They could really talk."

"It takes some skill," Claudine says, pushing away her wet hair from her face and lighting a cigarette.

"Yeah," Colin says. "Claudine is a brilliant listener, a genius when it comes to listening. Show us how you listen, Claudine. Is it like this?" He leans the palm of his hand on his cheek, then switches sides. "Or is it like this?"

How can he do this to her? Why is he doing this?

Sally laughs, embarrassed. "I know what you mean," she says, in a breathless voice. "When you're on stage, the most important thing is to really listen. Even though you've heard it a hundred times before, it's got to be like you don't know what's coming next. Like the audience has to feel you thinking and listening. That's the trick. Total concentration."

"Is that so?" Claudine says. "Tell me something, Sally. Is that your dog out there?"

Sally looks at Colin. Colin is watching his fingers doing a drumroll on the bar.

"I gotta be going," Sally says. "I work lunches at the Rivoli? And I start rehearsals tomorrow." She is standing up now. Her eyes are a deep brown. Claudine is fascinated by her face, the light on the planes of her cheeks, her arms, muscular in her cut-off T-shirt, the slip of a snake ring on her baby finger. She is seeing her through his eyes, it's a kind of erotic thrill she can hurt herself with in the half-blur of her drunkenness. But there's something about the dog. She wants to know about the dog. She doesn't want to let up about the dog.

"Is that your dog out there?" Claudine smiles. "Concentrate, Sally. Is that your dog?"

"Yes, that's my mutt."

"You shouldn't leave a dog like that out in the rain. It's not right. It's cruel."

"I didn't know," Sally says. "I didn't know it was raining."

They are looking right through each other. Sally swallows.

"Well, I'll see you," she says, and lowers her eyes, and then gives Colin a quick look, very precise, of you've got a sticky problem here and it's not mine and wash it yourself in whatever river you can find.

Colin watches her leave. Claudine looks for Dan to order another draft. Dan is wiping the bar at the other end.

Colin lights a cigarette, looks at himself in the mirror behind the bar. "That was ugly," he says, "really ugly."

"What?"

"'What?' You should hear yourself. Honestly. You sound like Jackie Kennedy talking to a servant. Pissing from a great height."

"Why are you doing this? Why? I just want to know why."

"Well, she's a dyke if you're bothered about that. Dan, bring us another couple of drafts."

"Don't say that, don't say dyke like that."

"Yeah, some of your best friends. Listen. I just met her, okay?

Right here. Didn't you see her T-shirt? I love dykes, I want to give them my balls for breakfast."

"I saw you, Colin."

"What? What did you see?" He's gone back to watching the TV, the big bold graphics of "The Journal" announcing themselves like the second coming. Barbara Frum is interviewing pollsters. They're predicting a majority for Mulroney in September.

"Good riddance," Dan says. "About fucking time, eh, Colin? That new guy Mulroney, he's going to get those Liberals, am I right?"

"It's not good, Dan," Colin says.

"Colin?"

He turns to her. He is slack-faced now. "I can't help you, Claudine, I can't live for you. You got to do that yourself. If I don't go with what I've got, I die."

Well die then, she wants to scream. Die.

"I don't know the difference," she says, "between loving and hating."

"Bullshit." He takes her face in his hands. "This," he says, "is loving." And tries to kiss her.

"Don't touch me," she says. "You're hell, you're low-rent hell."

He laughs. "Low-rent, eh? And what does that make you?"

"Stupid. Crazy."

"Stop fighting it. Look at me."

She looks at him. His drunkenness is taking him somewhere else now, to a floating place.

"We belong together, you and me," he says, gently, as if talking to a child. "It's a hard fit, but it's the only fit worth having. I'm going to watch you grow old and love your old bones. And we're going to have babies, lots of them."

"The world doesn't need more babies like us." She's shivering.

Odette
July
Jamaica

THERE ARE VOICES IN ODETTE SHE WOULD RATHER NOT hear. She doesn't know where they come from, these seizures of filth while she lies, brown, oiled, in a one-piece spandex royal blue bathing suit that moulds her "still good chassis," as Walter puts it. Still good at fifty-four, and she hasn't had thigh tucks and tummy tucks and eye tucks like all of her friends. "This is me," she often says to Walter, "without a stitch on."

She lies under a blue and white beach umbrella, on a rubbery navy pad, on a white-slatted chaise-longue. She is trying to drift back into the dream she had last night. Vague images flutter past her eyelids.

The beach of the Villa La Mar Condos is deserted, as it usually is in July. Much too hot for everybody except Walter, who insists this is the best month, but then sits in the air-conditioned condo most of the time. The others leave. Summer in Maine. In New Hampshire. In Vermont. In the Muskokas. Everybody but Odette dear. And the man in 38, Arnold Osmond, who practises the fox trot every day, alone, arms extended, ageing legs spidery on the edge of the waves. He has the grace of the blissfully unselfconscious. Arnold says he is curing himself of cancer by dancing. The cancer is in his palate. He whispers with inflection.

But Arnold is not dancing on the edge of the waves today. The beach has been freshly raked, the white chairs face the sun, the white tables have been wiped. From the beach bar, Odette can hear a blender, crushed ice mixing with bananas and sweet canned juices. It is a lovely morning. Nobody around but Odette and the black workers doing their chores. It is impossible to avoid hope on a morning like this, not to think yes, everything can start again. The air is fresh, the water inviting, the sky still pale with streaks of a sunrise. The groundskeeper has swept the terraces in front of the low-rises that make up the beach view part of the compound, and now he is watering the bougainvillea that cascades over the tall stone fences with a pink watering can. From where she sits, Odette can see the sparkle of water drops on the shiny leaves. He's young. He wears white pants. He is singing something that sounds like body move, everybody, body move.

It is Odette's favorite part of the day. By noon, the heat has killed hope of anything, the sand is too hot to walk on, the air smells of burning vegetation, the water looks like a mirage, the island dogs bark at the slightest provocation.

Listening to the waves rippling onto shore, Odette tries to find the thread of her dream. Something about losing her two babies overboard. Yes, that's it. She was on a big cruise ship with Roger. She didn't want to be with Roger. In the dream she knew she was with Walter and shouldn't be with Roger, it was a sin, a betrayal to go back there. Janine and Claudine were barely walking. Odette kept losing track of them, they were crawling through pipes in damp rooms in the hull of the ship. Roger wouldn't help. He was playing shuffleboard with an orange kitten.

The girls fell into the water just as Odette was emerging onto the deck and seeing that there was no railing on the back of the cruise ship.

She woke up crying mes bébées, mes bébées, sweating and crying. She thought her ribs would crack open from sadness. Mes petites filles, mes pauvres bébées. She could smell the baby in them again, the tender skin in folds, the small arms around her neck. In the dream there was so much guilt. Had she really broken the hold of their arms again and again? They wanted so much. Everybody did. Everybody had always wanted a piece of her.

No, she had always loved them like this, in a fit of grief. A good mother. A loving mother. Walter said so. Walter said you worry like a good mother.

But there was something here she had never wanted to face, that her tenderness had always been mixed with the grief she caused them. She had always wanted to gather them up against the slings of herself. The dream brought up this first form of loving — with guilt, with pity. "Je t'aime, Janine, je t'aime, Claudine, je vous aimes, si vous saviez comment je vous aime."

"You don't know," she said to Walter, who woke up, large, annoyed, "you don't know how much I love them. I love them so much it hurts. You can't know what that's like."

Walter did not see "good," did not see "innocence," did not see a mother's heart-breaking love. He saw a woman who was taking her suffering for a ride. On a carousel. Up and down. Lying about the horse she was riding on. Trying to find a way to blame him.

"Yes, Odette dear," he said. "You do love your two daughters. Now go to sleep."

And that calmed her. She lay her head on the pillow, and a goodness came over her face. But she couldn't sleep, had gotten up in the dark and felt her way to the living room and tried to call Claudine. Claudine would understand, she'd always understood her. As a child, she'd hold her hand and say pauvre Maman. So mature, she was.

It took a long time to get a line out, and then Colin answered, a gruff voice that opened up once he knew it was her, such a charming voice he had, and that had felt good, and it had drawn her out of her dread. He said Claudine was on the roof. The roof?

What roof? But he was gone and then the line went dead. When she tried again, the Ocho Rios operator said there was malfunction, ma'am. The electricity down. What did that have to do with phones, Odette wanted to know.

The waiters are sitting behind the thatched bar. They wear black pants and white shirts, and every once in a while one of them swats at a fly with a flipper. No one ever uses the snorkels and the flippers on this compound, they're all too old. They fear cardiac infarctions on the reefs, the last breath: a blue gurgle.

Odette is having a tired day. She shifts on the navy foam pad on the white wooden lounge chair. That's what she said to Walter this morning. "I'm having a tired day." He looked up from *The Gleaner*, the Kingston newspaper, and nodded. She is the youngest here, twenty years younger than Walter, thirty years younger than some of the retirees, but sometimes she feels older than all of them. What she's seen, what she's seen and felt compared to these people who've been living in bubbles, in perfect bubbles of charm most of their lives.

But people are always telling her that she looks good, and she knows that she's been in the bubble too these last twenty years and that it has had an effect on her, too, that she has worn herself down to an upper-class contour, smooth, polished, almost impermeable. She's worked very hard at standing off anything that stuck out, everything that used to cling to her.

She is still blond, but toned-down blond, old-money-silver-blond. Early on, she spotted the danger of being blond in upper-class Anglo Montreal, how you could be mistaken for Florida French-Canadian, brassy, brash, braying with loose sunburned breasts. Nobody ever looked down on Grace Kelly for being a blonde. That's the kind of blonde Odette had wanted to be. Pure, golden, transcendent, not the other kind. Why couldn't they see that? Why did she always feel like she was sticking out somewhere?

Still felt that, even after all these years of trying so hard not to stand out.

That was the cardinal rule. Never stand out, except on the golf course, where the men can wear floral pants and wild pink shirts, and the women can wear lime green culottes and crushed strawberry sockettes with pom-poms sticking out the backs of their white golfing shoes. She is used to it now, to the sight of these Wasps bright as Froot Loops walking through brilliant greens, but when she married Walter, she was flabbergasted. Oh my god, she thought, and it's these people been calling us Pepsis.

Ten o'clock. Too early for a drink. Odette shifts on the chaise-longue, skin sticking here and there on the rubber pad, and reaches down for a Marlboro in her see-through plastic beach purse. The morning is already partly ruined. The heat. The sweat. The smoke now, so good, filling up the hole her dream left in her.

Some people drink in the morning and are not alcoholics. They just like the taste. And then have a swim and pop a mint, and it's nothing, really, just a natural thirst in this heat. But she can't bring herself to call the waiters over, just yet. She's afraid of what they would think of her, so she just smiles at them.

She stubs her cigarette out in the sand, watches the pink lipstick stain around the white filter before pushing it all the way under.

In the house she came from, nobody ever hid collapse the way wealthy people hide it, smelling sweet, laughing with gold teeth on putting greens, colostomy bags hidden beneath bright pants. That is what is so strange about wealth, the way it contains and covers human misery. You'd never know it if they were rotting from the inside with gangrene the way her father did after two strokes. That was the summer he was having an affair with

Francine at the cottage on Lake Memphremagog. He had the strokes in August when the chill of fall was already in the air. Her mother had left by then, and it was Francine who found him, paralysed on the dock. Francine had done what she could, and then Julia had taken him in again, to nurse him, because the whiff of death had scared Francine off, and there was nobody else.

Near the end, he'd had both legs cut off because the poor circulation had invited gangrene. He sat watching TV with a clicker in his hand, in his big La-Z-Boy in the Cartierville apartment Julia had rented after selling the Sainte-Famille house. He didn't care where he was. He expected Julia to pick up the pieces. He expected to be served, even then. A buddy had given him a bar scotch dispenser, so between switching channels he could push a glass underneath it and serve himself. There was a lambskin under what was left of his legs. Nobody was allowed to touch the clicker. He kept on watching TV when she went to visit with the kids. The kids had never seen a clicker, they wanted to play with it, but he wouldn't let it out of his hand.

Odette had been ready then, ready for something, ready for the answer to what she'd done wrong.

But he just watched TV and threw his anger in their faces until he died the next fall. The poor man, angry to the bitter end.

She can feel herself coming to that, to a kind of death. Scared all the time now, of dying. It scares her, the force inside that wants to let go, the voices she hears out of the blue.

It is ten-thirty. Still too early for a drink. Her smile was mistaken for a summons and now one of the waiters stands before her, casting a shadow on her thighs. "I'm sorry," she says. "I don't need anything at the moment, thank you. So sorry."

The blue Caribbean flashes before her in a blink as she opens and then closes her eyes. It is hard to look upon nothing. And the nothing is guarded on either side by men in bamboo towers and by barbed wire fences that keep all other life out of the white clearing. Sometimes at night Odette hears shots, but nobody ever talks about it in the morning. "Something must have backfired," Walter says.

"It's a safe investment," he always says, "now that Commie Manley's gone." In town, someone has sprayed the walls with a red slogan: Seaga = CIAga.

*A*s a child, Odette spent a lot of her time imagining what it would be like remembering what she was going through. It was a habit like a tic or a stutter. She was always doing it. Whatever it was that she was going through, she would put herself somewhere else, imagine herself remembering what she couldn't bear to undergo in the present. She would think, I will be rich, I will be sitting on a beach in a white terry robe, rich, famous, married, and I will remember doing these dishes in this greasy water in this old house on Sainte-Famille Street. I'll remember the soap eyes ringed orange with tomato soup, my father's eyes on my back, the feel of my underwear through his stare. I will remember these things and they will mean nothing.

Many times she must have said I will be on a beach, because she is starting to remember a lot of things now. Most of them can't be true.

This afternoon she has to golf with Walter. Has to. Always this having to, snaking like a thread through the cloth he calls their life.

"You can do whatever you want," Janine used to say when she lived at home. On the very rare occasions when Janine calls now, she says things like "I'm so sick and tired of hearing you say you have to. You don't have to do anything."

"But Daddy says," Odette would say, and Janine would sigh, and in that sigh Odette would hear her own mother, spitting in a hankie and wiping tears from her cheeks. One time, Claudine, who was a cruel adolescent, screamed, "He's not your father, stop calling him Daddy."

"I know," Odette said. "What do you take me for? He's *your* Daddy."

None of them knows. None of them knows what it's like to live in jail.

Odette is too hot now. She needs a drink and she doesn't care if it's ten-thirty on a July morning in 1984, doesn't care what the waiters will think, what Walter will say smelling her breath.

The young man smiles. "Yes, ma'am," he says.

"I'm so thirsty," Odette says. "Could you, could I, please have a tall glass of orange juice with ice?"

He turns to go.

"Oh," she calls out. "Might as well add a tiny bit of rum. Not too much. Just a tiny bit." Smiling, she holds up an eighth of an inch between thumb and forefinger.

"Yes, ma'am," he says.

She watches him walk away in the sand, dust obscuring the shine of his black leather shoes. The waiters have made a little sandtrap on the beach by the bar, and one of them has a nine iron out, he's practising getting the ball out of the trap. The sand sprays up and falls down over and over again as the balls pop up and fly into the sea. Odette relaxes now, waiting for her drink. She lights another Marlboro. Life is good.

Some people have started complaining at finding golf balls in the surf. But it's the waiters who pick up the balls when they come back with the tide. So Odette doesn't get it. Why it matters. It's as if the sight of a black man with a golf club in his hand enrages them.

Odette must have been thirty-five the first time she went golfing at the Kahnawake Golf Club, Walter's golf club on the outskirts of Montreal. After they got married, he said you're going to have to learn to play golf. Blacks and French-Canadians couldn't be members of his club then. Being married to Walter took the frog part of her away, washed it clean, made it exotic, cute, Parisian. They didn't like Jews either, Walter's friends at the Kahnawake Golf Club, the kikes they called them, but they were more careful about saying Jews weren't allowed to be members.

Odette knew many Jewish people. They made a lot of the clothes she modelled in her pre-Walter career. The rich ones all belonged to the Montreal Golf Club. When she mentioned Kahnawake to Mr. Young, who made copies of Yves Saint Laurent suits, he made a face. "All the caddies at Kahnawake are Indians, I'm gonna pay for that?"

It was true. All the caddies at Kahnawake were Indians. Mohawks from Caughnawaga reserve.

But the golf pro was American. Dropped out of the PGA circuit because he couldn't take the pressure, Walter told her, "but he's got the sweetest swing you ever did see." Odette took lessons from sweet-swing, he was a handsome man, about her age, with a face reddened by excema, who wrapped his arms around her arms, standing behind her, legs apart, his hands wrapped around her hands, showing her the proper grip.

The proper grip. The sweat of that. Sweating through becoming the proper wife with the proper grip. They all laughed at her for trying so hard.

The drink so cool and delicious, and with the first sip she already knows that she will want another one.

The first times at that golf club. Must have been the middle of June, the peonies were in full bloom. The women's locker-room at Kahnawake was full of their heavy, layered heads falling down over the rims of blue glass vases. The scent of them in that pale blue room, icy with good taste, had made Odette dizzy. Her hands were already sweating in her new deerskin golf gloves, and she wondered how often you were supposed to change gloves anyway. Odette doesn't know when to change her gloves, she heard one of her voices say. They smell. Have you noticed how Odette's gloves smell?

She gripped and she gripped and she gripped and at night she showed her calluses to Walter. Sweet-swing kept saying relax, relax, let go, let your wrists go, loosen up your hands, loosen up your mind. It's just a game, let go of control, the ball wants to go. Oh sweet-swing could talk a blue streak in her ear, while he pressed himself against her. That was another thing. The way he thought, like most of the men there, that she should be available to him. Because she was blond. Because she was pretty. Because she had a French name. She couldn't say anything to Walter about it. And the women hated her for it. It's always been like that. The way the world is.

And sweet-swing couldn't do anything about the sight of V-Jay's name on all the plaques. V-Jay, Walter's first wife, had won a lot of tournaments; the women's championship and the doubles, the husband and wife championship, the costumed foursomes, whatever it was, V-Jay's name was always up there on a plaque. Hard not to grip hard, living with the ghost of V-Jay, her life imprinted in every corner of Odette's life, at the club, in every chintz cushion of the Westmount house, in every resentful fold of Walter's boys' minds.

Odette polishes off the rum. Always did everything to please those boys. Never got so much as a thank you. She'd had to be the heart, in that house, had to be the furnace that warmed things up.

"Odette!" It's like a command from the hot sky.

She turns, sees Walter waving from their balcony. His hands encircle his mouth. "Teeing off in twenty minutes."

So, she wants to scream. So?

"Better come in and shower."

Odette waves, closes her eyes. When she figures that Walter's gone back in, she smiles at the waiter and gets herself a refill.

Downs it in two seconds flat. Closes her eyes, feels the first swimming dizziness of the day, her limbs floating in the chair she lies in.

Getting hotter now. So hot the air shimmers. There is a film of salt over her eyes, the sweat between her breasts drips down, making a dark stain on her royal blue bathing suit. Her fingernails dig into her palms. So often now when she looks at her hands she is surprised to find tightly clenched fists. She has to tell them to unclench, as if they belonged to someone else.

So many voices. She tries to still them with rum and Valium, but they come out muffled and dark, dragging her down to the bottom. The voices want to pin her down, blame her. They emanate from Walter sometimes. Those voices tell her, I don't want to hear what you have to say. Odette can hardly breathe sometimes. When he moves, the air sours with ancient commands. "Don't make so much noise. So unseemly, so demanding, so annoying. So goddamn emotional. I don't want to hear about it. Be quiet. Stop breathing." Most of the time Walter is silent, but this is what she hears in his silences. And she has to stop herself from saying but I didn't do anything, I am innocent.

There's something in his silence, in his will to silence her, that drives her to fight him. She wants to penetrate that wall, bash into it with her fists, with her tongue.

"Are you angry with me?" she said this morning at breakfast.

"No, what makes you say that?"

The weight of it. Trying this and that.

"I love you," she said, getting up with a plate full of crusts.

It is her only form of punctuation.

"Odette."

"Yes?"

"You should watch the sauce."

Maybe she has time for another one now. And then she'll have a swim to wash it all out. She is lifting her glass in the sun, a tall pocked glass. The waiter nods.

So bad. She's so bad for doing this. Can't help it.

I can't help it. Wanting to scream that, when the girls said you're embarrassing when you drink. You drool, Mummy.

Janine and Claudine know nothing. They don't know what it took, what it takes to make these kinds of bargains. What it is to age, as a woman. They think women have power now, but they don't know how that beam of power gets weaker and weaker for a woman the older she gets, how sudden the discarding is. No matter what you've given, what you have not given. How you can turn around and be on the street. They don't know what it is to hold your tongue.

She wanted them to go to university. To be spared poverty. To have that power. To get an education in English. To be spared the pale bleached dresses of hand-me-downs by calling Walter Daddy. To climb the ladder, to be good, brave, climb that ladder, hold their tongues for the time, just for the time being, until they managed independence, she wanted this for them.

What was so wrong with that? What had she done that was so wrong? Odette sees it in their faces now, when she visits, once, maybe every two years, sees the refusal. As if nothing she had ever done had meant anything. Hard-hearted refusal. For everything she has done, in her wisdom, in her knowing.

Odette never went to university. Her father said that was for boys. Her father never laid a hand on Eddie, or on Doris and Kathleen, he took everything out on her. He hit her and shoved her against walls, against the newel post of the staircase, she remembers that time, looking up at the picture of the smiling cupid in an oval wood frame by the staircase, and feeling something wet falling in her eyes. She doesn't remember that much from the other times. Nobody knows this. There are things you just don't say. And her mother, rest her soul, made her apologize.

Say you're sorry to calm him down. Say you love Daddy.

And she did, she said I'm sorry, I'm sorry, weeping, I'm sorry. Crying, I'm sorry. And that made him hit her again, on her face, the face he said looked like a goddamn saint waiting at heaven's door.

Claudine and Janine know nothing.

They don't know about that, and they don't know about what Roger did. Everything she bought was repossessed. Houses, cars, even a second-hand boat she'd bought with her hard-earned money the summer she got the cottage on Lake Memphremagog.

I don't have any nerves left.

Roger always said tu te montes des histoires. And he hit her, too, and said he'd kill her and the children if she ever left. Nobody believed her, not the parish priests she went to for advice, not her mother, not her sisters. Nobody believed it. She believed it. She thought, he's going to kill me and my babies. If I leave, he's going to come after us and kill us.

And the children see him and talk to him and call him Papa. They don't refuse him. They resent her, and don't refuse him.

They never understood what she'd gone through after the separation with Roger, who didn't pay a cent of child support, who took his visiting rights on Sundays and brought the girls back tired, sad, unsure. She had taken any job then. Anything that came along. She was thirty-three, too old for modelling, except for the most menial things, which she did, like being a demonstrator for hospital beds. That was where she met Walter, who was on the board of the Montreal General Hospital. It was luck, really, he'd just happened to be there that day, part of the group watching her as she stood in white and pearls pushing the buttons of a bed that rose up and cranked down and scrunched into a snake shape right before their eyes.

He had watched her, listened to her patter, and smiled kindly. He was a tall man with grey eyes, a gentleman she thought, looking at his tall frame, his greying hair, at the peculiar smile he had, as if it were a surprising thing for him to smile, and that surprise worked its way into his smile.

The General bought the beds. Walter asked her out. He listened to her story, a woman, alone, having to support her two daughters, living in a small apartment, having to travel across the country sometimes to organize demos and other public-relations duties. Worrying about money all the time. What that did to her. He took her to Café Martin on Mountain Street, he took her to dinner at his golf club, he drove up to Summit Lookout in his Cadillac and pointed out the rooftop of his house just below the Boulevard.

His age made her feel young, and new. When he held her against him, she wanted to say take care of me, rock me, she wanted to be swept up out of the struggle. He found her endearing, she could tell that, he liked the quick way she had of laughing, of marvelling at the world of wealth he offered. He said he'd never met anybody like her, no woman had ever brought out what she brought out in him. He laughed at himself, turning up at her door with powdered candies with little messages on them, I love you, Be mine, bought her candies, perfume, made her wait in the restaurant while he went out to get the car and opened the car door for her. He did all these things as if they were simply normal. He had no idea that the regularity of his affection and his attention to detail were foreign to her. All that time, the time of their courting, she'd waited for signs of danger, for signs that civility could turn into rational savagery, romance into empty promises.

But it didn't. He talked to her in the way she imagined a good father would talk, telling her about things she'd never heard of, explaining things she'd never had time to think about. He pointed out the stars to her, showed her how to crack open a lobster, explained the stock market, revealed the secret of capital and interest, the river-flow of money that passed through his hands as the CEO of a large American subsidiary that made chemical fertilizers, how the company had branched out after the war, how the chemicals that had been developed for the war had been turned into first-rate agricultural enhancers. How the third world could be transformed by the wonder of high-yield farming.

It was the idea that he could love her small, disorganized self that she found most enticing, and that he could, because of his love, scoop her into another life, a life where money was never a worry, where she didn't have to leave the girls to go on trips, didn't have to think about what they ate, who they saw, about doctors' bills and dentists' bills, and all of the emergencies, real or imagined, that Janine and Claudine were prey to.

She had thought then, I will be free.

When they had moved into his house she had felt squeezed in a way she had never, for one moment, imagined. His old life had laid down tracks as intractable as steel, and she, who had dreamed of sleeping in, of shopping and reading, of having a second childhood, found herself hooked up to his engine, only allowed to watch his landscape on either side of the tracks.

And the girls. And his boys. Well, they'd done the rest. What they'd had, Walter and her, was a courtship and a three-week honeymoon, and that was all. When they'd come back from their honeymoon, they'd walked into a hormonal war zone with four teenagers riding around them like a posse, circling their intimacy and crushing it dead.

*O*dette walks to the water like a somnambulist. She is hot and slightly drunk, she wants to fall into the cool water and let herself go, let herself sink to the bottom. She dives, surfaces, kneels in the shallow water so as not to expose her skin to air. From the water, kneeling in the brilliant sunlight, stifling huge sobs, she sees Walter walking on the beach. Why should she be crying now, after all these years? She'd made her peace. A long time ago. Must be the drinks making her cry.

Walter is wearing a lime green alligator shirt and pink pants. His mouth is turned down at the corners. She can feel the weight of him as he walks with his cleats on the beach.

She waves. He turns his back on her. "Wait for me!" she yells. "I'm coming!"

Janine July

OH NO. HE'S STARTED. COLIN'S DRUNK AND HE'S STARTED, the big talk, the arguing, the flinging of hooks to catch a pound of flesh. Janine didn't think it would happen so soon, but Claudine and Colin came into her house looking just like a cartoon of a couple with black clouds over their heads, and now Colin is spreading the black cloud around. At first, Claudine apologized profusely for forgetting about dinner last night. As if apologizing and apologizing could make it better. If she'd noticed her new streaked hair, yeah, if Claudine had said something like your hair looks nice, maybe that would have made things better. But she was too much in herself, as usual, to notice anything.

Later, in the yard, while Janine was feeling good and strong cutting curly parsley with a pair of scissors, Claudine picked at her nails and said I think I'm falling apart. But Marie-Ange was still up, and right there with them in the yard, so Janine couldn't really pursue that line. It would lead to tears. It would upset Marie-Ange before her bedtime. All Janine could think of saying was, "Well, Colin sounded very lonely last night when I called." Claudine gave her a hard look and said what do you mean? And Janine said that when she called to find out where they were last night, Colin seemed lonely and unhappy. Maybe she should do her editing in the daytime. Men need a little coddling sometimes at night.

"You don't know anything," Claudine said.

"Pardon me for living," Janine said, "I just fell off a hearse." It had been their grandmother's favorite expression.

"I think he's having an affair," Claudine said, voice choked, pinching basil leaves between her fingers.

Janine took Claudine's cold hand in hers. "I don't think he's like that," she said. "It's not his style."

"I don't even know why I care," Claudine said.

"Because you're in love with him, that's why."

Colin and Jim watched them walk hand in hand over the yellowed lawn. Marie-Ange tugged at the hem of Janine's pink dress. Claudine, in a black jean skirt and a man's white shirt, walked with her head down, watching her running shoes. "A sight for sore eyes," Colin said when they came in.

And now the four of them are all sitting in the yellow dining room with the columns retrieved from torn-down houses, columns that used to hold up the roofs of porches but now hold vases of dried flowers. Marie-Ange is in bed, although not asleep, and demanding to be "checked" every ten minutes. And Janine is trying to keep a grip on things. She can't follow what's going on. She can never understand what Colin is on about. He's already drunk most of the wine, and now he's opening another bottle. He has to be the most articulate drunk she's ever seen. He never gets messy. He gets sharper.

There are fish bones and lemon slices on the big white serving plate that was piled high with salmon and ginger just twenty minutes ago. Janine knew that Claudine would forget about the Chinese food, and even if she didn't, Jim wouldn't eat it because of the MSG, so she picked up some frozen salmon steaks at Loblaws and made a pinker version of last night's meal. The orange poppies she picked from the garden are drooping from weakened hairy stems, the petals bright and delicate as tissue paper. It is hot as Hades again. Last night's storm did nothing to break the hot spell, just added humidity.

Jim, who's never been able to stand Colin, although he likes to smoke his joints, is pushing a piece of broccoli over to the side of his plate. Claudine's mouth is half-open, ready to deflate Colin's big talk. The appetite Claudine has for a fight can be frightening. Even when cowed, even when unhappy, Claudine can whip out a phrase that will cut through bone, so Janine's body has gone on red alert, the red alert of her childhood. Her body is stiff, wanting to control whatever is threatening to erupt.

"This country," Colin is saying, "can never decide if it wants to be a country. That would be too much trouble, getting out of diapers, going for a shit without the United States wiping our asses."

Janine waits, listening and absorbing the dark that comes out of Colin's mouth. Colin's hands fly in all directions, his head jerks from side to side, he goes blurry. He makes Janine dizzy. The polished cherrywood table is round, but Janine feels she's sitting at the head of it, the hostess responsible for everything that comes out of everybody's mouth. "It's international," Jim says.

Colin lights a Player's Light. He puts the burned match in the white serving plate, and Janine retrieves it as discreetly as possible. "What was that?" he says to Jim.

"The money market, it's all related," Jim says.

"That's exactly what I mean, man, I start talking about this country and all of a sudden we're talking about money. Not your money, not my money, but their money." Colin smiles at Janine. It is magnificent, this smile, so vital, so open, so conspiratorial. Janine smiles back. She can't help herself. Colin's smile makes you feel as if you're the special pupil in the class, the only one who really understands the complexities at hand. She doesn't understand his big talk, but she does understand his frailty, his neediness. He was the eldest in his family. They talked about it once, how the eldest gets broken up, breaking the parents in. He said when my brother was born, I remember being in the bath and thinking the little fucker had better not cut my grass. She'd been shocked a little. It's not what she'd felt. She wanted Claudine. She was so lonely before Claudine came.

"It's amazing, isn't it," Colin continues, "how when anybody starts to care about anything, somebody's got to bring up money?"

"It's all related," Jim says. His boyish cheeks are flushed with the wine he's drunk. He just seems to get younger. Since they've had Marie-Ange, Jim has grown more concerned about his looks. He's getting sixty-dollar haircuts at the Rainbow Room now. He never used to do that. When she met him, he was a Buddhist.

"What's all related?" Colin says.

"Everybody's money."

"Let me get this straight, the money's all related so we can't have a country?"

"I didn't say that."

"Yes, you did."

"I did not." Jim is nonchalantly tearing the pulp out of a lemon wedge, but his face is getting redder.

"How's the documentary going?" Janine says to Claudine.

"I'm stuck," she says. "When you go there, what you see is exactly the same conditions that created the problems in the first place. It's unbearable. It's a pen to control the rate of suicides. There's no programs, there's nothing. Nothing."

Claudine is smoking now, too, smoking and looking at the sky through the dining-room window. She had asked to put Marie-Ange to bed, and would have stayed there until Marie-Ange fell asleep if Janine hadn't put her foot down.

The sky is framed by lace curtains Janine has just this week soaked in the bathtub with bleach. It was so satisfying to see the lace go from dusty grey to bright white. But Claudine would never have noticed that; she has contempt for anything domestic. She is so pale tonight. Her green eyes look glassy, her hand shakes as she lifts the cigarette to her mouth.

"Do you want me to check on Marie-Ange?" Claudine says.

"No, it hasn't been ten minutes."

"But she sounds so sad."

Marie-Ange is crying out "Mummy, mummy, come check," from upstairs.

"The routine is," Janine says, with exaggerated firmness, "that we check every ten minutes, and she usually falls asleep after the third check."

"Sounds like luggage."

It goes right in like a blow. As it was meant to. A payback for something, but what? Janine stands and starts piling the dishes. "I'm sorry," she says, "but you don't know anything about it. Kids need rituals. This is her ritual."

"You know what I'm starting to think?" Colin says. "I think people get what they fucking deserve." He looks at Janine. "Where are you going? We haven't even finished the wine. Sit. You don't need to do that."

Trembling, Janine puts the dishes back on the table and sits down.

"I don't think I can do this any more," Claudine says to no one in particular. "Point a camera, like that."

"Listen, Jim," Colin says, "you want to be colonized by Americans and technology and live with swallowing the shit that comes with that, then fine. We get what we deserve. I don't care any more. You can't care about the guy who makes his own noose, know what I mean? When I hear this shit, it makes me want to kick the chair. To boot it out from under, and see the whole fucking country hang."

"Don't you think you're overdoing it just a tiny bit?" Claudine says.

"Yeah, you escalate so fast," Jim says.

"I can always count on you to back me up," Colin says to Claudine. "That's what I like about you, your unshakable loyalty."

"Ah come on, not everything is life or death."

"That's where you're wrong," Colin spits out. "It is life or death, and it's clear what side you're on, isn't it?" His face has gone slack.

Janine looks at Jim. Jim looks away.

"Sure feels smug around here," Colin says. "Pass me that there bottle of wine, Jannikins, I'm going to the back yard. I need some air. I need some *life*."

Claudine gets up to go with him.

"Don't fucking come near me," he says. There is so much violence in his voice that even though he's addressing Claudine, Janine feels like she's been smacked on the back of the head.

None of it makes any sense. These fights are never about what they're about. "Are you okay?" she says to Claudine.

"I'm fine, just fine," Claudine says.

Janine takes the dishes into the kitchen. She wonders what Colin means by "this country." Being from Montreal where mon pays was something sandwiched between a bunch of islands to the east and what she imagined as a big flat plain to the west, she's never said "this country" in her life. In Quebec, they talked about "the rest of Canada" sometimes, as if it were a plate of unappetizing leftovers. They were vendues, Claudine and her. That's what their father called them, mes deux vendues, because Maman had taken them out of French school and remarried English. Vendues. Sold-outs. Worse than assimilated. They didn't have a leg to stand on in either place.

Colin's passion for "this country" makes Janine feel guilty. A part of her always ends up feeling whipped when he goes on his rants. She's never cared about stuff like that. Has been trying to keep her head above water so desperately that it hardly mattered what pond she was in. Maybe Colin has to care. He's a writer and nobody reads him. Janine tried to read him, tried to read the novel he wrote about a guy who went on drunken druggie escapades with other guys. Maybe it was because she was pregnant at the time, but she couldn't stick with it. She did read *She*, and was slightly appalled at seeing her family history twisted and braided into his romance with Claudine and laid out for all the world to see. It was like watching something from the wrong end of a telescope. What had been huge and blunt as a club had been whittled down by clever phrases that had nothing to do with real life.

One time Claudine said that their trip to Jamaica was ruined because Colin's novel wasn't in the airport bookstore. The whole time they were in Negril, she said, Colin kept going on about Danielle Steel. There he was, said Claudine, on the most beautiful beach I've ever seen, and he was foaming at the mouth because all the women on the beach were reading Danielle Steel. It made Janine ashamed of loving Danielle Steel, as if she should hide this appetite, the way her mouth waters when she opens one of her books.

She'd never admit this to Claudine. There are so many things Janine no longer admits to Claudine.

They used to be one. Together they laughed at their mother, who never felt real, who kept saying a woman this and a woman that and a woman can't and a woman must. They had to laugh at her. They had to invent something better. Together they moved to Toronto in the mid-seventies for no other reason than to escape the weight of betrayals they were always asked to commit in their parents' orbit. It would never, ever stop, the pulling and pushing, the current of anger and hatred they had to carry from one to the other. And they helped each other get used to the new city, a strange city, a city that was, through newspapers and magazines, always exhorting you, guiding you, telling you what to do, explore, exploit. They tried to find downtown Toronto. They sat in the apartment they shared on Yonge Street and read piles of stuff about what to do, what to see, who to know, where to get stuff repaired, what to buy, what to eat, and felt like orphans left out of this huge repast. None of what was offered ever materialized. You could walk in Toronto and feel nothing at all. Toronto was like a blank tape, like something that had been erased, nothing called out to be answered. They thought they could start again. And they had, each in their fashion, but they suffered from the blankness of it all. Until time created its own shadows. Now things were wrong here, too.

Such silence. Janine walks upstairs to check on Marie-Ange. She has fallen asleep, hands clasped around her stuffed monkey. Looking at her child's pale, delicate eyebrows, watching her small chest rise and fall, Janine is filled with tenderness. She would like to fall asleep, too, curled around a new life. When Marie-Ange was a little baby, and she carried her around in a Snugli, chin grazing the top of her delicate, fuzzy head, Janine felt strangely sated. It was if her daughter's weight on her chest covered up a hole she hadn't known was there.

Tiptoeing to the window, she sees Colin sitting on the grass in the back yard. She can hear Claudine and Jim quietly scraping the remains of the meal in the dining room. What can she do, how can she make things better?

Walking back downstairs she thinks, I could make him apologize to Claudine. Her hand feels warm on the stripped wood of the banister. She fills the kitchen sink with hot water and soap, dumps the dishes in, grabs her glass of wine and goes out into the yard.

"You look gorgeous," Colin says, and then sticks out his tongue as if he's about to lick her. He is sitting by the flowerbed, cross-legged, the bottle of wine leaning on his left thigh. His long hair, which is usually dirty blond, is getting lighter, bleached by the sun. His soft denim shirt looks pale blue against the yellow zinnias. There's not a trace left of the black anger that just rattled the dining room.

Janine sits down, drapes her pink cotton dress over her bent knees, which she hugs with her arms. He watches her do this as if it was the most fascinating thing in the world, as if he was watching a great blue heron land on a rocky shore. It makes her a bit self-conscious, this being watched so closely, but the soft breeze fluttering the pink cotton of her dress around her ankles feels nice.

"Sorry about the explosion," he says. "Things are tense right now. Claudine's not happy with her documentary. She always takes it out on me."

Janine sips her wine. She wants to say tell her you're sorry, but the evening air has erased what she came here to do.

It is getting dark now, and in the half-light she can make out Marie-Ange's bright sand-toys in the sandbox at the back of the narrow yard. She thinks she should cover it so cats don't shit in it, but she's too tired to move.

"Your hair," he says, "is different."

"I was sick of being a frump, I streaked it."

"You look soft," he says.

"I was really blond when I was a kid, and then I was dirty blond, and then it got really dark after the pregnancy." She laughs, thinking for some reason that he would find the word pregnancy embarrassing.

After the heat of the day, the breeze is like a blessing. It makes them feel innocent, able to really see each other for the first time now, in the grey-blue half-light, sitting on the grass, caressed by a wind that feels like a breath. It reminds Janine of how the world seems so full of strong color, after sweating through a fever.

"I've always had a thing for blondes," Colin says.

"I don't," Janine says. It's a passing loyalty to Jim, who has dark brown hair, but her eyes are smiling. She sees his hand, pale, freckled, with long fingers leaning on the grass, and all she can think of is wanting to touch it, all of her is trying to will his hand to lift itself from the earth and take hers. Must be crazy, she thinks, must be imagining this. This is not real. I'm a mother, I should cover the sand-box.

"Say that again," he says.

"What?"

"Say you don't have a thing for blondes."

She laughs. "I don't." She's half-drunk, half-transported, it is like being in a Danielle Steel novel all of a sudden.

"Again."

"I don't have a thing for blondes."

"You're just like your sister. You can't stand the truth."

Something in Janine plummets, it's like an elevator dream, she's plummeted to the ground floor.

"I'm not," she says. Her heart is beating very fast. "I'm not like Claudine. We're very different. She's the smart one. I'm . . ." She wants to say I'm the kind one, but it doesn't seem weighty enough.

"Really?"

"Claudine is so competitive. I'm not like that."

"I like mothers. You're so . . . " He can't think of the word for a second. "Soft." And then he takes his hand and touches her cheek. She covers his hand with hers and makes his hand touch and feel her entire face. It is like a convulsion, the need for her face to be touched, it's as if she could never get enough of this.

"Oh god," she says. And then they are kissing, and his lips feel as hungry as hers, and the hunger scares her, stops her.

"What are you doing?" she says.

"What are you doing?"

"Nothing." She laughs. "Really I'm not doing anything."

"There's a lot going on in this nothing."

"We can't do this." Her lips feel swollen. She takes his hand and puts it on her belly.

"You're right," he says. "To do what feels good is a slap in the face of common sense."

"My mother always said I was the one with the common sense. Just like her. Claudine used to say the thing about common sense is that it's sooo common."

"Your mother's sweet," he says. His hand climbs to her breasts. "Oh no," she says, and stands up quickly, and starts smoothing the creases of her dress to make the feelings go away.

"Come back," he says.

"I've got to cover the sandbox. Can you help me?"

*T*he light in the kitchen is very yellow when they come back in. Jim is doing the dishes. He's wearing yellow plastic gloves. He's singing "Why'd you do what she said," mimicking Marianne Faithfull's voice, which is blasting out of the cassette player on the green Formica table. His face is set in a slight snarl that takes on her anger, "Why'd you let her suck your cock," he sings, baring teeth, circles of soap bubbles round his arms.

It shocks Janine, coming in from the soft dark and hearing this, and smelling marijuana, with its skunk-like after-smell.

Claudine is sitting at the kitchen table, and she's singing along while drawing with Marie-Ange's crayons. Her drawing looks like orange and red faces of women stuck in the bottom of a turquoise swimming pool.

"We've just covered the sandbox," Colin says. "I didn't know that cat shit was dangerous. Janine was telling me that they can carry microscopic worms that can get into the sand and if kids eat this they can carry this kind of parasite . . . "

Claudine doesn't even look up from her paper. Jim carries on singing.

"I read about it at the Children's Storefront," Janine says. Her voice feels loud. "They had this article tacked to the bulletin board. It really scared me."

She knows that they both sound good-tempered, that her body has gone into some sort of overdrive, and she doesn't know what to do about it, so she walks over to the freezer, takes ice cream out and says, "I forgot dessert. For dessert, there's strawberries and ice cream."

"I'm not hungry," Claudine says. She yawns. "I'm pretty tired, actually."

"Nice guy," Colin says to Jim, "smoking my joint without me."

"'There's a good-size roach left in the ashtray," Jim says, still scouring the clay pot.

"Are you going to have some?" Janine is holding out the strawberries like an offering.

"I'll have some ice cream," Jim says. "And then I'm going to go check out this listing on Howland."

"Oh. This late?"

"Yeah. There's this agent from Royal LePage, he's going to show me the house I was telling you about."

"I wouldn't say no to ice cream," Colin says, and sticks out his tongue. He looks at her as if they were still in a circle of conspiracy. She breaks the stare reluctantly and, grateful for something to do, searches for the ice cream scoop she stole from the kitchen store on St. Clair where she worked years ago.

Colin sits beside Claudine and lights the roach. She looks at him smoking. Her eyes are dark and dead.

"What's your problem?" he says. She doesn't answer. "Have a toke, relax, the night is young."

"No, thanks."

"Hey everybody, Claudine is sulking. Everybody watch Claudine sulking."

The tape clicks and goes dead. The word sulking hangs in the air. Janine stares at the two scoops of vanilla ice cream in the bowl she's been filling, at the strawberries in her hands. She's never noticed before that those spots on a strawberry are seeds. Jim wipes his hands on the dishtowel.

"I've got to go now," Claudine says, standing up. "I've got to go now. Oh my god, I've got to go." She picks up her large black leather bag and walks out of the kitchen. They watch her, stunned by the weak, collapsed sound of her voice.

"Wait," Janine says. "Wait." Claudine's slender shoulders are up around her ears as she walks down the hall to the front door. She doesn't look back. She keeps on walking. She slams the door.

"You've got to go after her," Janine says to Colin. Her face has settled into a serious mother mask, she's conscious of that, and of the large smile that wants to split that mask in two.

Claudine July

*I*S SHE MAKING THIS UP?

No one would make this up.

She can't be. You can feel these things, surely to god you can. He'll flirt with anything, even her sister.

Claudine is walking on College Street. Her temples are sweating, her jaw feels wired shut. She expected steps at first, and looked behind her, down tree-lined Brunswick Avenue, but there was nobody, just some kids on skateboards. Now she is walking past the red brick building Colin used to live in, up above Quality Bakery and Four Star Drycleaners. Across the street, the clock-tower by the fire station says ten-thirty. She used to rely on that clock when she went over to Colin's place all those years ago. She was cheating on Ben, she had to parcel out her lust to the tick of that clock. Weak-kneed, stomach pitted with guilt, she'd spring from his bed and look at that big clock-face and gasp oh my god, it's one o'clock, and she'd run to the shower, and dress while he kissed the back of her neck and her shoulders, while his hands roamed all over her body. "Stop," she'd plead, laughing, wanting to fall back into bed. He would walk her down and they would kiss on the last steps, leaning the full length of their bodies against each other.

Later, back at Ben's apartment, smelling of Lifebuoy, bright and chipper with invented stories, she'd crawl into bed with Ben and replay her time with Colin to float above the plague of guilt and self-hatred. Replayed it, and replayed it.

Never once did she think of Ben, of what it did to him. She had simply been angry at him, angry that his existence created complications. Maybe that's how Colin feels. No. It's not the same. Not the same at all. It's a habit with Colin, it's part of his male prerogative, that's what she can't stand.

What is it Colin says, when he's feeling high and mighty? Oh yeah, *not everything is about you.*

I don't think everything is about me, you asshole. It comes out with a snarl. She's said it aloud. The Portuguese woman in front turns and gives her a look.

You asshole.

Turning into a bag lady.

Claudine walks to the curb. Lifts her arm high. Taxi, she says, to no one in particular. A yellow cab on the other side of College makes a U-turn. "Thank you," she says. The driver is Jamaican. "No problem," he says. The car is spotless, the suspension smooth, the sound system exquisite. He's playing Marley, Bringing Down Babylon one more time. Claudine puts her head back on the brown vinyl seat, and yawns.

*M*oving about the loft she hardly lives in is like walking on a beach at low tide. There are pools everywhere of what came in and settled in their comings and goings, but in her eyes now, everything is his, his mess, his papers, his clothes, his overflowing ashtrays, his books, his bits of receipts, his stray pennies and socks, his western ties with buffaloes and Indian heads. It's as if he'd been shot and trailed his guts all over the place. In the days when she thought the pathology she was involved in was an ordinary relationship with ordinary expectations of shared housekeeping, she used to accuse him of domestic imperialism. Saying can you try and be neater would have no effect. The word imperialism might inspire guilt. He himself used the word with impunity in all his political arguments, but he just laughed when she lobbed it his way. So she created corners for him, a corner for him to write in, with his table, his lamp, his filing cabinet; a corner for him to read in, with his inherited chairs and a stand-up lamp. The place was big enough for this. But he couldn't keep to that. He spilled over everything. It wasn't that *she* was so neat. With Ben she'd been the messy one. It was just that somebody had to draw some line.

At one point, she became fixated with keeping the blond wooden table by the big windows free of debris. Every day she piled all of his papers in neat stacks and put his pennies in jars, and his receipts in an old peach basket she'd painted bright colors in brighter days. She wiped the table, put seasonal flowers in a glass vase, fruit in the blue bowl her mother had given her for her twenty-first birthday, and spread shells and stones around candles in wooden candlesticks. Every night, he dumped his pennies all over the table, pulled out shredded receipts from bars and restaurants, took a beer out of the fridge, put his feet on the table, took his latest manuscript and spread it all over the blond table. He made a deletion or two, left everything on the table, and talked about his work. When she said something, he looked at her with dark eyes. "I either live here or I don't," he'd say. Or, "For fuck's sake, what is this? Why don't you get some design magazines and make a nice spread on your table. If that's what matters to you, I'm outta here."

In that first year, when she'd rented the loft because she was sick of the smell of yeast and dry-cleaning fluid that seeped through the floors of Colin's place, the table had taken on the aura of an altar. He desecrated it, she cleaned it. Eventually she had given up on the altar, and on everything else. And what a giving up it was. If there was no equality, there would be nothing at all. He would have to live in his own fouled nest. Trouble was, she had to share that nest. If she cooked, it was with the understanding that he would do the dishes. If he didn't do the dishes, the dishes could sit soaking in the sink for a month. The water turned rusty, bubbles of mildew grew on the surface. Once, in the middle of a fight about housekeeping, he threw an entire set of dinner plates against the wall. She swore he broke the dishes so he wouldn't have to wash them.

"I'm doing it for you, too," he said.

"Sure you are. Teaching me non-attachment to worldly things, are you?"

And then, as sometimes happened, in the confusion of drugs and alcohol, truth like a great angel descended into him, and spoke. "No," he said, eyes serious, "I'm having the tantrum you never had." That's what Janine used to imply, when she had her hysterics. "I'm doing it for everybody," she'd say. Claudine felt herself wavering. "What do you mean, what do you mean?" she said, crying, picking up pieces of cheap white stoneware. But she knew exactly what he meant. He was the piece of herself she'd put away for a rainy day.

Claudine stands by the table, palms pressed against the blond wood, leaning towards the dark of the windows. There are three dried oranges in the blue bowl. A postcard from Anne, who is in Montreal editing a Film Board documentary about the daughters of mothers who took DES. "Wish you were here" is scrawled on the back. "It's dark, and airless, and the junk food is delicious." The postcard is of a mother chimpanzee picking nits out of her offspring's head. It is one of Jane Goodall's photographs. There is so much tenderness in the gesture, such intelligence in the mother's eyes.

It reminds Claudine of Marie-Ange's stuffed monkey, which she has to hold against her chin to go to sleep. The plush on the monkey's head is all worn down where she rubs it. Claudine noticed that tonight when she put her to bed. How loving Marie-Ange's face is, how open and loving. Can't have that. Not with Colin the way he is. There's no better form of birth control than not wanting to repeat a history.

Colin's change sticks to her palms. His journal is on the table.

Claudine's hands are cold, her neck compressed. She opens the journal, closes it, opens it again and reads. The last entry is a poem, it is addressed to "S." It starts with a quote from Ginsberg's "Howl." "Yes, yes," / that's what I wanted, / I always wanted, / I always wanted, / to return to the body / where I was born."

Claudine reads on.

She sleeps, small bones
warm between the sheets
while I write to you
   In her dreams
the sky falls like a roof
and buries the woman she dreams
I am writing to,

buries you who waits for
my shadow to wake
her from her sleep

Frozen by the table, Claudine doesn't hear the lock turn, doesn't hear Colin come in. She rereads the lines, trying to decipher an ancient language, meanings shifting with the blink of an eye.

"Stooping to snooping now," he says.

"God, you scared me," she says, whipping around, spinning to the ceiling. "I didn't hear you."

Colin walks to the fridge and grabs a beer. He looks taller than usual. He wears black cowboy boots he just picked up at the Sally Ann. He opens the beer with the opener he always leaves on the table and lets the cap fall beside it. It bounces to the floor.

"So how do you like it?" he says.

"What? That you're flirting with my sister now? How do you think I like it?" Claudine suddenly notices that her shoulder bag is still on her shoulder. Her mouth is dry with fear.

"How do you like the poem?"

"Who's S?"

"What?"

"S., who's S?"

"Christ, you're paranoid. It's part of the Sisyphus series I'm writing. It's a poem about waiting, about people who take the same rock uphill, over and over. About people who can't get over the first pains. I'm thinking about calling it *Sisyphus poems for my country*."

His eyes are round, dead, expecting to be challenged, but he's warming up to his theme. "We're always waiting for deliverance to come from somewhere else."

"This is such bullshit," she says, plopping herself down in the chair by the table. "You're trying to make me crazy." She lights a cigarette. "Tu vas me rendre folle," she says.

"What?"

She's too tired to answer.

He drinks his beer. They listen to the buses go by on Spadina.

"All you ever do is attack, attack, attack," he says. "Do you know what it's like to be on the receiving end of this?"

"Please," she says, "don't bother going into your martyrdom schtick. Spare me, okay?"

"Just tell me what you want," he says.

"I want —" She just has to say it, but she's terrified, as if it will bring violence to say it. "I want this to be over."

She sees it for one brief second, the panic of loss on his face. He clutches her arm. "This cold thing in you," he says. "This cold thing."

"You made the cold thing."

"I did a lot," he says softly, "but I didn't do that."

The phone rings, cutting the thick air between them. She gets up on the third ring, grabs it on the fourth.

It's her father. Nice of him to call just then. She hasn't heard from him in months. He had gotten through to Janine weeks ago to tell her he was going to have an operation. "C'est tu sérieux?" she'd asked Janine. "C'est toujours sérieux," she said, "mais c'est jamais sérieux."

He doesn't mention the operation. He's phoning from Quebec City, from "a top of de line 'otel, dans une belle chambre, y a un bar, la télé en couleur, pis une belle vue des plaines d'Abraham." He says he's driven there with his wife, Jeanne, so they can watch the Tall Ships coming in from all over the world.

"Viens-t-en," he says. "Viens nous rejoindre."

She tells him she's working.

He says he needs to see her. "On va avoir du fun. C'est un moment historique," he says, "on reverra jamais ça."

"Okay," she says. She's hypnotized, can't refuse his voice full of need. "Okay, Papa, je m'en viens."

"You're so weird," Colin says, "when you talk to your father."

"Yeah?"

"Like young and breathless."

It goes in like a hook. She stops herself from biting. She can pack her bags. She has somewhere to go.

Christmas
1960s

*T*HE CHRISTMAS AFTER ODETTE LEFT ROGER, SHE BOUGHT her first artificial tree. The trunk looked like a green broom handle, shiny and full of tiny holes. The girls stood in the living room of their small apartment in Ville Saint-Laurent and took on the job of unpacking the synthetic branches and plugging them into the holes. They put them in every which way, not paying attention to the tagged numbers that insisted on a symmetry of long branches at the bottom and shorter ones on top.

Odette was in the kitchen, where she was taping fake holly to the handle of a glass pitcher full of viscous eggnog from a carton. She came into the living room and poured them each a glass. The girls tried it, made polite noises and put their glasses down on the mantel of the fireplace that didn't work.

The living room was a small rectangle with pocked walls and ceiling. The furniture from their old house in Notre-Dame-de-Grâce looked much too big for this room. The cold room was crowded with stuff, reminding the girls of their diminished state. Behind the pale blue curtains, which were too long for this room, a door led to a small battleship-grey balcony with a wrought-iron railing. The way Odette said "the balcony," you would have thought it wrapped the length of the building like a penthouse balcony in a forties movie.

The girls felt a responsibility not to crush the false cheer of

Odette's fantasies. They had to agree to Odette's version of things, otherwise Odette would cry, and the sound of it, like lungs going through a wringer washer, was too much to bear. But the balcony scared them both so much that they hardly ever went on it.

Claudine didn't understand the construction of it. It looked glued to the building, there on the third floor, with the view of other balconies from other apartment buildings. In nightmares, the balcony cracked from the façade of the building and sent her toppling down onto the roof of a car. Over time, she became obsessed with rehearsing the fall, imagined herself hanging on to the railing and jumping the gap from the falling balcony to the doorstop. If she couldn't manage that, she thought that if she remembered to bend her knees at the last minute, she could perhaps bounce off the roof of the car like a trampoline and be saved.

Sometimes she thought she had the capacity to survive anything. She was an emissary from another planet, sent to bring on the evolution of the human race. She had been chosen, and as a chosen one, was marked for survival. At other times she thought she might be dead already, and what she witnessed as the world was le Bon Dieu's limbo, a region reserved for half-sinners and pagans, grey, flat, without a sense of her body's gravity. Just last month, right after Odette had picked them up from school in a taxi and brought them here to this apartment, she'd seen an episode of "Twilight Zone" that had shaken her, the story of a man who'd encountered an absolute replica of himself in every respect. The man became obsessed with killing his double. He did manage to kill him, with a knife, but suffered a gash to the wrist while doing so. He looked at it. He was standing in the middle of a highway. He lifted up the gap of flesh on his wrist and saw the electrical circuitry where his veins should have been. He was a robot. The double he'd killed had been his human self. Claudine took to watching her wounds very carefully.

"*Il* faut recommencer," Janine said. She looked pale, and dark-circled. Her navy blue school tunic was shiny from wear. The tree branches stuck out every which way like a TV antenna. She was trying very hard, which gave Claudine the freedom to say "c'est niaiseux." And it was niaiseux, their first Christmas without Papa, and a broom handle for a tree. Odette said, "Ça va durer longtemps un arbre comme ça." She told them she couldn't carry a real tree up three flights of stairs.

Claudine did nothing. She sat on the couch, tongue coated with eggnog, watching Janine and Maman rearrange the branches of the tree. Odette called out the numbers, and Janine found the appropriate holes. Every once in a while both of them would walk away from the tree to admire their handiwork. Maman put her arms around Janine's shoulders and told her she was going to be an engineer.

Claudine picked at the skin around her thumbs, bit tiny strips and chewed them. It was already dark, and she could smell the cooking from downstairs. Fried onions. Sour cabbage. They themselves had eaten turkey TV dinners. Odette had put orange slices and maraschino cherries on top to make the aluminum trays look more festive.

"J'ai oublié la musique!" Odette said, and threw her head back and rolled her eyes. There were little bits of dry skin on her orange lipstick, and gold bangles clinked on her wrists. She hurried over to the RCA Victor and put on Chubby Checker.

"Come on, les girls, let's twist," she said, and started to sing, "Let's twist again, like we did last summer, do you remember when? Allons, Claudine, lève-toi."

Claudine put on her shoes with the slippery soles. "C'est ça,"

Odette said. "On écrase une cigarette avec nos pieds, est on s'essuie avec une serviette."

Janine was twisting up a storm with a synthetic branch in one hand. "Like we did last summer," she sang.

Odette couldn't bend all the way down like they could, and this was very satisfying. They always laughed at her dancing. They were laughing now. Odette tried everything, and she was the one who'd taught them the twist, and brought home a limbo bar with crepe paper the color of fire, but now the twist was passé and the girls were learning the new dances, and teaching Odette. Privately, Janine and Claudine often talked about how she just didn't have it, she moved to the rhythms of another time, she tried to make everything sexy.

"Ouf," she said now. "Ouf, j'en peux pus," and sat down, laughing. Claudine stuck it out to the end of the song, to show her how effortless it was for her.

"Viens ici, Claudine," she said and grabbed her from the couch. "Ma p'tite t'as l'air triste, donne-moi un bec, pitoune."

"Maman," Claudine said. And tried to get away. But Odette brought her hand down and stroked Claudine's hair. "Maman," she said, and suddenly felt sleepy.

The song ended and Odette got up and put on *The Chipmunks' Christmas*. High-pitched voices leapt out of the gold-flecked speaker, and Odette went back to her job of reinventing the tree. Her pleading face said this is fun, this is even better than a real tree, isn't it?

Claudine started to unpack the Christmas balls. Some were ridged with blobs of artificial snow, which they'd used for the first time last year. Their father had gone crazy with the stuff because it came in a spray can. He had been smitten with aerosol cans for months. For a while their house had been alive with the sound of little balls being shaken in cans of spray paint. He was especially fond of Scotchgard, which was supposed to coat furniture so it wouldn't get stained. In a rare moment of domestic involvement, Roger had Scotchgarded the couch and chairs of the living room in the Notre-Dame-de-Grâce house. He sprayed everything, mosquitoes, windows, boots to protect them from salt, garden chairs to protect them from mildew. It was the spray era, and after Roger's interest in pushing the button and spraying died, everything came to a sad standstill. It had satisfied something in her mother, had brought on a truce of sorts. Odette had stopped hiding bottles from him. They went to see *Days of Wine and Roses* together and talked about it, and she got the money together to send him to the States to a place called Wildwood, which was said to help people "dry out." Janine and Claudine had blossomed in the truce, had helped out with things, had walked as softly as they could through the no-man's-land of their parents' rapprochement. But then something worse even than drinking had happened and the house heaved with the convulsions of that, night after night. And the bottles came out again.

Claudine wondered if her father would have an artificial tree, too. She was hot, hands sweating on the silver ball that reflected her face like a kettle. She took her school tunic off and threw it on the couch. Her mother gave her a look that said a couch is meant to be looked at without a navy blue tunic on it. So Claudine retrieved the tunic, folded it and took it to her room to the chipmunk sound of Rudolph the Red-Nosed Reindeer.

Her bed was squeezed in with Janine's. She fell into it the way she fell into water off the dock of the the cottage their mother had bought last summer, their last summer as a family.

*S*o sleepy, so tired in the radiator heat. Claudine brought her knees up, close to her chest, and closed her eyes. In that darkness, she saw her father's face in his apartment on Côte-des-Neiges.

Was he listening to the Chipmunks, too, was he decorating his tree by himself? What did he do without them? Was his apartment full of what he called "his chums?" The chums argued together. Roger would get all heated up about not being able to be answered in French at Eaton's, and a chum would say, "C'est vrai, Roger, on est pas maîtres chez nous." And they would swear together, calvaire, d'hostie de sacrament, and then the chum would apologize for doing it in front of his "belles filles." Claudine hated the awful men in his apartment building, all of them drinking, away from their wives, their children. A drinking building, that's what he'd found.

He'd nailed the wooden cabinet in his bathroom shut. Claudine and Janine both knew that there were women things in there. They could sense that a woman lived there, too, her traces removed for their Sunday visits. Was it the woman who had made her mother call him "un maudit cochon," whom Papa said Odette invented because she was crazy and green with jealousy? At night when you heard these things you saw pink pigs and green faces dancing before your eyes. All Roger said when they asked questions was, "Dis pas ça à ta mère." Don't tell your mother. And when they went home on Sundays, exhausted from worrying about Roger's drinking and driving, Odette grilled them for the bits they couldn't give without betraying him.

Last Sunday he'd taken them to see *The Sound of Music*. He left them there in the middle of the movie. He said he was going to the bathroom, and she and Janine held hands after that, afraid suddenly, while Julie Andrews raced to the top of the Austrian Alps. He didn't come back until the movie was over. They were putting their coats on. He herded them to the car and took them to the Black Sheep bar at Ruby Foos, where they sat on stools while he talked to the woman behind the bar. "J'ai des belles filles, hein," he said to the woman. And the young blond woman smiled and said, "Oui, Monsieur Beaulieu, vous avez des belles filles." And he said, "J'aime ça quand tu m'appelle Monsieur Beaulieu," and stuck out his tongue like he'd known her a long time.

The Black Sheep bar had a stuffed black sheep with curly horns guarding its entrance. He'd taken them to this bar for years, but Roger never failed to point it out to them, to deem it sufficient amusement while he drank. They'd exhausted its entertaining possibilities years ago. They were almost teenagers, almost eleven and twelve, and they wore pearly pink lipstick and nylon stockings with elasticized garters under sleeveless synthetic shifts, they teased the back of their hair a little so it stuck up in what they called their bubble cuts. They rolled their eyes at the Shirley Temple cocktails and were starting to look down on younger kids, boys in short pants and girls in frou-frou dresses. But he didn't see any of that, he didn't see they were growing up.

After eating Chinese food, he took them back to their apartment and parked the car. He started to cry, then, saying, "C'est-tu beau *The Sound of Music*." And they both begged, "Pleures pas, Papa, pleures pas." He told them their mother had stolen them from him. His special girls. Claudine, who was going to be une artiste, and Janine, who was going to be une bonne mère de famille.

"Je vous aime," he said, "si vous saviez comment je vous aime. Ça fait mal, aimer comme ça."

Odette July

THE GAME WENT BADLY. SHE SLICED THE BALL, AND HOOKED it, and two of her drives ended up being dribble balls. She was carrying a dead weight around, as if there had been a shift in gravity, as if the fairways were trying to trip her and flatten her body against the green grass. She hardly said a word to Walter, who drove the cart with boyish gusto. She declined to play the last nine holes, pleading tiredness, and watched him play in his pink pants and green golf shift. She could never get used to the sight of palm trees on a golf course. It was like playing on a hand-tinted postcard.

Walter is napping on the large white bed with the wooden ceiling fan circling above him, the blades throwing shadows on the white sheet that covers his body. The last thing he'd said before falling asleep was red snapper disagrees with me. Mrs. Bryce, the housekeeper, had made it for lunch, smothered in onions and curry with rice and peas. Almost hallucinating with Valium and booze, Odette had seen his face arguing with a red snapper.

After the golf game she wanted to write letters to her daughters, and she did, sitting on the balcony, watching snowy egrets swooping down into the dun-colored grass by the watchtowers. But what she wrote is a blur. Then she took a shower.

Naked now, she walks to her white-louvred dressing room,

unhooks her royal blue bathing suit and puts it on. She takes a bathing cap she's never worn, it is covered with flowers and yellow shapes like fish scales, and puts it in her see-through beach bag. She slips on her straw sandals, folds the letters she wrote to Janine and Claudine and puts them on top of her chest of drawers, by her wedding ring. She sets out for the beach.

*J*enny stands behind the bamboo poles of the bar, straightened hair pulled back tight into a pony tail wrapped with a flowered scarf. Beyond her, the sea sparkles in the four o'clock sun, the blue sky stretches to infinity. She is wiping the counter of the bar. Usually, Jenny works at the desk inside, managing the time of cleaners and gardeners. But there is so little beach traffic in the off-season that the men who usually tend bar have the afternoons off, and Jenny spends part of her afternoon waiting there for the occasional Villa La Mar denizen to drop by.

"You alone today, ma'am?"

"Yes," Odette says. Odette likes Jenny, who is Mrs. Bryce's daughter. She reminds Odette of herself, young. Jenny is always immaculately dressed, and solicitous and cheerful. She is saving up her money to study hotel management in Kingston.

Sometimes Odette can hear the phrases ticking away in Jenny's head, phrases from her era when she switched to public relations from modelling, when she promoted soft drinks and cigarettes in order to make a living. She had battalions of cigarette girls working for her in promotional campaigns. They swarmed into the prestigious balls of the Anglo winter season, the St. Andrew's ball, the Heligonian ball, where debutantes with broad shoulders and too much face powder found their husbands. Those were heady days for Odette, mastering the lessons of Dale Carnegie, teaching the young women whom she hired how to listen, how to think positively, how to marry a product to human flattery. It was so easy for her to fool the world, but afterwards, she couldn't help but have contempt for the men who paid her to delude them. Such fools, all of them.

Jenny's got it, she's got the moves and the put-on lacquered face. Put on a happy face, the customers are always right, make them feel special, be a good listener, nod and smile. But there's something soft underneath, something soft in her body. The air around her gives. Odette always thought she would break if she stopped trying to please.

"A rum and orange juice, ma'am?"

"No, not today. Jenny, I want to go snorkelling."

"Alone, ma'am?"

"Yes."

"Not recommended alone, ma'am."

"I'm not going far. I'm just going to the reef."

"I dunno, ma'am."

"Well, maybe I won't go that far, maybe I'll just stay by the shore. Practise my breast stroke." Odette demonstrates a feeble breast stroke, even though she is a strong swimmer, always has been.

Jenny is looking at her funny.

"I need the snorkelling stuff, Jenny. Can you please get it for me."

Jenny walks to the big wooden padlocked box behind the bar, takes her huge key ring out of her belt, selects a small key and opens the lock. She looks back at Odette. She takes out black flippers, a blue mask with snorkel. Odette looks at Jenny's feet in yellow espadrilles.

The sun on the sand is blinding. Did she say thank you, can't remember now, hurrying, feet burning, rushing to get to the wet part of the sand. The sun works at erasing her head, swiping her head off with the glare it picks up from the white metal tables dotted here and there on the sand.

Odette wants water to surround her limbs. That's all she knows. She longs for the tingle of salt around her mouth, the way she has of letting in a little salt water and spitting it out, like a clam, breathing. She looks back to see if Jenny is watching her. Jenny is on the bar phone, oblivious to Odette's struggle to adjust the black straps of the flippers.

They are huge and ridiculous on her feet. Bending now, spitting into her mask and then rinsing it, Odette feels the sun beating on her back. She adjusts the mask over her flowered bathing cap. Time to bite into the mouthpiece. Now, walk, she says to herself, walk into the water. She walks in up to her knees, bends, and embraces the water in the shallowest of dives.

The shock of the cool water on her face wakes her up a little. It gives her a burst of energy. She swims fast, with strong strokes to get beyond the surf. She can hear her breath as she sucks the air down into her mouthpiece. She can hear it in her ears, her breath is inside her skull. Her flippers have stirred the fine sand, at first she can't see anything, then she sees the clear sandy bottom all around her.

Her legs are awkward with the extra pressure the flippers exert against the water. For the longest time, her breath sounds like someone else's breath in her ear. For the longest time, she sees herself as one-dimensional, flattened between sky and water.

She has swum beyond the surf so she can relax now, arms extended, clutching the blue Caribbean in a slow crawl. She lets herself drift, feels her body relax, give in to the water. The water is as warm as bathwater. She closes her eyes, bobs in the small waves, just like the small waves you can make in a bathtub. She sees her grandmother's face, vague now, some silvery halo, long teeth, her face when she was very little, yes, she was in a bathtub and her grandmother was standing above her. She was little and her grandmother was saying your mother's gone back to Halifax.

The heaviness there, the sleepy heaviness while she bobs up and down. She could go to sleep, right here, right now.

Swimming towards the reef, using the breast stroke, Odette bites down hard on her mouthpiece. She thinks of all the ships that must have foundered there, split hulls spilling chained human beings into the waves. She saw an engraving of a scene like that in a museum in Kingston last year. It was not something that belonged in a picture, not something that could be cross-hatched and framed.

The sandy bottom is gold from the sun that streams down through layers of water. But suddenly a curtain has dropped, the golden light vanishes. The sandy bottom turns grey, almost muddy. Confused, Odette looks up. The water streams from her mask, the shore bobs into view, white sand and green vegetation shot through with dots of dull color, palm trees with rusty-colored coconuts, roofs, umbrellas, satellite dishes. The tinny sound of reggae carries over the waves, as does the smell of vegetation burning. It is dark without the sun. The darkness brings the chill out of the water and breeds fear. She imagines a huge hand grabbing her legs and pulling her down into the darkness.

Should she go forward or backward? She thinks of drowning as a seizure, as something sudden, uncontrollable, a seizure of doubt about belonging, as if a bird suddenly lost faith in its wings and plummeted, that's what it must be like, to doubt buoyancy for one second and then panic and thrash and swallow the ocean for air. I will bring it on, thinking this way, breathing too fast. The hand in the water. A huge hand. She is gasping, can't seem to get enough air. The mouthpiece feels like a hand across her mouth.

The sun reappears, floods the water with benign golden light, bounces off the whitecaps forming at the reef to the east of Odette, illuminates the brightest ribbon of turquoise around the shore.

She floats, her breathing returns to normal. Too many bad pictures. Craning her neck, Odette checks the distance to the reef, puts her head back in the water. The bottom has dropped. She is floating over a huge bowl of darkness, sleepy again, letting go of her stiff fear.

She snorkelled here once, the first winter they stayed at Villa La Mar. She came out to the reef with Walter in a glass-bottomed boat. She had been so afraid then, of sharks, currents, lampreys, of brushing against the sharp spines of unknown molluscs. Walter had stayed in the boat and all the time she swam above the reefs she had been conscious of him watching her, waiting to laugh at her awkwardness. He had not laughed, as far as she knew. When she got back in the boat, telling the young skipper that she had thoroughly enjoyed herself, she had seen herself in Walter's mirrored sunglasses. A squashed version of herself, with a huge belly, against white clouds.

She had not wanted to snorkel then. She had wanted something else, to float in a boat by herself, small, protected, lying down soaking up the sun in a shell, yes, that was it, she had had this childish fantasy of being a Thumbelina set adrift in a walnut shell.

Now she watches the bubbles forming around her fingers, the water like jelly in her hands, hears her own breath sucking air out of the blue sky into her mouth, her lungs, filling her chest with buoying strength. Sometimes she can hear her feet crashing against the surface in the webbed slap of flippers, sometimes the passage is smooth, all is warm jelly.

The bowl of darkness ends in a wall of black coral. She is afraid of scraping her belly open, but the wall is farther down than it appears. Here is another bowl, defined by perimeters of coral, all kinds of coral, coral that grows in twisted branches, in coils like brains.

She lets herself float above it, bobbing with the waves that have picked up from crashing against the reef. Then she takes a deep breath and dives through layers of cool water. It is as if the pressure of her body in this bowl flushes out every bright fluttering creature that has found its way here. Schools of parrot fish dart before her eyes, swim with great speed away from her looming body, then, suddenly used to her, circle back. The water is teeming with translucent fish, their tiny skeletons visible beneath their scales. Electric-blue fish separate and dart away as she swims towards the bottom, amazed at the plants growing with all the ease and decorative spacing of a botanical garden. Holding her breath, ears popping a little, Odette thinks, all this hidden away, no one can see these riches without going down.

Then she sees it. Tries to blink it away, but it's still there. Something brown and orange, like a bloated hunchback caught on a coral alcove.

She pushes herself off coral and swims as fast as she can to the surface, legs thrashing, gasping for air.

Oh my god, oh my god, oh my god.

Not that.

No.

The water in her mouth, full of death.

But before she realizes what she's doing, she's gone back down straight for it. It becomes more angular, the closer she gets, less like the bloated body of a man. She is almost out of air by the time she gets to it. But she touches it with both her hands, grasps it, and pulls it from the coral. It's nothing but a rusty old anchor covered in orange tarp. She has broken the coral behind it. She picks up the piece of coral and ascends, holding it with one hand, swimming with the other.

Panting, she breaks the surface. In the sun, the piece of coral is pale and pink and layered with spirals. Skeletons. She had thought she was going to see a dead body, and she'd brought back this, the skeletons of tiny creatures, sharp and beautiful in her hands.

Claudine August

*H*ER FATHER HAS A SCAR ON HIS THROAT NOW, SINCE THE operation. He wears it like jewellery. It is pale and crooked and begs for a question. But otherwise it's the same. The two of them, father and daughter, tongue-tied, with Jeanne fussing in between.

*O*n the train from Toronto to Quebec City, Claudine read *A Passage to India* to escape the dread she always felt going back to Quebec. She wanted to like the book because it was supposed to be good, and she tried very hard not to succumb to the hypnotic telephone wires looping up and down along the track, to that hypnotic marking of time above sad, dusty chicory and limp goldenrod. She tried hard to stay in the prejudiced intrigues of colonial India, but the passage where Miss Quested went into the caves kept confusing her. What had happened in the caves? What was the terrible echo she heard? Why wouldn't Forster say?

Claudine still expected to find out how to live from books, but she no longer read in French. Had not for years. In French the words exploded, leaving her sad and defeated, the same feeling she had when she went back to Montreal. It wasn't really Montreal she was afraid of, not the real Montreal floating in the St. Lawrence with its network of bridges, its mountain peaked by an electrified cross, not the real Montreal of Sherbrooke Street and Sainte-Catherine Street or even of the Main, all spiffied up with boutiques and restaurants now, but still smelling of slaughter and sawdust and gravestones. Montreal wasn't a real place anymore for Claudine. It was more like a plain with a crater at the centre. A collar around the neck that tightened as soon as she saw the tin roofs shining in the sun, the steeples, the sorrowful backs of Saint-Henri houses leading into the heart of the city.

It was her tongue, tied. The way it had been on the phone with her father. She could say the words, she could think the thoughts, but her tongue was numb, big, twisted in the wrong directions from speaking English all these years.

They had gone over the border now, you could tell by the churches and the flashing tin roofs. Claudine put her book away in her black bag. She closed her eyes. She let the train take her away, let herself feel the pleasure of moving without willing anything. In the babble of French and English around her she thought she heard her father's voice saying, c'est un moment historique, un moment historique, to the steel rhythm of the train. That was the last thing he'd said on the phone to entice her to come and see ships from all over the world sail into the harbour of Quebec City. "C'est un moment historique, on reverra jamais ça."

For her father, history had always been something that other people organized. Something borrowed. Something that dragged you out of the house. When the Queen first came to Montreal he had dragged the girls to an Outremont street and made them wave Union Jacks and fleurs-de-lis at a crowned dot in a convertible.

Years later, after Odette married Walter and they lived in his Westmount house and the bombs started going off in neighboring mailboxes, Roger went into a separatist phase. Made bombs of his own rage. Told the girls that Walter should watch himself "dans son gros Cadillac." It was always like that, he took things from the world and wrapped his needs around them. Everything became urgently his, a manifestation of himself in the alchemy of the world.

Claudine slept right past Quebec City and woke up at Sainte-Foy with the word histoire in her mouth.

Her father stood on the platform with Jeanne. He was wearing a navy blue blazer with brass buttons, a white turtleneck that stretched over his belly, and white polyester pants. Jeanne, blond and grassette still, wore a red cotton dress with little anchors on it. The wind made the dress cling to her thighs.

"Allo, Claudine," he said, and kissed her on the lips with tight, held-together lips that made her go dead. And then he looked at her face and said, "Why did you cut your hair, mon pitou?" And then he looked at her legs and her feet in sandals and asked why didn't she wear des bas de nylons. And then he looked at her from top to bottom and said, "T'es bien mal emmanchée."

And they got into his car with the spring bouquet deodorizer, and the VacLite handy for ashes and crumbs and the magnetized token holder for the booths on the autoroutes.

Claudine sat in the back. They drove in silence, cushioned by the soft velvety interior. Her father was breathing hard from putting her suitcase in the trunk, and it reminded Claudine of how he used to sound when he took them to church on Sundays, so hung-over, breathing hard, rolling on the balls of his feet. Odette always slept, Sundays. He fixed roast beef and Shirriff instant potatoes, shaking shiny flakes like detergent into a bowl. He made them chef hats out of teatowels. "On a du fun avec Papa, hein, les p'tites," he said, again and again, and they fake-laughed, greedy for attention.

Jeanne turned the radio on, fiddled and found an easy-listening station, lots of string, a brass section that had been poured through a muffler. "C'est un big band sound, ça," Roger said to Jeanne, and snapped his fingers and laughed. He turned to Claudine. She fake-laughed. He looked at her. His soft sore eyes drank her in, draining her, like a glass.

*I*t is hot on the terrace with the pink tablecloths flapping like sheets in the wind, the wind annoying Jeanne, who had wanted to sit inside.

"C'est moche, ça," Jeanne said when they walked down the three steps to the terrace of this Grande-Allée restaurant. "Laisse faire, Jeanne," Roger said, "ma fille est icitte. On est en famille." At that declaration, Jeanne sat down very quickly at the first table, removed a pink serviette from a wine glass and set about polishing the cutlery.

Her eyelids droop, her mouth is set in a moue. She is not that much older than Claudine. Roger is twenty-odd years older than Jeanne, but her grande bourgeoise pretensions weigh her face down as surely as her slate-colored eyeshadow and dark lipstick.

Claudine reads the menu. The wind rattles the sheet of paper listing today's specials. Potage cressonière, entrecôte au poivre, saumon grillé au beurre d'anchois.

Holding the menu with one hand, and the corner of the tablecloth with the other, Claudine feels precariously perched. Above their small pink table on the green carpet of this terrace, thin clouds race in the evening sky, their swift forms stretching to breaking point in fields of pale green and pink.

The wind has made them invisible to one another by dizzying their inner ears. Or so Claudine thinks, perched on her chair, holding down the pink tablecloth. Unaccountably bereft is how she feels. She wants something, the way a child wants something, with swamping intensity, dizzy with the anticipated disappointment. It comes to her that it is her mother she longs for, here in this windy restaurant. She wants her mother and father to sit together and look at her and see her.

The wind dies down, suddenly, as if to give them an opportunity to order. Roger says he can't eat salad with his new teeth. He sounds angry. The waiter, whose skinny wrists stick out of enormous white cuffs, smiles with perfect understanding. Jeanne says, "Tu pourrais prendre un bonne soup." Roger sighs.

After grilling the waiter about freshness and quality, Jeanne decides that the potage aux asperges is suitable for Roger. Roger agrees that yes, he has been known to like asparagus soup in the past even though today he is not particularly drawn to it, but is willing to have it because there is nothing else suitable for his new teeth. He orders his consolation, a virgin mary, "dans un grand verre, avec beaucoup de Tabasco, pas de céleri, du sel, du poivre, et ben de la glace."

He stopped drinking years ago. He always said it was Jeanne who got him through. He joined AA and drank up others' lives, jack-knifed out of bed when buddies found themselves trembling on the edge of a drink and called him on the phone. And then Jeanne had put a stop to that because it wasn't just men who called.

It was too late for Janine and Claudine. All of that.

Jeanne closes the menu with a flash of red nails and sparkling rings. She orders the saumon grillé, without the anchovy butter. The way she says beurre, you would think it caused leprosy. Claudine tries to make up for Jeanne's snotty tone by ordering a simple salad Niçoise in an overly familiar way. And then it is as if this ordering of food has completely exhausted them. They stare at the people walking along the Grande-Allée, at women in white blazers with gold buttons, at men in captain's hats. Evidently, the naval trend is building to coincide with the arrival of the Tall Ships into the Port of Quebec.

Suddenly, Jeanne looks like she's about to spit. "Moi, là," she says, "j'aime pas ça être servie par un pied-noir." Claudine has never heard this expression before, pied-noir, black foot.

"Pardon?" Claudine says.

"Ils sont partout maintenant," her father says. They both look distraught. That Roger imitates Jeanne imitating what she thinks the upper classes do and say, horrifies Claudine.

Claudine drops the word racist on the table.

It is like turning on the light in a cockroach-infested kitchen. Roger and Jeanne scurry with tales of incompetence and laziness and how they are ruining everything now that Quebec is finally aux Québécois. Both talk at the same time, red-faced, veins throbbing, defending, attacking, competing. Claudine has set a jack-hammer in motion and it is out of her control now. The litany is fierce. Québécois, pure laine vieilles souches families are being pushed aside, and financially drained to make room for these newcomers who have loyalty to nothing and nobody. Montreal is unrecognizable. It is not like les Juifs, ou les Grecs, Jeanne says with finality. "Les Juifs, les Grecs, eux-autres, au moins ils sont propres."

Roger takes a sip of water. "Listen, Miss Big-shot from To-ronto," he says. "You don't live here no more. You live here, you can talk."

Exhausted by their outburst, Jeanne and Roger fall silent. The air between them has formed a wall. Claudine swallows. She doesn't want to argue. She wants to go home now.

The silence is oppressive. Occasionally, they each lend a hand to stop the wind from flipping the pink tablecloth. Jeanne is now cleaning grains of salt out of the cut-glass grooves of the salt shaker with her long red nails.

"Ta mère," Roger says, finally, "comment va-t-elle?"

"Ah, tu sais Maman." She doesn't have the heart to say the booze, the Valium. She tells him they are in Jamaica until the end of the month.

"Elle va pas bien, hein," he says.

Jeanne looks up from her cut-glass task.

"She's always been un peu crazee, ta mère," Roger says.

"Elle est folle quand ça fait son affaire," Jeanne says.

They want Claudine to jump in, the way she always has, by listing all of Odette's sins. She's never realized this before, how it is their form of communication, Jeanne and Roger, to exploit her wounds, to cheer her on while they get to shake their heads on the sidelines.

Roger waits. Claudine looks away. Church bells are ringing, full of promise, and in the restaurant there is the frothy sound of milk being steamed for cappuccinos. The wind has died down, and the patrons of the restaurant are adjusting their voices to this sudden stillness.

"Bon," Roger says, "on va laisser faire les bygones." He grabs his virgin mary and jerks it to his lips, drinks, puts it down on the table, and takes it up again for another gulp. "She took everything," he says.

"Roger."

"Papa."

"Ben oui. Try and stop me. You can't stop me. She kiss me goodbye, Odette, in the morning, she kiss me goodbye, just like une bonne femme kiss her mari off to work, and when I come back at night, the house is empty. Rien. Nuttin. Pas un lightbulb, not even a curtain rod. You know what dat was called, hein. La technique choc pour alcoholiques. Shock technic. I was shock, all right, I was shock. A même pris mon stéréo."

Roger is shaking. "She took everything," he says, "she took mes filles," and here he grabs the salt shaker and moves it to his right, "she took ma Corvair," he grabs the pepper mill and moves it to the left, "and she took mon stéréo." The stereo is the sugar bowl. Roger looks at the neat row he's created. "C'est de la folie, ça. De la folie."

The waiter comes with the asparagus soup, the saumon and the salade Niçoise. Roger puts everything back in the middle of the table.

"Bon, on va manger," Jeanne says, and squeezes lemon on her salmon. Juice squirts across the table.

"I don't remember," Claudine says, wiping her face with the pink serviette.

She is chewing an egg yolk. Her father is slurping the soup so fast the bowl looks like a sink, draining. Jeanne is happy with deboning her saumon, brandishing delicate bones up to the light with her beautiful nails.

"You were too young. Now you can understand," he says.

"I was not too young. J'avais dix ans. Somebody picked us up at school by taxi and we went to an apartment, and we never saw our house again."

Odette made things vanish. She made herself vanish with her rage. Claudine has never seen it before, the rage she must have felt to punish him like that, to not even care about her children enough to temper the joy of inflicting pain on Roger. Claudine is beginning to understand this. Living with Colin has taught her that at least.

Roger is almost finished his soup.

"Pis that grandmère," he says, "she was furious at what your mother did the summer before."

He is speaking English because he thinks it has more force, more factual weight.

"Quoi?"

"Les pillules, là. Comme Marilyn Monroe."

Claudine's body turns to ice. The heat of August is a movie screen sham; it is really February, and she is on a terrace, hands frozen to silverware, feet paralysed on a foot of snow.

"Tu dois te rappeler de ça," he says, slurping the last of his soup. "It was the summer Marilyn Monroe died."

Claudine says nothing.

Jeanne says, "Elle était une belle femme, Marilyn Monroe."

"Oui," Roger says, "c'était une ben belle femme. Une belle blonde."

Jeanne is a blonde, just like Odette.

Claudine feels sick. "Excusez-moi," she says and spits egg yolk into her napkin and bolts to the bathroom.

Roger rented two rooms in the Concorde hotel, a tall tower behind the Grande-Allée.

They spent most of the afternoon at the port looking for a parking spot. Claudine had wanted to walk, but her father had insisted on driving, and there was much traffic, and few spaces. From the parking lot, they saw the masts of a Tall Ship flying the Dutch flag.

Her father started to curse the City of Quebec and the government of Quebec for not providing enough parking spaces for such an international event.

"Arrête de t'énerver," Jeanne said. Roger finally stopped a policeman and said he was here with his daughter all the way from Toronto, and he couldn't find a parking space, it was a national disgrace. The policeman advised him to go back to la Haute Ville and take a taxi.

Roger said he was too tired to do that. He needed un p'tit café pour se remonter. So they drove to a café near the port and sat on black metal chairs in a greystone courtyard. When Jeanne went to the bathroom and they were alone for the first time since Claudine arrived, he turned to her and said, "Ma pauvre p'tite, t'as pas l'air heureuse."

She couldn't say anything. He said a father could sense things like that, that's why he'd called. She could always talk to him. He'd always been a chum, not like a father. He would rather be a friend, he said, at their age they could be friends.

He took her hand and squeezed it.

Her throat felt tight, paralysed.

"Dis-moi," he said, "qu'est-ce qui se passe?"

"Papa," she said.

"Moi," he said, "je t'ai toujours compris. T'es sensible comme moi, tu a l'âme d'un artiste."

Jeanne came back just then, lipsticked and powdered. "Les artistes," she said, "ils faut qu'ils mangent comme tout le monde."

Roger said that was the reason he had not become a musician. His father had said ça se mange pas de la musique. He had wanted to play the drums when he was young, he said it was the only time he had ever been totally happy, when he had sat behind les gros drums and bashed out what was inside of him.

"C'est pour ça, la jeunesse. Mais il faut grandir, n'est-ce pas, Claudine?"

He said to Jeanne that when Claudine was young she made the most beautiful paintings, she had so much talent. He said he didn't understand why she made those films, ces trucs, là, with so much ugliness in them.

"Les gens veulent pas voir des trucs comme ça," Jeanne said.

"Mais non," Roger said. "On veut pas se faire garrocher ça en pleine face."

"Mais c'est mon travail," Claudine said. "Mon travail."

She wanted to rush out of there and call Colin and say you wouldn't believe, you wouldn't believe what they said. And call Janine and hear her laugh it away, saying what did you expect? On the phone, she'd said, "I don't know how you can go there. It's beyond me."

Her father could tell she was angry. He took her arm to walk back to the car. She watched her sandals on the cobblestones. He said, "Abandonne-moi pas, Claudine." She looked up. He had tears in his eyes.

She starts calling Colin at ten-thirty that night from the piano bar downstairs in the hotel. Jeanne and Roger went up to their room after dinner. She went up, too, but came back down, and now sits at a table in the dark maroon bar and orders a beer. The place is almost deserted. A woman with kohl-rimmed eyes is singing Claude Léveillée songs while playing the shiny black piano at the far end of the room. There are small mercies, Claudine thinks. At least I don't have to listen to "Send in the Clowns."

The singer ends her set with "Georgia," which sounds wonderful with a French accent, Georgeea on my mind, and the light is beautiful on her pale face. Claudine orders another beer and takes it to a phone booth at the entrance of the bar, and makes a collect call. There is no answer, the operator says, over and over again, no answer, please try again.

She has another beer, and then goes up to her room because a guy sitting at the bar is sending her those aren't-you-lonely looks. Tries calling again. No answer. She sprawls on the big bed with its orange and yellow-flowered bedspread. Her room has an autumnal theme. Everything in it is rust or mustard. She turns on the TV and stares at a man with a huge forehead and a tiny goatee. He is explaining how Tall Ships are constructed. He has diagrams. He is an expert. Of course, he says, the original Tall Ships had none of these amenities. The interviewer concludes the segment by saying that the history of this continent began with "le vent qui avait gonflé les voiles de ces grands navires." And on the soundtrack a voice sings, "Il était un petit navire, qui n'avait ja-ja-ja-mais navigué, ohé, ohé."

Her father used to sing that on car trips. He was the only one who could ever lead them out of the first verse.

There are bits of peanuts between her teeth. She'd eaten them in the piano bar, while drinking her beer. She undresses, looks at the time, one o'clock, the bars are just closing, he should be home soon. She walks to the bathroom, brushes her teeth, looks at herself in the mirror. She is pale, like she was as a child. She lights a cigarette. She's smoking too much. She's got to stop, her lungs feel like charcoal.

By three o'clock, she's still dialling. She's past the embarrassment of having to go through the operator at the front desk. She puts in a call every fifteen minutes. By four o'clock, she's spiralled down to imagining Colin's death, tried to grieve for him, but it was hard to do while plotting his murder.

She had told him she wanted it to be over. But something in him had been scared, and he'd held on in the morning before she left and said don't go, we can work this out. Call me as soon as you get there. Why does he say these things, why does he always do something to keep the hope alive?

By five o'clock she is lying down on the bed, still as a statue, the hum of the air-conditioning like cotton in her ears. The beers have worn off. She is in the throes of imagining scenarios for Colin. She has been split in two, part of her on the bed, part of her living out a phantom life. That's what her documentaries are, phantom lives. That's what living with Colin is like, his lies, his secrets, phantom lives she has to imagine, so that she can feel part of something. He used to call her a voyeur, and she is, but it is not a choice. She's always had this, and only this, the ability to see inside other people's skulls, and predict what will happen by becoming them.

She can see him now, and Sally. Maybe he's unhooked the phone, or else he's letting it ring. They've been there all day. They're tired now. She can see it all.

*S*ally is sitting cross-legged on the bed. They've been in bed most of the day. They went out for lunch around three o'clock, spring rolls and beer at the Rivoli, where Sally waitresses part-time, when she's not acting, which is often enough. They took her dog with them, Sally never goes anywhere without it, and now it is tied to the doorknob, sleeping peacefully in the heat of the hall. Colin didn't want any dog hairs in the loft and he had to think up some excuse about allergies.

Would he even think of that? Probably not.

Now that it's almost nighttime, Colin and Sally are weak-kneed from spending so much time in bed. They've gone from flushed to enthralled to giggly, to sad. As if they couldn't absorb one drop more but are determined to be together until some very bitter end.

The sky is bright pink through the large casement windows, and the place is full of bluebottle flies, huge ones, iridescent, buzzing around Sally's sweaty head. Colin can't be bothered to install the little half-screens Claudine bought at the hardware store. The sound of the traffic through the open windows is almost deafening, with buses exhaling like tired dinosaurs, and streetcars grating on steel tracks.

Colin is eating a pear, cross-legged, facing Sally on the bed.

"Pretty soon," he says, "Twinkies will be healthier than fruit."

"I don't think in that way," Sally says. She's twenty-three, and almost completely devoid of humor. "I," she says, "eat symbolic fruit." A fly lands on her hand. She looked at it for a while, as if it were a visitor from another planet. The tickle of its movement gets to her and she flicks her wrist up in the air. "I mean," she continues, "and I know it sounds crazy, but I think that if you banish toxins from your mind, they don't affect you."

"That's the silliest thing I ever heard."

"Are you calling me silly?" The fly lands on her breast.

"No. I mean. Yes. I mean, what you said, not you."

"Don't call me silly."

He looks at her as if she was very far away, a figure that should never have ended up in the foreground.

"I just meant," he says, trying very hard not to sound condescending, "that it's silly to pretend that physical reality doesn't exist."

She nods, then looks away. "I didn't say it didn't exist, I was talking about transforming physical reality."

"And how do you propose to do that?"

"Through energy, through feeling, thinking energy. Things can change without our will. There can be chain reactions in the universe that may not seem connected to us, because we are changing, too, and can't see the connections. But everything is connected, and what we think and feel has an effect on material reality."

"Sally."

"Yeah."

"Kiss me. Kiss me here, and the energy will come out there. You are so beautiful, Sally. So beautiful. Long tall Sally."

"The way you talk," she says, "makes me feel like I don't exist." She looks embarrassed. She wants to laugh. He's like her father, who is forever quoting movie lines, or humming Gershwin while breaking the shells of lobsters on his wife's special gourmet nights.

"Sorry," Colin says, and closes in on himself. He can't help it. It is true that the lines come out of him like ticker tape, that he has no control over what was put in his psyche. Saying you are beautiful to a she is supposed to soften a she. This she, however, is young and prickly; she has yet to be defeated. Unlike older women, she doesn't carry a lot of baggage that can be used to climb on. Her favorite words are clean and clear. That doesn't leave Colin much room to manoeuvre.

"You don't get it, do you?" she says.

"Yeah, I get it. I get it, Sally." He wants to say rewarmed physics platitudes are not beyond my capabilities. There isn't a soul on Queen Street who isn't applying theories of physics to dance, performance art, theatre and poetry.

"No, you don't get it," Sally insists.

Ah shit. If it's going to be this hard, he'd rather be writing. About her and what she does to him, about this moment here, with the pear slimy in his hand, with her sitting cross-legged on the bed, a strand of her blond hair falling over her mouth. He'd rather be imagining her as a schoolchild, sucking on a strand of hair in a classroom, mesmerized by the minute hand of the clock over the door.

And then he realizes what it is about her that attracts him so. She looks like a Havergal girl. Now that he's identified it, he can almost see the kneesocks, the bloomers. She has the snub nose and square jaw of those upper-class girls, the blunt look of privilege, teeth white and orthodontic, bones set by good food and expensive camps.

He'd grown up with those trappings, going to school at Upper Canada College, dating girls from Bishop Strachan and Havergal, but the secret inferno of his parents' marriage, his father's drinking and shady financial dealings, the violence of his temper, had made a mockery of privilege. Dancing against those girls so long ago, he'd felt tainted somehow, not up to their pure, untouchable standards.

While he had wanted to melt into them, he couldn't cope with the other side of his lust, the side that anticipated rejection. His anger made him want to erase those straight white teeth and rip the gold charm bracelets full of baby booties and royal coins from their big field-hockey wrists. It had proved so easy to tarnish their clarity with the lies he carried.

Is that true? Is that it?

"What's wrong?" Sally says. Her eyes are serious.

"What do you mean?"

She gets out of bed. She finds, then puts on, her white cotton underwear and her orange bermuda shorts. "Your aura is very angry." Now she's buttoning a short-sleeved white blouse with pearly buttons.

"My what?"

"You know what I said. Your aura. Do you know how broken it is? It's full of holes, and right now your aura is, like, black and blue."

He laughs. "Sally, I had no idea. Must be the drugs. Must be all the acid I did."

"Don't make fun of me. I know things you'll never know. I could do things. To you." It is dark now, there is something sad in the white light of the furrier's workroom across the street, it is like an old winter feeling creeping into the August heat. Just as Sally starts to wrap a long black western belt twice around her waist, the phone rings.

"I'm a witch," Sally says.

"I'm not here," Colin says, "I'm not answering."

"I remember," Sally says, over the ring of the phone, "being tortured. They made me chew and swallow a long rag because I wouldn't confess. I had to swallow and swallow, and when they pulled it out of me, inch by inch, it was like being turned inside out."

"You remember? What do you mean, you remember?" The phone is still ringing, it's the sixth ring, it must be Claudine checking up on him. "Excuse me for a minute," he says and walks over to the phone, unplugs it, and crawls back into bed.

He can feel Sally looking at him, it makes him conscious of his nakedness, his age, compared to hers.

"I shouldn't tell you these things," she says. "You're stuck in one version of the world."

"I'm a writer," he says. "I believe in versions."

"There's something dead in your eyes, you know."

Ah Christ. "I'm just tired," he says. This is bullshit. He wants her to go away now, so he can relive the sex in peace. If she doesn't stop this witchy bullshit soon, he's going to have to start cutting her up in little pieces. He can feel himself going to that place with the paring knife and the crushing vocabulary, the place where his mind is cold, superior, elegant, dangerous as a trap waiting for delicate ankles. Only Sally is not delicate. He can see that now. He wanted the Havergal girl, and the Havergal girls are not delicate.

Sally has suddenly gone white. She's shivering. "Something stops in your eyes," she says. "There's eyes you can look into and it's like opening one window after another. I thought you had that." Her teeth are chattering. The dog starts whimpering from the other side of the door. "I've got to take her for a walk," she says, turning away while adjusting the straps of her straw bag on her shoulder. "I've gotta go."

"Do you want me to come with you?" he says. Now that she's going, now that her face is pale and vulnerable, he wants her to stay a little while longer. There's something so sad and tired in both of them, something he doesn't want to be left alone with. He grabs a roach from the ashtray by the bed.

"I have to go and be by myself," she says.

His body feels glued to the bed as she walks towards the door. She seems to get bigger, not smaller, as she does this. He lights the roach, inhales deeply. He could turn it around, in the old days he would have had the energy to turn it around.

"Sally?"

"Yeah?"

"Where you from? Originally, I mean."

"Leaside," she says, and starts closing the door behind her, but then opens it again. She's transformed, there's color in her cheeks, she's beaming with the friskiness of her dog, who is leaping up on her. "You should answer your phone," she says, "you never know what you could be missing."

She slams the door. And then, in his stoned state, Colin thinks he hears her skipping down the hall, like a little kid. But it isn't skipping. It's her dog's claws clicking and sliding on the cement of the hall.

Colin is exhausted now. Never used to get so exhausted. If he'd said the right things, or done the right things, he could have kept Sally from going, he could have kept her enthralled, the way he had in the beginning, with his shiny intelligence, his experience, his burning honesty, but mostly with his uncanny ability to stick pins and burrs into her confident exterior. She always came back because he was the only one who could remove what had hurt and stung and scraped by offering the flip side of the equation, the most idealized glamorized portrait of herself Sally Richfield could ever have wished for.

Who are we talking about here?

But he's getting sloppy now. Thirty-five. Too old to care that much one way or another. It was all material. All of it.

He used to be able to do anything, used to be able to turn any situation around. Nowadays, though, things are tougher. Everything looms large and heavy as a tanker, and everybody knows how long it takes to turn a tanker around. Turning a tanker around is one of Colin's two most favorite analogies for life. The other is how the Viet Cong would lie down across barbed wire as a causeway of flesh their comrades could cross. He often sees himself as that human causeway, flattened and bleeding on the barbed wire, a sacrificial offering to Canadian culture, a creator who is making it possible for future generations to thrive, generations who even now, if Sally is any indication, have no inkling of how empty and dull and dead colonial Toronto used to be before his generation, well maybe not his exactly, but close to it, seized the day.

Lying in bed, sweating, Colin can sense something stirring in him, a wave of words swimming into the yellow light of low-wattage bulbs around him. With a lazy arm and hand, he feels for the Player's by the bed, takes one, lights it. Feeling the short panting breaths of his stoned lungs, Colin takes out his green spiral notebook, uncaps his pen and writes Witches of Leaside at the top of the page. He underlines it. He takes another drag if his cigarette, inhales, and realizes he's exhausted. He got the title. He needs a little nap now, to dream the story.

Sally's parting words have stuck in his mind. He plugs the phone back into the jack, crawls into bed, bunches up the sheet into a ball, hugs it to his sweaty chest, and drifts off.

*L*ying on her hotel-room bed, Claudine dials one last time. It is five-thirty in the morning, the light is pearly white outside her hotel window. She got it all wrong. There's still no answer.

Odette August

WESLEY IS A JUMPY DRIVER. HE HAS A SKINNY NECK AND LONG skinny limbs and puffy eyes that fail to read the protective coloring of Odette's wealth. Instead of waiting for a red-plated regulated taxi to come from Hotel Americana, Odette hailed the first gypsy taxi she saw while standing at the Villa La Mar gates, and now she regrets her impatience. She's stuck with Wesley in a car that pumps exhaust through the floor, and the heaviness that's plagued her for the last while is back, pinning her limbs to the car seat. So tired. She wants to mail the letters she wrote to Claudine and Janine, cheery letters telling them she misses them. They never write. They never phone. They never even remember her birthday.

She has not slept well. She dreamed that a big man was smashing the delicate louvres of their condo with big fists, and there was nothing she could do about it. In the dream, she kept trying to scream help, but nobody heard her. Nobody protected her. She shook Walter awake. "Something's happening," she said. "I don't feel safe." He told her to go back to sleep in a flat, groggy voice. "Maybe they poisoned the dogs," she said. "And that's why they're not barking." She'd read about it in *The Gleaner*, about thieves putting arsenic on raw steak for the guard dogs.

But this morning everything looked normal.

This morning she'd looked at the piece of coral she'd plucked from the reef, and felt a kind of secret pride there, that she'd swum with it all the way back to the beach. She decided to go somewhere, anywhere, without Walter. Walter never goes out of the compound unless he's armed with a list that has at least five items on it. This morning he sat on the bed in his blue boxer shorts and held a large canvas shoe out in front of him. "Need new shoelaces," he said. "These are frayed." And then he wrote shoelaces in his big script on a steno pad. That was the third item on his list, after nose drops and Pepto-Bismol, which he guzzles any time the housekeeper uses spices in her cooking. When there are five items on the list, they take the rented silver Toyota into town, which gives Walter the opportunity to scream at Jamaicans with impunity. In Montreal, he cursed the Pepsi pipsqueaks; in Jamaica, he curses the goddamn lu-natics. On these outings, Odette keeps her foot on an imaginary brake, pressing as hard as she can on the floor when Walter passes buses and mini-vans.

But now she's got the gypsy taxi to worry about, and Wesley, who is the first Jamaican she's instinctively disliked. They are bouncing through the outskirts of town, behind a bus belching black smoke, stopping for chickens and goats and carts of melons and bananas. Wesley drives on the stop-start model, braking and accelerating his way through the peopled road. Odette looks for his eyes in the rearview mirror. Her neck is whipping back and forth, surely he can see what his driving is doing to her. He is looking at her with bloodshot eyes, eyes that don't see her, so she looks down to the long plush thing hanging from his mirror.

She does not want to know what it is. It is all a dream, all of it, a technicolor dream magnifying her every fear. In this dream place, where everything grows at an alarming rate, where vegeta-tion has to be burned, fought back, Odette survives by trimming down her own reality.

Today, before leaving the compound, she had to talk to Mrs. Bryce about her cooking. Mrs. Bryce was sitting at the kitchen table listening to the obituaries punctuated with organ music on the radio. Mrs. Bryce looked up. Odette said, "Mrs. Bryce, my husband." She couldn't go on. She suddenly felt naked in her bathing suit. The kitchen is like occupied territory, full of mysterious bits of things wrapped in clean rags, bits of coconut flesh and packets of herbs. Odette tried again. "Mrs. Bryce, if you could please try and cook plain food for my husband." Mrs. Bryce nodded. "Yes, ma'am." And then she said, "Di master, ma'am, di master i' full o' bile. Pepperleaf wi bruk you bile," and she handed Odette a packet of herbs. Pepperleaf, presumably. Odette smiled and said thank you ever so much, Mrs. Bryce.

Odette closes her eyes, grateful for the Valium she took after her shower, leans her sweaty head back, and pretends she is in a carriage, going down an alley of poplars. She tries to imagine something fruity and fall-like in the air, to imagine anything that will cut through the cloying heat, anything that will take her out of her sad, heavy self — the memory of leaves burning on Sainte-Famille Street, of apples falling in the neglected orchard on the road to the Magog cottage. The smell of those apples, and how as children they loved to walk on them, to crush the rotten fermenting apples beneath their feet; it was as satisfying as cracking the thin ice of puddles in winter.

She has her plan, a perfectly reasonable plan, something any normal woman could do, she could not be reproached for it, even though Walter made her feel that it was strange to set off on her own, some strange quirk she will cure herself of if she knows what's good for her. She is hot and she is going to the caves to cool down. She is going to take the tour and come back up and have a couple of rums in the cool of the cave bar. She is going to tip well, and make it worth the tour guide's time. And then she is going to take a real taxi back, with a real driver, one certified by the Jamaican government.

She opens her eyes, sees that they're going by the farmers' market. The vegetable and fruit stands are deserted in the heat. Small girls in pretty cotton dresses sit on the laps of tired women. One woman is braiding her daughter's hair, and the little girl shoos flies away from her mother's face with a palm leaf.

The car's sudden braking pitches Odette forward. "What," she says, and then sees an elderly white man standing in the middle of the road. He is cursing in patois, banging on the hoods of slow-moving cars to make them stop. The old man has liver spots all over his neck and face, and he's carrying a small basket full of red snappers.

"Dem is backraw," Wesley says.

"Pardon me?" This old man must play baccarat, although she can't imagine it, can't imagine what this old, stooped, cursing man has to do with a game she associates with Ian Fleming, who lived here, and whose writing Walter admires.

"Baccarat?"

"Yeh mon," Wesley says, accelerating now, dodging a few of the goats who are heading towards the trash cans in front of the Ocho Rios Burger King. "We call dem backraw. In slavery days, dem whites used to whip da slave. And da slave can take no mo, an say, no mo, mastah, mi back is raw." Wesley shakes his head. "Dat's why we call 'em backraw, dem white Jamaicans."

Wesley's eyes in the rearview mirror are vacant, he's intent on getting up the steep hill. The car strains and groans in too low a gear. As they reach the top of the hill, they can see the pale blue-green water of a bay. It flashes in the sun, light hitting the crests of waves.

"Discovery Bay," Wesley says.

Odette nods, and closes her eyes again.

"Discover dis, discover dat, o'body move, everybody body move. Body move." Wesley stops singing as suddenly as he's started. "You wonderin' what dat ting is?"

Odette opens her eyes and sees his brown eyes in the rearview mirror. His buckteeth make him look hungry. Odette wipes the sweat from her eyes, tries to swallow, but her mouth is too dry. Wesley grabs the long plush thing dangling from his mirror.

"It's advertisin'," he says. "It's trut' in advertisin'."

"Pardon?"

"It's trut' in advertisin'." He laughs, flicks the long plush thing with his fingers, and then reaches for his crotch.

At first, what he says hardly penetrates her fog. And then in glimmers, as the sunlight flashes on fields of sugar cane, bounces on the hood of the car, she realizes that he must think she's one of those white women who come down south to get what they can't get at home. Odette has seen them in the bar at Hotel Americana on calypso nights, the yearning in their eyes, their pale skin, and then within a week, a look of frayed abundance on their tanned faces. Some of them stay on. Grow hopelessly freckled and despondent. "I'm not," she says, but then she is afraid of saying anything, afraid of assuming, of creating a situation. So often, she doesn't understand what Jamaicans are saying, so she smiles and tries to build bridges of affable ignorance. This doesn't seem to be called for, at the moment.

"Money back guaranteed," Wesley says. "A good ride, mon. Wesley king of the good ride. You wantin' a good ride?"

"No," she says, as simply and as gently as she can. Must never make them angry, men. Be polite, but firm. She is fifty-four years old, a grandmother, this is what she's got to get him to understand, it's all in the eyes, those messages.

Wesley's watching her, his eyes serious.

"Are you wantin' da good ride, missus? Mi know you wantin'

da good strong ride. Wesley know. Wesley de best. Wesley make you say yes."

"No," she says. "My husband." And now it's as if she is losing herself, retreating into some very old part of herself while her body sits there, hollow.

"Fifty American dollar. Money back guaranteed. I know da ladies, I know da ladies want Wesley. Sometimes a lady say no at first, but Wesley stir it up."

His eyes are mechanical and mean. He's pushing now, pushing way beyond the sale. He can feel her fear. She can tell he can feel her fear, but there's nothing she can do.

"No, thank you," she says.

She is holding on to her hands, because her hands want to reach up and hit the back of his head. Hit it and crush it. She holds on to the vinyl seat. He is so young, still a boy, she says to herself. Look, look, this is just a hungry boy.

"Mi needin' da ride," he says. "Mi needin' it bad."

The rearview mirror reflects his brown eyes. It has nothing to do with her, this cold hate in his eyes, it is what lies beyond the threshold of not caring about anything. He's stopped caring about the game of his sale, he's stepped off the edge of the deal into something ancient in himself.

Odette is shaking now, it starts in her knees and creeps up to her shoulders. Nobody would know if he dragged her off somewhere, nobody knows she's in this cab, nobody saw her leave. She can see herself in the hot sun, flies on her wounds. Nothing more. Coming to this. Her death spelled out in a tawdry headline in *The Gleaner*, picked up by wire services, carried worldwide, accountable for a small dip in the tourist industry, then forgotten. She sees everyone at Villa La Mar asking why didn't she know, why didn't she get out of the taxi, why didn't she run. And the shame on Walter's face. Only it is not Walter's face she sees now but her mother's shamed face, her mother talking about the devil, the devil.

She is heaving now. Can't help herself. Dry heaves into her hands, the tape in her head saying I'm going to die, I'm going to die. She can feel herself floating up and up beyond the roof of the car, watching herself from far away, watching the flowers of her print dress spread over her body like a funereal mantle.

"Please," she says, "please stop the taxi. I'm going to be sick."

The roof of the car is turning into a pale white ceiling, the ceiling of a room when she was so little. Something wants to come out, but she can't allow it to come out. Because it can't be true.

"Stop," she says in a dead voice. "Stop it."

Wesley stops the taxi on the dusty shoulder above Discovery Bay.

They are not far from the caves. Odette can see the sign, up the hill, above the white pillars of the gate. Slowly, pushing herself through an underwater world, she opens the car door.

Wesley opens his door and steps out so that he stands directly in front of her. His cut-off shorts are held up by a piece of twine. He is playing with the ends of the twine.

The heaving stops. For the first time she can see his face full on, a lean, young, dormant face. His dark eyes are spinning with possibilities, looking at her through a kaleidoscope, her body jumping like colored chips.

"Get away from me," she says. And then she is screaming into his face, so hard her face feels distorted, raw. "Get off of me, now, get off !"

He brings up his hands slowly. He doesn't seem to know why he's stopped here, on top of the hill. He's backed off from his game, and now he's trying to make it seem like she's crazy.

"Don't you look at me like that," she says, and crumples a ten-dollar bill and throws it in the driver's side.

"Chill out, mon," she hears him saying. "No problem." But she's already walking away, in the sunlight, feet on the ground. And after a while, when the thud on the back of her head doesn't materialize, she looks back and sees Wesley turning the car around, heading back towards town. Shaking, she walks towards the gates.

Janine
August

THE FEVER STARTED IN THE AFTERNOON. MARIE-ANGE HAD been playing in the sandbox. At first Janine thought Marie-Ange was hot from the sun, but no, she was much hotter than that, and limp, and her lips looked chalky.

Jim was out of town, giving an estimate on a renovation. Claudine was in Quebec City. Audrey, who lived across the street with her husband and twins Marie-Ange's age, was away at her mother's place.

Janine bundled up Marie-Ange and took her upstairs and lay her down on her bed. Marie-Ange was crying now, hiccupping and crying, and Janine could feel the crying in herself, and the heat of her own body. She took Marie-Ange's wet, sandy shorts off, and peeled off her T-shirt, a gift from Odette that said If You Think I'm Cute Wait Until You See My Mother. It was so embarrassing, but Marie-Ange liked it because it had a picture of a smiling cat on it.

"What hurts, honey, what hurts?" she said. But Marie-Ange looked at her blankly and pointed to her neck.

Janine gave her some Tempra and stroked her moist forehead. She started to cry again when Janine left the room to get the electric fan from downstairs. Of all things, she didn't want to be alone with this, alone with a sick child, with cries she couldn't interpret, with her mind going to meningitis and rheumatic fever and all the things that could go wrong.

"Mummy, Mummy," Marie-Ange cried.

"I'm coming," Janine yelled from downstairs, carrying the fan.

She plugged in the fan, watched the blades going around behind the silver grille, watched it turn from left to right, a giant head turning this way and that.

She lay down beside Marie-Ange and Marie-Ange clung to her pale yellow shirt with her tiny fists. It took a long time, but Marie-Ange fell asleep, a facecloth on her forehead, the fan's motion blowing back the wet tendrils of dark hair from her face. Janine gently unclasped Marie-Ange's hands and went downstairs to fix herself something to eat and to look up diseases in Dr. Spock.

*A*t ten-thirty that night, Janine is in a panic. Marie-Ange has woken up many times, and has had to be walked back to sleep. Now she is asleep, but her face is red and her chest is heaving too quickly.

She dials Colin's number. The line is busy. She tries again fifteen minutes later. It rings only once.

"Hello," she says.

"Darlin', I just got in," he says. "I missed you at the Rivoli."

"It's not Claudine, it's Janine."

"Oh, sorry, I'm confused, I just got in."

"I'm sorry. I just didn't know who else to call."

"What's wrong?"

"Marie-Ange is sick and Jim is away, she's so hot, she's burning and I don't know what to do. Should I take her to Emergency? I'm so scared, Colin. She's burning up and her breathing — "

"Okay, okay, hold on a minute here. What's her temperature?"

"She won't let me. I mean, I can't take it. I mean, she, I don't know. Tell me she's going to be okay, tell me she's not going to die."

"She's not going to die, Janine. Where is she now?"

"She's in my bed, asleep, but she's going to wake up again. She didn't sleep well last night either, I didn't know this was coming on, I'm completely exhausted."

"All right, this is what you're going to do. You're going to make us a pot of tea, and I'll be right there."

"Thank you."

Janine goes upstairs to the bathroom. Something is nagging at her, the Rivoli, that's it, he said something about the Rivoli. Is Claudine back and at the Rivoli? He would have said if she was. Strange. She takes off her yellow shirt and looks through the hamper for her white lacy camisole, which is not really dirty, just has a stain at the bottom. It can be tucked into her pearly grey skirt. She brushes her hair and puts it up loosely, like a Gibson girl, and applies a little mascara. She looks tanned and fresh. Maybe she should look tired.

Oh god what am I doing, she says to herself, smoothing her eyebrows with a finger. She tiptoes past her bedroom, peeks in at Marie-Ange. Her whole body is straining to keep Marie-Ange asleep. Please, just an hour.

In the living room, she looks around for what she should be reading. She hides the Danielle Steel in Marie-Ange's toybox, picks up Jim's book on tesselations in Escher's work, lies on the couch, plumps a pillow behind her, opens the book. The pictures make her dizzy, all those cubes and diamonds and frogs turning into salamanders. Her fingers, turning the glossy pages, are moist.

The tea, my god, she's forgotten the tea. She puts the book down and rushes into the kitchen. Can't be all made up and not have the tea ready. What would he think? It's been at least half an hour since Marie-Ange has woken up. Maybe she's all right after all. Maybe the worst is over now.

Colin has a fresh shirt on. Must be a fresh shirt, it is pale blue and not wilted and crushed by heat. He smells clean. That feels better. He's trying, too. When he walked in, after knocking softly, she had this moment, standing by the door, of feeling like a courtesan, rouged and powdered and wearing silk pyjamas. Now that they're in the kitchen, and she's pouring tea, she feels calmer, more like herself.

"I guess I kind of panicked," she says.

"It's understandable," he says. "Kids get such high fevers. But it means nothing. It means their bodies are fighting like crazy to get rid of something."

"I know. But when you're alone, your mind can go to some pretty awful places."

"Why are we whispering?"

"Not to wake her up." She pulls a chair out from the kitchen table, sits down beside him and pours two cups of tea.

"Feels like church," he says.

"I always fainted in church."

"Why?"

"You were supposed to wait three hours before swimming, I mean communion, or is it the other way around, three for swimming, one for communion? Anyway I was hungry, always so hungry, and I'd faint, my knees would buckle and I'd pitch forward, an awful feeling, isn't it, fainting, all hot and cold afterwards."

"Janine, are you nervous?" He pushes his hair back and looks straight at her.

She looks down at her tea. "No. Yes. Well, maybe a little." She feels naked in her white camisole.

"Poor darlin'," he says. "You're all worn down." He warms his hands on his tea mug, stands and walks behind her chair, puts his hands on her shoulders. "Here, here, let me do this. I think the mum needs more attention than the kid."

Her neck feels delicate, she can imagine the back of her head as it looks to him. "Oh," she says. He caresses the top of her shoulders, slips his fingers under the camisole straps and spreads them out so that they catch on her shoulder. She has gone completely still. She never ever wants this to stop. Just as she begins to relax to his touch, a slow massage carrying warm waves down into her belly, he stops, and runs a finger along her neck.

"You have a mosquito bite on your neck," he says. "Right here."

"Oh yeah?" She has to pretend it's just a massage. "I don't know when that happened, must have been when I was out in the yard."

He's caressing the back of her head now, and her hands on her lap are sweating.

"Sorry," he says, "I have to kiss it better," and brings his head down on her neck and kisses her, and then before she knows what's happened she is standing up, and he is kissing her against the kitchen counter, running his hands down her back, her breasts, her belly. She feels lost now. His hands are caressing her thighs underneath her grey skirt, and he brings one of her legs up, around him, so that she is standing like a swooning stork.

"I can't," she says, "I can't do this."

"You're so soft, so soft."

The smell of him is so familiar, some aftershave, his lips are so hungry, as hungry as hers. "Oh, we can't do this," she moans. But he takes her hands and brings her down so that they both end up sitting on the floor and she is sitting on top of him, her legs wrapped around his waist. They are pushing against each other, breathing fast now. "You're so beautiful," he says, "so beautiful." "Oh god," she says.

And then they both hear it, and she stops and goes still, but he's still pressing himself against her, saying so good, so good, so good. "I'm not like this," she says, "this is not me." He holds her away from him. "This is you," he says. And looks right into her eyes.

They are breathing so hard it's difficult to hear. "I think she's crying," she says. "Colin, listen. Listen. I've got to go up."

"Hunh, hunh," he says, hanging on to himself. "Please. Can I have a rain check."

She gets up, quickly and awkwardly, and now she's standing above him, smoothing her clothes, and she doesn't know what he means, rain check, what rain check? Marie-Ange's crying has made her body switch tracks. All of the feelings of wanting him have turned into panicked guilt. "Ah, I don't know," she says. "I don't know. I got to go."

She runs up the stairs, rounds the top banister, pulled faster and faster by Marie-Ange crying Mummy, Mummy, Mummy. The room is dark. She turns on the light. Her guilt takes in Marie-Ange, red and crying, twisted in a white sheet. "Oh, my poor baby," she says. "My poor, poor baby."

*T*hey didn't go to Emergency. Colin said that if they took her to Emergency they would just have to wait in that awful harsh light, and they'd probably just take her temperature and send her home. Marie-Ange wasn't complaining about her ears or about her throat, so it couldn't be an ear infection or strep throat. She must just be fighting off a bug.

Janine thought Colin would go home, and at first she wanted him to go home because she didn't want his eyes on her, she didn't want those kinds of eyes distracting her from giving Marie-Ange what she needed. But he didn't go home. He stayed and helped.

Marie-Ange turned into a baby, she needed to be carried and walked like a colicky baby. All night, Janine and Colin walked her in their arms, back and forth in the upstairs hall, walked her until she fell asleep. She would wake up and cry as soon as they tried to put her down on her bed. So one of them would take her into their arms and start walking again, back and forth along the hall. They had to switch because she was heavy enough now, at three, to weigh down their backs until it became unbearable. They sang to her. Janine sang "Les Anges Dans Nos Campagnes," Colin sang Bob Dylan songs without putting the angry whine into them.

She was so sick, she didn't balk to be out of her mother's arms. As long as she was moving, she was all right, pressed against a living, breathing chest that moved up and down as she had moved once, carried in the warmth of her mother's womb. When she fell asleep and they tried to lay her down, she would moan and start crying again, her arms would reach out to her mother's neck. "Mummy," she cried, "Mummy."

Janine disappeared into her, walking in the upstairs white hall, white camisole soaked with her daughter's fevered body. Colin helped by just being there, so that she couldn't spiral down into her feelings of inadequacy, of being a bad mother who didn't know what she was doing. Having him there stopped the panic. As the night wore on, it was as if they stopped seeing themselves as having any relationship beyond the one of keeping Marie-Ange moving through her fever. When they switched her from arms to arms, they nodded silently. Colin seemed grateful, in an odd way, to have a reason to forget about himself.

At six o'clock in the morning, Marie-Ange's fever broke as suddenly as it had come on. She looked up from Janine's shoulder and said down. Janine looked at Colin, who was slumped against the door of the bathroom. His hair was stringy. Sweat stained his shirt.

Janine put Marie-Ange on her feet and she ran to Colin and said where's Deen, her name for Claudine. "She's away," Colin said. "She's in Quebec City." And then Marie-Ange said she was hungry, and they all went down to the kitchen and Janine gave her a bowl of Rice Krispies. She ate that, and then pieces of apple and a banana. Then Marie-Ange crawled onto her lap and fell asleep there. Her forehead was cool to the touch.

Janine carried her upstairs, Colin following. She lay Marie-Ange on her bed and covered her. Her dark bangs were still wet from the fever and the washcloths they'd taken turns applying to her forehead. Her white skin was translucent, showing pale veins around her temples.

They watched her sleep in the early light of morning, listened to the birds singing in the chestnut tree that had been in full bloom just weeks ago.

*I*n the full morning light, Janine makes a pot of coffee, pours them each a cup, and then decides against drinking it so she can get some sleep and be fresh when Marie-Ange wakes up.

She feels shy, sitting opposite him at the kitchen table, thinking of herself as she was hours ago, moaning against his body. And him saying this is you.

In the diffuse light of the pink kitchen, he looks pale, drawn, almost hollow. Yes, that's what's in his eyes when he stops talking and gesturing and reaching for something, his eyes are hollow. She looks at him over her steaming cup of coffee and descends right down into those eyes, down to the very bottom of him, and at the bottom is a frightening emptiness. He is, she thinks, what people need at the time. Nothing else.

"I've got to go," he says.

"Thank you."

They walk to the front door. She opens it.

"Good night," he says, and tries to kiss her on the cheek, but in the awkwardness of not knowing what she wants, she twists her head and his lips end up on her ear. "I guess I should say good morning," he says.

She watches him walk away. The Portuguese woman across the

street is shaking her throw rugs as she does every morning. Janine waves. The woman looks at Colin, waves back. Janine feels an odd rush of wanting to explain, it's not what you think. But the Portuguese woman has gone back to beating her rugs on the wrought-iron railing of her porch, and Janine closes the door and goes up to bed.

Claudine August

CLAUDINE WAKES UP IN A SWEAT. THE ROOM IS PITCH DARK except for a grey band of light between the drapes of the hotel room. In her dream, Odette was drowning, and Claudine had to watch, helpless, from the shore. There was nothing she could do but watch. A tidal wave had come and taken Maman away, a wave as big as a highrise, and Claudine had almost been swept away, too.

The bed is hard, the room smells of processed air and synthetic rugs, and she is so thirsty her dry lips are sticking together. Didn't something like that happen? In the darkness of this foreign room in Quebec City everything seems upside down, unknown, shadowed. The breeze from the air-conditioner blows against the curtains, shifting a band of light on the ceiling. She could be underwater, she could be anywhere. One time Claudine had asked Janine about it, do you remember, she said, the time Maman drowned? "What are you talking about?" Janine said.

"The summer before they split up. Didn't Maman almost drown?"

"You know what happened that summer," Janine said. "Nobody drowned."

Claudine rolls onto her belly. So soft this bed, a soft siren call for more sleep. But no, she's wide awake now. She feels around the bed for the phone, because that's where the phone ended up last night.

Sitting up naked in the dark, Claudine looks at the glow of the digital clock radio on the bedside table: 7:48. She wants to call again. Why is she stuck here, with an ice pick in her belly, dialling for no answer?

She lets go of the phone, kicks the mustard-colored blankets back, puts on the oversize white T-shirt she was wearing last night, and walks to the window. She parts the curtains, and there it is, like an old deserted soccer field, the Plains of Abraham. The plains are shot through with black hoses, from which sprinklers shoot sprays of water at regular intervals, soaking the grass in the pearly light of early morning.

Soon the calèches will start moving along the road that cuts across the plains. Soon the sun will be hot and high in the sky. Soon, sleek grackles will look for worms under the wet drizzle of the hoses. Somewhere on the outskirts of the city red-winged blackbirds will trill and dart from bush to bush in the blazing light of drying marshes.

The heat will come through the cobblestones of the old city, will soften the tar of flat rooftops, bounce off the slate tiles of mansard roofs, will heat the water of the St. Lawrence, will cover the horizon in white clouds.

To walk in this great big world. To find a way of untying the knot while walking in this great big world.

Claudine opens the curtains wide, turns and sprints to the bathroom.

In the shower, she gulps the warm water to assuage her hung-over thirst, washes her hair, her armpits, her neck, her breasts, her belly, her pubic hair, her thighs, her knees, her calves, her feet. The train travel, the bad meals, the beers, the peanuts, the awful encounter with her father, the obsessive night of phone calls, all of it swirls down the drain with the water pooling at her feet.

The shower curtain has grey mermaids and pink scallop shells on it. She can't see herself in the steamy mirror. She brushes her wet hair back on faith.

*J*eanne must have heard her moving around, because there she is, face sticking out of her door, when Claudine starts walking down the hall.

"Où tu vas, là?" Jeanne whispers.

"Prendre une marche."

"Es-tu correct?"

"Oui."

Jeanne looks young and open without her make-up, without her stepmother mask. She wears a turquoise negligé, smells of Jean Naté. She smiles, and, surprised, Claudine smiles back. For one brief moment, they are simply women chatting in the early hours in a hotel hallway.

"Claudine?"

"Oui."

"Prends ton temps."

*I*n the coffee chop, Claudine eats a rancid croissant with marmalade from a package. She reads *La Presse*, leaving fingerprints of butter over a report that Lévesque is suffering from bouts of amnesia.

The waiter takes her money, says merci, à la prochaine, as if they'd spent the night dancing. Bienvenue, she says. He looks just like Jean-Pierre who used to live next door to them in Notre-Dame-de-Grâce. Dark, dark hair, and eyebrows reaching to join over the bridge of the nose. Or like Jean-Marc, her older cousin, who used to flirt at eleven years of age by giving her electric shocks with Christmas tree icicles at the Beaulieux' house in Outremont.

This city is not a city either, it is all statues and cannons, all embalmment and defence.

Even Duplessis, whose corpse used to stink of corruption, has been cast, and is now displayed on the green lawn of l'Assemblée Nationale.

Claudine walks past l'Assemblée and down to the promenade that overlooks the St. Lawrence. The city is Sunday-quiet, the sky blue. The clouds are the puffy white clouds of childhood, mysterious shapes waiting to be named lamb, angel, dragon, shapes and beings nobody over three feet could ever see. Claudine sits on a bench by a statue of Marie Rollet and her children and watches the river that figured in all of her drowning nightmares as a child. It was the only water, the only river. Les courants would take her away, they said, would take you from the shore if you so much as put a foot in, take you down to the depths where you would be dragged across lacerating rocks. You would die, never see your family again. Le fleuve tue, they said, and it did every summer, the river killed the children, just like abandoned Frigidaires did, in basements, in garages, in the pages of *Allo Police*. And the adults talked about those poor children in hushed tones, like they were little martyrs God had decided to take, and you could feel the fear of death in their voices, and it was left to you, the child, to live with the horror they tucked into their warnings.

But it is still blue, le beau fleuve St-Laurent, and it flashes silver in the sunlight, seagulls darting here and there over the moving water. There is something awesome about it, a giant artery carved into the earth, pulsing with currents.

And then Claudine sees a tall ship coming in, with huge masts and sails straining against the wind. Watching the slow progress of the ship in the river, she thinks of what it must have been like to see these ships arrive for the first time. Those who lived here did not see Tall Ships, they saw hairy bears on the leafless trees of moving islands, hairy creatures from another world coming to their shores with crosses and swords. Those creatures brought diseases, a baptizing God and a way of looking at the world that split it in half, into the good, the bad, into les européens, les sauvages, into les blancs, les peaux-rouges, the spirit, the flesh. They sanctified the spirit and raped the flesh. Salvation and damnation, that was the stubborn template she had been taught, year after year. The hatred she still feels for Catholicism surprises her. She never thinks about it in Toronto.

Claudine stands, looks up at the passive, suffering face of Marie Rollet. She remembers her name but not what catapulted her to bronze-hood. She hardly remembers the history she was taught year after year by the nuns. What she remembers is the peculiar smell of lies in the chalky rooms, suffocating lies that smelled of convent wax, the caramel-colored wax that nuns used on the wooden corridors of schools, nuns on their knees spreading the smell of purpose and hate, of control, of martyrdom and rage. And children soaking it up like thirsty, dry wood, waking up night after night with nightmares of les sauvages surrounding them with tomahawks, scalping them, skinning them alive, eating their hearts.

Claudine walks down the staircase to the bottom of the cliffs. The shops are opening now. Artisanat. Weaving for profit in colors assigned to the past, brown, beige, brown, beige.

She walks right to Place Royale as if she knew where she was heading. The church, Notre Dame des Victoires, the ice cream and souvenir shops, the restored seventeenth- and eighteenth-century houses all create an airless square tomb there at the bottom of the cliffs. No car sounds. Just a humming, as if the square were air-conditioned.

She finds a table on the terrace of the café by the church. She orders a coffee and looks at the church. It is small, grey, the kind of plain church sailors always ended up with. It rises up, singular, light blazing on either side of it, unlike the other buildings in the square, which are joined together in restored façades. Above the portico of the church is a statue of the Virgin Mary with cast-down eyes and open hands. She looks like she has just dropped something, frozen in an attitude of regret. The sun beats down on the cobblestones. When the coffee comes, she cradles the white cup in her hand, watches the dark blue shadow of her head on the white metal table.

Somebody has left something on the table. A pamphlet. From the pamphlet she learns that the remains of Champlain's habitation were found underneath this spot. They've painted white stripes over the pavement to indicate where his house was. The life below was a life of mud, of frozen ruts, a life made bearable by the steaming breath of domestic animals destined for slaughter. And below that, there was something else, too, Stadacona, an Iroquois village, a granary of corn.

So many layers. So many bones. Paved over and painted with white stripes so you can't feel the bones.

But humming like a crypt anyway. Just like memory, humming in her cold body.

August
1962

THE SUMMER MARILYN MONROE DIED, ODETTE RENTED A cottage on Lake Memphremagog where she'd spent some of her childhood summers at her rich uncle Jean's place. The girls were happy to get out of the city, it was like going outside for the first time after being sick with a fever, everything looked sharp and clear and clean. It was going to be a summer of ferns and white pines and cedar smells, of long days spent in swimming shivers and sun.

Their grandfather and grandmother were at Jean's place that summer, a white clapboard cottage farther down the lake. By the time August hit, Béribée was in the full throes of an affair. The affair was carried out by seventy-five horsepower Evinrude; every afternoon the girls watched as their grandfather's wooden boat honed in on Francine's cream and green cottage.

Francine had a daughter, Lucie, who was Claudine's best friend. All summer Claudine, who at ten was still young enough to collect crayfish in tin cans, weighed complex loyalties against the shame that had crept into Lucie's eyes. Francine's breasts were so dark that her cleavage looked black. Claudine's grandmother blanched every time someone mentioned her name.

Before they'd gone to the cottage, Odette had threatened to leave Roger, Roger had said he would kill her if she left, and then he'd threatened to leave himself, and the girls had dropped to their knees and hung on to his legs screaming stay, Papa, stay. It filtered down to the girls that they were going to a cottage with their mother so that their parents could rehearse a more devastating outcome.

Béribée, Julia, Francine, Odette, all grieved for Marilyn Monroe. Sympathy poured out of them like milk from huge milk cans, their eyes grew soft and teary, their faces opened with love. Even the priest at mass in the village of Austin had made them bow their heads in silence for her. The girls didn't get it. They looked at her pictures in *Life* magazine and saw babyflesh squeezed into tight clothes. In movies she toddled, she squeaked, she looked like she had a baby's bum on her chest, her lips pouted like she wanted a bottle. What was so important about her, what did she have that they didn't have?

*T*he weekend after she died, Roger came to visit by hydroplane. That's what started it. "Le maudit de show-off," Odette said as they all stood on the verandah, watching the hydroplane hovering over the lake. She inhaled her cigarette with a tragic mouth. Her face looked cloudy, at odds with her Tammy outfit. It was the summer the movie *Tammy and the Bachelor* came out to the small dusty cinema in the town of Magog. And Odette had taken the girls to see it three times. They all braided their hair after that, and wore red and white gingham shirts and rolled-up jeans and sneakers, and chewed pieces of grass self-consciously, offering their profiles to the sunset.

Odette looked like a girl, braids tied with bits of yarn, gingham shirt tucked into what the girls called maman-jeans. But her face was set against the hydroplane. "A big shew," she said in her Ed Sullivan voice, "a really big shew," and slammed her mother-of-pearl lighter down on her pack of Craven "A"s, and sat down on the wicker rocker by the railing of the verandah.

Janine and Claudine ran down to the dock, and all the way down the dirt path they felt pulled back by their mother's disapproval. It was like running with an elastic band tied around your waist. By the time they got to the dock, their father was already standing on one of the skis of the plane, hanging on to the wing, laughing. He had a bottle of Gordon's gin in one hand and his eyes were as glassy as the lake.

The pilot was a big man, his face flushed with broken capillaries. "Des belles filles," he said to Roger, while tying the hydroplane to the dock so Roger could unload his suitcase. Roger asked him up for a drink. The pilot said no, but Roger insisted. "Un bon p'tit coup," he said, "ça va te remettre." He made a fist when he said that, and punched it up in the air, as if a drink were so magical it could kick-start the universe itself. Then he picked up the girls and kissed them on both cheeks.

All the way up the hill, Roger looked for Odette. The girls could sense it in his sweaty palms. It was not the meeting they'd spent days imagining. Claudine thought the hydroplane would bring mother around, but it only made her angrier.

Odette sat on her chair, a forlorn Tammy, self-consciously absorbed in the black-eyed susans the girls had picked for the visit. All day, when they'd been cleaning, the girls had urged their mother's decorating spirit on as she arranged blue mason jars and antique irons on the mantel of the fireplace. But all of it was coming to nothing. They could see her face now, as they mounted the steps. She looked at the three of them as if they were a package. She stubbed out her lipstick-stained cigarette. When she finally spoke, it was in her cold voice. She said, "Combien ça t'a coûté, ça?"

But when Odette noticed the pilot, her blue eyes lit up. "All-o, Yvon," she said, and kissed him on both cheeks, very French-French gracious. Her cloudy face had opened, and she was suddenly launched into one of her French-French impersonations.

For the girls, her French from France impersonation, which surfaced intermittently, was the safest of her many impersonations because it was modelled on her friend Louise, who was kind and loving. Louise had pots of money, summered in St-Tropez when it was still a fishing village, picked lovers from Parisian boîtes à chansons, drank red wine with lunch and did yoga first thing in the morning. She was Odette's only French-French contact, even though she wasn't French-French at all, but a rich Montréalaise with bohemian tastes.

Odette's American impersonations were not so safe. She could go from Joan Crawford in *Mildred Pierce* to Marilyn Monroe in *Some Like It Hot* in two seconds flat. The mid-range was not so bad. There was Doris Day for avid innocence, and Debbie Reynolds for bouncy. But the worst thing that ever happened in Hollywood as far as their father was concerned had to be Grace Kelly's marriage to Prince Rainier. When Odette was in her Grace Kelly phase, Roger was nothing but a frog who should have been a prince.

Yvon the pilot blossomed in her French-French effusion.

"Un p'tit drink?" Odette said.

"Je ne dirais pas non," Yvon said, and smiled.

Odette went into the kitchen and came back carrying glasses with life-buoys on them.

They all sat at the little table on the verandah, drinking gin, the ice tinkling in their glasses, smoke rising from their cigarettes like distress signals.

Odette told the girls to do some découpage on the floor of the verandah while the grownups "talked." They cut out pictures of movie stars from Odette's *Photoplays* and *Screen Gems*. Janine and Claudine had to share scissors and Janine grabbed them first and started to cut out a picture of Dr. Kildare. There was an ornate frame of curlicues around Dr. Kildare's face. Janine took her time, driving the scissors with minuscule precision around every curl. Her tongue was sticking out. Claudine sat, cross-legged on the green-painted verandah, looking at the picture of Ben Casey she wanted to cut out. The frame on Ben Casey was plain.

She might as well listen to what the adults were talking about. She might find out something that would protect her later on.

"She was too good to live," her mother said.

"C'est vrai," her father said. "Too good, like an angel."

"La beauté," Yvon said, "c'est tragical. Ça fly du monde."

"En tout cas, c'était une belle femme." Her father took a big sip of gin. "Hein, Yvon, une belle femme, ben sexy, hein, pour un homme it was something, Marilyn Monroe."

They were silent after that. And then her mother burst out, "She couldn't breathe. You understand that, Yvon, don't you, a woman like that couldn't breathe. People were on top of her all the time. Wanting something she couldn't give."

Yvon looked embarrassed. His English wasn't so good and he didn't want to be left behind. "Ouais," he said, "she couldn't breed."

"Ben respirer, c'est respirer," her father said, "arrêtez-donc."

"Tu comprends rien," Odette said with a sigh. "On parle psychologie, là, Roger."

"Ah, la psychologie," he said. "She was rich, she was sexy, you're going to tell me dat's hard? She was crazy. I know dat kind of crazy."

Claudine caught her mother's eye, the sadness there, and pushed it away.

"Yvon," her mother said, "don't you think Claudine looks just like Elizabeth Taylor dans *National Velvet*? And Janine, elle, she's a young Ingrid Bergman, look at those lips. I could kill for those lips."

"Elles te ressemblent beaucoup, Odette," Yvon said.

Claudine pretended not to hear. She was sick of waiting for the scissors. She told Janine that Dr. Kildare looked like something that came back from the drycleaner's. Janine dropped the scissors. "Ben Casey, là," she said, "he's full of hair. C'est laid ça, du poil sur les mains."

"Maman," Janine said, "c'est qui le plus beau, Docteur Kildare ou Ben Casey?"

"Bien moi," their mother said, "je préfère Docteur Kildare."

Claudine waited. She felt nothing. And then something exploded in her chest. She raced across the verandah, hit her leg on her mother's chair, fell, got herself up again and screamed down the stairs. She heard her father say, "Mais, voyons donc," and Yvon say it was time he was going, and her mother say that this was a dramatic age, and then all she heard was her own heart pounding as she raced into the woods.

She hid in the woods for a long time, imagined that she would spend the night there and give them all a big scare. She walked, stirring dead leaves and scaring birds from trees. Her throat felt sore, she was shivering, even though she was sweating from running up the hill.

After a while, sitting on a stump, scratching a piece of tree fungus with her fingernails, she heard Yvon start up the hydroplane, and saw it rise in the late afternoon sky.

She would have liked to go up in the sky like that, to get out of the swamp of what she felt. She knew things were going to go wrong, could sense it in her whole body, the way animals could sense an earthquake.

Claudine decided to follow the ridge behind the house and then find a way down to the little beach with the big rock covered with green moss. The rowboat was beached there. If she could get to it without being seen, she could row out onto the lake, watch the reflections of the birch trees undulating in the water, feel the strength of her arms on the oars, the water dripping from their tips when she pulled them out, let her self drift out of the picture.

She got bigger as she walked. She had a plan. It surprised her how quickly she got to the beach.

Problem was, they were there.

She hid behind the cedars that sheltered the beach.

Her mother was leaning on the big boulder that straddled the beach and the water. The moss on the rock looked lime green in the last rays of the afternoon sun. From that rock, Claudine and Janine had fished and caught little perch with pale yellow bellies.

*H*er mother's face was washed-out in the sun, her arms were crossed against her gingham shirt, her jaw set against her father, who had picked up a stick and was making lines in the sand, lines that radiated from his feet. He'd taken his shirt off, and his plaid bermuda shorts were too loose, they hung below his navel where the dark hair grew in a line.

"Odette," he said.

"I paid for the house," she said, "with my hard-earned money, and I want you out. Tu comprends? Roger. *Out.*"

"Ton argent, c'est toujours ta maudite argent. I paid, too. J'en ai payé, Odette des affaires. You're not the only one paying and paying and paying. And money's not the only thing I paid. De te voire flirter avec Yvon, comme ça, c'est humiliant, Odette."

"Maudit menteur. You can't stop lying, can you? You just can't stop. Just answer this. Is it me or is it you who bought the house in Notre-Dame-de-Grâce?"

"C'est toi. Mais je suis encore père de famille, Odette. C'est encore moi qui porte les pantalons icitte. It's me that wears the goddamn pants in this house."

"Then try and keep them on!" she screamed.

"Pardon?"

"How is she, la p'tite cocktail waitress qui travaille au Black Sheep bar chez Ruby Foos? Hein, a va bien, elle? Elle a pas d'enfants, elle, hein. Elle s'en fout, elle, des enfants."

"You're not going to start that again. C'est fini, ça. Baby, I tell you it's finish."

He walked over to her, and was about to take her chin in his hand and lift her head up when she screamed, "Touche-moi pas, touche-moi pas! Don't come near me." She was shaking. "The detective," she said, "he didn't say it was finished, c't'affaire-là."

"Maudite chienne. You had me followed? Maudite cochonne."

Claudine stopped breathing so she wouldn't have to hear. She wanted to run away.

Her father grabbed her mother by the shoulders and started to shake her against the big boulder. "I'll kill you, I'll kill you!" he shouted. Odette was crying, terrible cracked sounds were coming out of her chest.

"Maman, Maman," Claudine moaned, but they didn't hear her. They struggled against each other, until her mother crumpled crying on the sand.

"C'est fini, Odette," her father said. "Fini. You killed it, satisfied? It's over." He walked right past Claudine.

"Roger, laisse-moi pas toute seule, Roger."

He turned around, for one split second. "J'en peux plus, Odette," he said. He was crying, but he kept on walking.

Claudine had done something wrong, she was doubled over with the pain of having watched. After a while her mother stopped crying and stepped down to the water, and washed her face there.

Claudine ran as fast as she could back to the cottage. She was feverish, she was dying of thirst.

*A*fter gulping down the rest of the gin from the bottle, their father said he was going to take them over to their grandfather Béribée's house to eat. His hands were shaking. Claudine looked at the label on the empty bottle.

What about Maman, Janine asked. He said she wanted to be alone. "On va prendre le bateau," he said, "on va avoir du fun."

Roger was weaving a little as he walked down the path. Claudine and Janine followed. Claudine said I don't feel well, to Janine, to the trees. She kept thinking about those nightmares she had where she could hear kittens mewling in the basement and she couldn't get to them, they were buried in rubble. It was an awful sound. But in the dreams she forgot about the kittens and left them behind, just like she was forgetting about something now, and leaving it behind.

Roger had trouble starting the engine, he pulled and pulled on the cord and it flew back without a sound. He swore. He pulled the choke out. It still didn't start. But then he squeezed some black bulbs from the lines going to the orange gas tanks, and when he pulled the cord this time, the engine started.

And so they went to their grandfather's house, bobbing in orange life-jackets that fit over their heads like stocks, and their father gunned the boat through the dark water, and the wind whipped tears from their eyes.

Roger manoeuvred the turquoise steering wheel with a crooked baby finger. "Woooah," he yelled, and slalomed through imaginary buoys.

Claudine looked behind her to see if her mother was on the verandah. She wasn't. The motor cut through all of the reflections in the water, ploughed through the wavy zigzag of birch trunks, ripped through their dark foliage and left a white scar behind.

There was music coming from the large white clapboard cottage, but the car wasn't in the driveway. Soft big band music broken up by insistent horns and the child-like sound of a xylophone drifted to the lawn of their great-uncle Jean's cottage.

The music stopped suddenly, and something else started up, a man's voice, deep and phony to the girls' ears.

"C'est Mel Tormé," Roger said, bobbing his head to either side and snapping his fingers. "I'm getting sentimental over you."

"C'est dégoûtant," Janine said.

Claudine was so feverish, she wanted to lie down on the lawn and go to sleep.

Standing by the screen door now, they could see their grandfather with his arms around a woman who wasn't their grandmother. They were dancing. It was Francine, but not a Francine they'd ever seen. This Francine had long dark hair falling onto her shoulders instead of her usual French twist, and she wore a light print dress instead of bermuda shorts with a stained sleeveless white blouse.

When they heard them shuffling at the door, Béribée and Francine parted so abruptly that it was as if time had changed gears, what had been slow and syrupy turned jerky and speedy. Lights were switched on, Mel Tormé was whipped off the old Victrola with a good scratch of the needle, Francine adjusted her hair, Béribée poured drinks, and then settled into his usual posture on the armchair by the table where he kept his war magazines with pictures of Nazi soldiers tearing blouses off the shoulders of women with pained faces.

They learned that their grandmother had gone to Montreal for a few days.

Francine took the girls into the kitchen and made them

Campbell's tomato soup and toast. The overhead light in the kitchen was very yellow, and the linoleum floor smelled like grey Spic and Span water. Francine put cream in the soup, and it turned pink. Claudine tried to eat it, but ran into a viscous jellied lump. She spat it out.

"Je me sens pas bien," she said.

Francine put her cool hand on her forehead and said she had a fever.

In the living room, Béribée and Roger were discussing their mother. Claudine and Janine's ears were burning with fear. They were going to have to go back in the boat in the dark, and Roger was on his second rye already.

*I*n the haze of her fever, propped with cushions on the living-room couch, Claudine heard them discuss Marilyn Monroe. Her grandfather said that Francine thought she had been murdered by the Mafia, that maybe she knew things and that they gave her pills to make it look like a suicide.

"Whatever she knew," Béribée said, laughing with a wet wheezing cough in his armchair, "it was safe in her pretty pea brain."

"Qu'est-ce que ça veut dire, pea-brain?" Francine wanted to know.

"Petite, là, comme un pois," Roger said.

"Elle avait la cervelle dans ses seins, hein, Roger?" Béribée said, and broke up laughing.

"Her brain in her tits, elle est bonne celle là, Béribée." Her father was laughing so hard he had tears in his eyes.

"Je trouve pas ça drôle," Francine said. "Pas drôle du tout."

Béribée looked at her hard. "Fait pas ta grande Catholique là, franchement. Je l'aimais Marilyn, you know that."

"Moi aussi, Francine," Roger said, "je l'aimais Marilyn, a beautiful woman like that. Une vraie déesse. On joke, mais on l'aimais au fond."

Things got quiet after that, and the silence pried Roger loose.

"Tu veux ma grosse flashlight?" Béribée said.

"C'est une pleine lune," Roger said, and so it was, huge and silver, bouncing light on the lake like bits of quartz in a dark stone. But he took the big flashlight anyway, and Janine got to shine it all the way home.

*T*he cottage was dark. Not a light on.

Claudine thought, Maman's gone. But the car was still there, parked by the back of the cottage. Claudine grabbed the flashlight from Janine and shone it on her father's footsteps up the hill.

Roger opened the kitchen door and turned on the light. There were toast crumbs on the counter and there was a note on the kitchen table. Roger crumpled up the note, and the girls followed him through the dark living room and into their mother's room.

Claudine was still holding the flashlight, it felt like a game, like she was a robber flashing a beam of light here and there looking for money and jewels. The beam lit up her mother sprawled naked on the bed, sheet wrapped around her, eyelids soft as moths. She was snoring.

"Maudite sans-coeur," Roger said, and grabbed the flashlight and turned on the bedside lamp.

"Les filles, out," he said. "Janine, mets la bouilloire, et prépare un café pour ta mère. Deux cuillerées de Nescafé. Ta mère a pris des pillules."

Claudine sat on the kitchen floor. Her knees were shaking, her teeth were chattering. She watched Janine make the cup of coffee, in a dream, Janine moving so slowly, the kettle taking hours to boil. From a great distance, she could hear her father shouting, "Réveille-toi, Odette, réveille-toi," over and over like a needle stuck on a record. It sounded like he was slapping her.

And then everything moved very quickly again. Claudine grabbed the cup of hot coffee from Janine's hand, and she was walking outside, following her father down to the dock. He was carrying her mother on his back, holding her hands around his neck. A heavy, lifeless body. Nobody's body. Her feet dragged on the ground. She was naked and her skin shone phosphorescent in the moonlight.

Janine walked behind Claudine, moaning, "Elle va mourir, Maman va mourir, Maman va mourir." Claudine wanted to tell her to shut up, but her jaw clamped shut. She was stiff from being scared of tripping on a cedar root and splattering hot coffee on her mother's back. If only Janine would stop moaning. Her moaning could pull death out of the dark. The moonlight looked metallic now.

She'd left her mother behind. She should never have done that. It was her fault, all of it. Her father cursed her mother all the way down to the dock. "Maudite sans-coeur, tu vas marcher, ma maudite sans-coeur." Claudine could see his anger stabbing her body, the knives in it that made her mother's body twitch and lurch on his back. And she started her own chant, "Arrête Papa, arrête Papa, arrête Papa." She wanted to crush his killing voice and her sister's dirge. They were calling death down from the trees. They were going to make it happen. But there was nothing she could do to stop it.

"Tu fais semblant, Odette, avec tes mélodrames," he said as they walked out of the dark trees onto the moonlit dock. He lay her down on the dock. Her head fell away from her body like a rag doll's. Her eyes were closed, her breathing shallow. Her white breasts gleamed in the moonlight. Claudine took off her kangaroo sweatshirt and covered her mother with it.

There was mist on the lake now, bats flung themselves around the light of their neighbor's boathouse, swooping and squeaking.

"Bon, écoutez, les enfants," Roger said, "il faut pas la laisser dormir. C'est dangereux. Il faut la réveiller."

He unzipped his bermuda shorts and stepped out of them. In his underwear, he jumped off the dock and landed waist-high in the dark water.

Janine went crazy. "Il va la noyer!" she screamed, "il va la noyer. Claudine, il va la noyer." Roger hoisted himself back on the dock and slapped her face. "Tu es hystérique," he said, and she was quiet after that, tears streaming down her face.

Back in the water, Roger scooped some of it in his hands and splashed Odette's body on the dock. Her eyelids twitched. Goosebumps rose on her flesh. "Odette," he said, "the joke is over." He was pleading now. He splashed her and splashed her, like a priest baptizing a newborn, speaking her name over and over.

"Maman," Claudine said, "Maman, réveilles-toi." The mist was breaking up. The wind came up from nowhere and shook the leaves of silver birches behind them. It sounded like rain.

Odette opened her eyes. And sat up. Her hair was wet, her face was wet, and she wiped the wetness with Claudine's sweatshirt. Her shoulders shook from the cold. In a faint voice, she said, "I want to die."

And then yelled it, I want to die, I want to die, yelled it from a place so dark that everything around her died.

"You should be ashame of yourself, Odette Beaulieu," her father said, "ashame of yourself in front of the children. Tu fais ta Marilyn Monroe, hein? Ben t'es pas Marilyn Monroe, tu m'entends là, t'es pas Marilyn Monroe."

"Mes bébées," their mother said, "mes bébées," and reached out to hold the girls in her arms.

Claudine looked at her, hard. And then she started to yawn. She couldn't stop yawning. She was cold as ice.

Odette August

FROM THE BRIGHT SUNLIGHT, ODETTE STEPS INTO THE PALE electric light of the caves. Plaques on both sides of the entrance explain that the caves served as hiding places to the Arawak Indians, who were killed off by successive waves of conquerors, and to the Maroons, or runaway slaves, who were hunted down by the British with the help of wild dogs.

Odette turns away from the plaques. She knows this, has read this before. In *The Gleaner*. And she remembers reading something about the wild dogs, that they weren't really dogs but an animal indigenous to the island. The Arawaks had hunted them once, and now both of them were extinct.

Odette's heart is still pounding, as much from the steep walk uphill as from her encounter with Wesley, who already seems far away now, a paper ember, swept by the winds that have brought her here. The heat has erased him, but not the traces of rage that distorted her face, there on the dirt shoulder above Discovery Bay. Her fists are still clenched from wanting to pound his chest.

Stepping into the cave, past the needy eyes of a girl selling straw hats and coral earrings and necklaces, Odette makes herself open her hands. The voices are back. Voices that make her feel like a ventriloquist for someone else's wrongs, someone else's pain. *I'll kill you if you come near me. I'll kill you. I'll kill you dead.*

She is fighting the words that want to come out of her mouth with a clenched jaw, with whatever remains of the Valium coursing through her tired, rigid body.

A drink is what she needs. A nice cool drink. A tiny drink. Just one. She deserves it. Especially now. She really deserves it now. She would like to go right to the bar carved out of rock in the very heart of the cave, and have her complementary rum punch, but she knows that she has to go through the tour first, that it would look very bad to go right to the bar. Mustn't ever look like I can't do without. *I need, I need, but I must never look like I need. Never.*

For a moment, standing at the entrance, watching her lime green sandals on the smooth rock floor of the cave, Odette feels compelled to tell somebody, anybody, about what just happened. She wants to go up to the girl selling hats and say this man, this man who took me by taxi, he tried to do something to me, you've got to help me, but the girl would not know what to say, would not know what to do, and what if she dreamed it all, what if she imagined this, what if Wesley was not saying the things she thought he was saying, what if she hadn't seen or heard properly. Her self is untrustworthy. She is untrustworthy. She imagines things, always has. *You imagined it. You dreamed it.*

Stunned in the half-light, Odette stands, shredded lipstick-stained kleenex in one hand, ticket in the other. She is stuck there at the entrance with a ticket she doesn't remember buying. She must have bought it, before reading the plaques. On the other side of the girl selling hats a woman leans against the cave wall, watching her. She wears navy blue. She looks official.

Walking towards Odette, the woman says, "My name is Angela, I am your tour guide." The way she says tour guide makes it sound like the most special thing in the world to be. Her voice is devoid of inflection, rinsed clean of any traces of patois. Angela is wearing a navy blue Dacron skirt, a white shirt and a red, white and blue polka-dot silk scarf around her neck.

Odette says, "Thank you very much, you are very kind," and follows Angela into the cave.

The caves are pale orange in the electric light of the bulbs strung along their corridors and alcoves. The color must have something to do with the iron in the rock. The red rock is streaked with pale green. All of the walls are moulded into smooth protruding shapes; years and years of trickling water created this.

It is like walking into the jaws of a domesticated animal to walk through this cave with Angela, stopping every few feet to look at the formations of stalactites dripping from the ceiling and stalagmites rising from the floor. Angela's steel-tipped heels click on the smooth floor. She approaches every designated alcove with dignity, stands to the side of it and rattles off her rehearsed commentary.

"Notice," she says now, "the formations to my right." Odette looks, sees the intricate accretions of water and salt lit up by a single electric bulb. Odette waits politely. "Notice," Angela says, in the flat voice of officialdom, "how the formations look like the three wise men, bearing gifts. Can you see the star of Bethlehem?"

Odette looks, sees nothing resembling three wise men. She sees three spear-like formations. "Yes," she says. "I see."

As she follows Angela to the next alcove, Odette thinks this is like doing the stations of the cross in church. Tastes come back to her, the taste of vinegar and blood, the imagined taste of the wooden rosaries of the brothers who walked the church, robes sweeping, wooden rosaries knocking against waxy-smelling pews. The taste of old olive pits, that's what she imagined those rosaries would taste like, like the olives on the mount where Christ was crucified, drinking from a sponge of vinegar and water proferred by a centurion. She had stood at every station, feeling her lisle stockings bagging at the knees, the heavy cotton of her underwear bunching between her legs, stood and waited for the bright flash she had imagined revelation to be.

Angela turns on her heels, walks at a quick pace towards the next alcove. Odette follows her. They have turned a corner, left the light and heat of the entrance far behind. Odette is afraid now, in the dark of the cave, afraid of the sound of waterdrops falling in hidden pools, of the black flitting lines of bats overhead.

Sensing her fear, Angela says, "The bats are harmless." Like a child, Odette repeats harmless, the bats are harmless. Her whole body is a limb that has gone to sleep, tingling, heavy, she can hardly feel the pressure of the rock on her feet. She must be floating away. She wants to say to Angela I feel faint. She is staring at a formation that looks like a robed man.

Her mother called the priest. That's what her mother did, afterwards, after the girl she was had seen blue and red circles breaking in her tightly closed eyes. She had not wanted to see the dark tornadoes coming out of his eyes, his mouth, so she closed her eyes. And her eyes stayed closed for a long time after that.

Angela keeps walking, and Odette follows her in a dream, stops at each alcove and listens as if her life depended on it. Buckingham Palace, Angela says, Santa Claus and his reindeer, she says, Bob Marley's profile, with dreadlocks.

Her mother called the priest. That's what her mother did, afterwards. Odette couldn't open her eyes. She had closed her eyes not to see his face. She had left her body not to feel the pain between her five-year-old legs. She left her body and her thin spirit floated to the ceiling of that rooming house in Halifax, with the view of grey waves, with the sound of wind whistling through the cracked windowpanes.

They are walking again, Angela is leading her to another alcove.

Don't tell. Not supposed to tell. You will die if you tell. Tu vas mourir.
"I am," Odette says.

Angela looks up. "Please follow me," she says, "we will now go down to the underground pool."

"I," Odette says. "I can't." But her voice is drowned out by Angela's clicking heels.

Afterwards Mum cut up a piece of cotton and put it between her legs and called the priest. The priest sprinkled holy water on her body, talked Latin to her limbs. Later there was blood on the cotton, rusty brown, the color of scabbed knees.

On the train from Halifax to Montreal, she had a fever. The cows grazing outside had dancing spots, her heart was wanting to come out of her mouth when she threw up in the swaying toilet of the train. Her sisters ate cinnamon hearts out of paper bags at the railway stations. They stayed behind. Her hands turned red holding on to her cinnamon hearts.

When they got to the city, her mother put her to bed in the house that smelled of cats and lemon oil. They put her to bed and talked, Granny Mattie, Grandpa Stephen, Mum. She heard them talking. She knew she was bad. Her mother never said anything. She left the next morning. She left her there all alone. Mum. Stop crying, they said, stop crying, stop crying.

She follows Angela down the steps to the underground pool. Angela takes her hand so she can step into the yellow rubber dinghy that will take them into another part of the cave. Odette sits down and cries.

"Are you all right, ma'am?" Angela says.

"My mother," Odette says.

"A recent bereavement, ma'am?"

"My mother. I would like to talk to my mother."

"It is good to cry," Angela says. "Good to cry, ma'am, grief need crying like earth need rain." Her paddling echoes in the dimly lit cave.

Odette brings her hands to her face, sees her mother's face, her fierce blue eyes, so beleaguered and alive. What else could her mother have done? There was no one then, no one. If she had not brought her to Montreal, he would have done it again. She had no money, no place to go. She must have threatened him so he wouldn't do it to the others, must have found a way. There was no divorce, the priests had seen to that. So she did the only thing she could do, she took her away to a safe place, and went back, and hoped she would forget.

And she had forgotten. All that time with this inside her. Is it possible? Are such things possible? And her mother, all those years saying I did my best, and then looking at her with guilty eyes. Odette had never understood those eyes, the eyes of a woman who bleached and ironed her clothes, who laid out everything for her with infinite care, who said I do my best, I did my best, eyes that said nothing I can ever do will be good enough. How angry Odette had been at her, for no reason she could tell.

Odette wipes her face with a kleenex from her purse. She has always known it, but never known it. His crime, not hers. His crime. All this time, carrying his crime.

They have gone over to the other side of the cave, in a lagoon lit from above by a natural skylight. The water is pale green. Odette grazes it with her hand, and then tastes it.

"Not quite fresh," Angela says. "Brackish water."

Claudine August

THE KEY TURNS SOFT AS BUTTER IN THE LOCK. CLAUDINE PICKS up her suitcase and walks into the loft.

Colin is standing at the round table with a fly-swatter in his hand. He turns. A dead fly sticks to the yellow plastic. The round table is clean, with a pot of yellow chrysanthemums in the centre.

"Sorry," he says, "the place is full of flies." And so it is, full of bluebottle flies buzzing around the flowers, bouncing off the glass of the windows overlooking the lighted billboards over the Spadina bridge. "I don't know where they came from. It's like they're hatching in here."

"I didn't expect you to be here," she says.

"Why?"

"I don't know," she says. It's only ten o'clock, the mauve sky through the windows is just beginning to darken, but she's suddenly very tired. She would like to unpack, to make everything tidy, but she's always found it impossible to do the simplest things with Colin around. It's like there's a current coming from him that she has to attend to. So she stands there by her suitcase, like a character in a badly directed play who can speak only while standing still. "I don't know," she says. "On the train, I kept thinking of coming in here and finding a note, one of your cryptic poem notes, you know. You'd be gone and I'd . . . "

"Burn the note?"

She laughs. "I didn't get that far." She had gone far, but not in that direction.

"I'm here," he says. "Have a seat, grab a beer. You look like Lot's wife. How was it, anyway?"

"It was awful. It was what it always was. But I saw it for the first time."

"Saw what?"

"That it had nothing to do with me."

"What?"

"Just that."

"I don't follow."

"I don't want to talk about it."

"Talk about it."

"That's how you . . . "

"What?"

"Get me."

"I'm not doing anything."

There's something different in him, something proprietorial. He started to live here while she was gone. That's what it is. All of a sudden, it's like she's visiting him. She walks slowly to the kitchen area and puts the kettle on. Takes her sandals off and savors the wooden floor under her feet. It is nice to touch the floor, nice to touch the pink cup she puts a teabag in.

"Everybody," he says, "is saying it had nothing to do with me."

"I didn't say it had nothing to do with you. Who's everybody, anyway?"

"Janine, she said something like that."

"Oh."

"Marie-Ange got sick, she asked me to help, I went over and she had a terrible fever." The fly-swatter is sticking right up like a flag in his hand. His hand is starting to shake a little, even though his voice has grown deeper with some fond remembrance of altruism.

"When was that?"

"Last night."

"Really? That's weird. Don't you think that's weird?"

"What?"

"That she'd call you."

"No. Jim was out of town. You know how scared she gets about things."

"Last night, I tried to . . . "

"What?"

She wants to say call and call, and you made me go crazy. But she can't be bothered. She looks at him. He doesn't look like the monster who makes her crazy, who pushes her to those awful places. He looks like a boy with a fly-swatter who has nowhere else to go. Claudine sees the just now in it. He has nowhere else to go just now, and what he builds around this moment she'll have to carry, because he will have tried, will have said the things he thinks she needs to hear, will say them until someone else comes along, fresh with promise, fresh as untracked snow.

She sees all this, waiting for the kettle to boil on the red-hot burner. And what's more, she sees the hope she's always carried, the hope that he would change. It tastes bitter now.

"I'm tired," she says.

"It's so tiring living with a bastard. That's what my mother used to say. And you know, she was right. He was an asshole, and I'm an asshole. I know that. I know I don't deserve to live." He's smiling. He's spotted a fly on the table. He brings the swatter down. "And neither does he, the little fucker."

The kettle boils.

"It's not my job," she shouts, "to figure out whether you deserve to live or not." She scrunches the teabag against the side of the cup and flicks it into the garbage. She opens the fridge, finds some milk beside a twelve-pack of beer, pours some in the cup, and slams the fridge door. She stands by the kitchen counter.

"I did some shopping," he says. "I bought that milk, I bought some groceries, I carried two bags of groceries up here. I even got you flowers. Maybe I deserve to live a little bit." He's smiling, a big wide smile.

"I didn't say you didn't deserve to live," she says. And takes a sip of tea. It scalds her tongue. "Did I get any mail?"

"This isn't interesting. You've gotten dull, do you know that, Claudine? You've gotten really dull."

"Good," she says. "Now you can pack your stuff and find yourself something interesting. Maybe my sister. Maybe you'll find that interesting. There's a husband, there's a child, she's related to me. There's lots of complications that you'll find interesting."

"Your sister didn't do anything wrong," he says.

"I'm sure she didn't. She's too good, she's too nice to do anything wrong." Claudine puts her tea down on the floor and kneels to unzip her suitcase, then sits down cross-legged in her jeans. Fingers tight on her clothes, she sorts through them to make a laundry pile. "She probably told you I wrecked her life, that's what she tells everybody." She flings a bunch of T-shirts in a pile. "She's always tried to wreck anything I had by making me feel guilty. I made myself so small, I almost disappeared." She can't even see what she's doing now, the piles she's making have no rhyme or reason. "I'm so sick of wearing black, look at this stuff, it's all black."

"My god, Claudine. You're getting interesting again."

"Fuck you. Fuck you all." She's shaking as she walks to the window. She watches the cars go by on Lake Shore Boulevard. She hears him behind her, he's waiting for her to turn. Then his arms come down on either side of her, as he leans on her back, chin resting on top of her head.

"You can't stay out of it, huh, you just can't resist it," she says.

"I'm a writer."

"You're not a writer, you're, you're a, you're a robber-baron." It's the most ridiculous thing she's ever said.

"I love you like crazy. I've always loved you like crazy."

"I don't want to be loved like crazy. I want you to go."

"Okay," he says. "Fine. That's just fine. I'll go, but I want you to know I'm never coming back. This is it. This is your choice."

"My choice? My choice?" How can he stand there and say that? "You're really something, you know that? You lie, you cheat, you play around with people, and then when they can't put up with you, you go that's your choice."

He walks back to the table and rummages in his pile of papers. "I finished my book of poetry," he says, all business-like now, as if he'd just finished pruning a tree and had to move on to the next one. "I just wrote this poem about Marie-Ange's fever, about carrying her. It's the last poem in the book. It's about the future."

"Is she okay?" It comes out like a croak.

"She's fine. It's a beautiful poem." He's found what he was looking for, his address book.

He shoves his papers into his black satchel.

"You're going to be miserable," he says. "With me or without me."

"Thanks."

"I'll get my stuff later," he says. "I'm leaving you the poem." His face is dark, detached.

He's walking away now, towards the door, leaving a track of something she wants to follow. I'm going to die, she thinks, I'm going to die. She stands by the kitchen counter and turns the tap on. Just as she's about to say did you love me, really, tell the truth, did you ever love me, he turns around. "Do you mind," he says, "if I take the beer?"

She can't look at him as he squeezes between her and the fridge and takes his beer.

*I*t was Janine who called, finally, who said what's going on, I haven't heard from you in so long, are you mad at me? Nothing's going on, Claudine said. I had to finish editing the documentary. Now all I want to do is clean this place. I can't believe what I've been living in.

Janine offered to help.

*S*he comes in bustling and business-like with a whole basket of cleaning supplies, holding a mop in one hand and Marie-Ange's hand in the other. Claudine, who has just been cleaning windows from her perch on the round table, suddenly feels dizzy there at the door.

"Are you all right?" Janine says. "You don't look so well."

"I'm fine. Come on in."

Janine, tanned in a white camisole with lace along the neckline, puts the cleaning stuff down and looks around. The sun has bleached her hair and her streaks, and she looks as blond as when she was a child.

"You look great," Claudine says, and bends down to hug Marie-Ange, who's wearing a sweatshirt with a map of Jamaica on it and No Problem in black letters above it. Odette must have sent it.

"It's weird," Janine says, "I feel so strong, I've never felt stronger in my life. Maybe it's the sun." Sidling up to Claudine, she brings her arm alongside hers and says, "Look at my tan." She presses her finger down on the skin of her arm to show the contrasting white under the tanned layer. But the contrast doesn't seem to satisfy her totally, so she keeps pressing down, leaving white impressions of her finger along her forearm. Claudine looks at her own pale arm and then at her sister's face. "It's a golden tan, eh," Janine says, avoiding her eyes.

"Yeah, you tan just like Mum." Claudine climbs back on top of the round table to finish cleaning the windows.

"It's not the same thing," Janine says.

Claudine takes a rag from her bucket of vinegar and water, wrings it and wipes the windowpane. Janine takes Marie-Ange into the bedroom part of the loft where the TV is, and Mr. Dressup's theme music suddenly fills the loft.

Janine comes back in and starts cleaning the kitchen counter.

"I did that already," Claudine says.

"Oh."

They work in silence. Janine has settled into scouring the top of the stove with Comet. Claudine is sickened with vinegar fumes. She can't reach the top of the windows, she'll just do everything she can from standing on the round table and then figure out how to reach the top.

"So," Janine says, with exaggerated concentration, "are you moving?"

"No."

"So what's all that?" she says, pointing to boxes and bags by the door.

"It's Colin's stuff."

"Oh."

"Look at these windows, doesn't it look great?" Claudine can't believe it, the buildings across the street look etched now, such precise lines with the sky so blue above them. All the murky summer air has vanished, the squeaky-clean windows are filled with crisp fall light.

"You've broken up? Ah, Claudine, I had no idea. That's awful. I'm so sorry."

"Why are you sorry? You always hated him."

"I did?"

"You kept saying he's bad news."

"That's true. Do you want me to do the oven? I've got the stuff here."

"It's okay, that stuff stinks. I never baked anything anyway."

"All right." Now Janine is scraping something on the stove with a fingernail. "It's just that I saw another side of him, he was good to Marie-Ange, you know. Oh, did I tell you? She was sick and Jim was away? What *is* this gummy stuff here? Anyway, he came over and I saw that side. There was a good side to him. There's a good side to everybody."

"Yeah, Hitler had a good side." Claudine's done everything she can from her perch. She climbs down and empties out a milk crate full of old newspapers. She lifts the crate up on the table. Then she takes her pail to the sink and empties it. "He got a poem out of it, that's what he got out of it," she says.

"What do you mean?"

"He wrote a poem about carrying Marie-Ange, how it woke up the old nomad in him. I shouldn't laugh. Actually, it's quite a lovely poem. Really tender. It's a real testament to Marie-Ange's powers, if you ask me."

Janine dumps some more Comet out and starts scrubbing the rings around the elements. Claudine fills the pail with fresh water.

"Do you know where he is?" Janine says. "I mean, so he can come and get his stuff?"

"No."

"You didn't give him much of a chance, you know."

"What?" Claudine's not sure she's heard this right. She turns off the taps.

Scouring and scowling, Janine says, "I don't mean to criticize, but you don't give people much of a chance." She walks by

Claudine and rinses her rag in the pail that Claudine's just filled with clean water.

"Hey," Claudine says. "Hey."

"Claudine, I'm saying this because I love you. I know it's hard to hear, but this keeps happening. Do you know how many times I've had to do this, help you pick up the pieces?"

"I can't believe this. You? You, help *me* pick up the pieces? My god, Janine, I've seen you through the Emergency rooms of two major cities, I've lent you money, I've given you money, I've let you stay at my place for months at a time. What the fuck are you talking about?"

Janine sighs. Claudine empties the pail once again and turns on the taps.

"I'm your big sister, I've always supported you, I've always had to rescue you."

"This is such bullshit. You say the words, but they're just words that make you feel good about yourself, that make you feel superior."

"You're the superior one, not me."

"Yeah, yeah."

"Colin wasn't so bad, you know, but nobody can take that, how you cut people up, show them their flaws all the time. I never did that to you. Never, ever."

"You do it in your way, which is all underhanded, that's the way you like it." The pail is full. Claudine picks it up and walks back to the table. She's muttering now. "You've never had the courage of your own meanness."

"I don't know what you mean. I don't know what you're talking about." Janine follows Claudine to the table. Ignoring her, Claudine climbs onto the table and then onto the turned-over milk crate. It's wobbly, but she can reach the top of the windows.

"You know what I'm talking about," Claudine says.

"Maybe we should stop talking now. I think it's upsetting Marie-Ange. I don't want to fight. I really don't."

Marie-Ange is still in the other room watching TV.

"That's so typical. That's so fucking typical of you. To shut it down when it gets close to the truth."

"What truth? We only had each other and I took care of you. That's my truth."

"You're a liar." The warm water drips down Claudine's arm.

"I am not!" Janine shouts. "How can you say that to me?" And then she starts to cry. "How can you do that to me? How can you do that to me? Why are you doing this to me? Why? Why? Why?"

"Please don't cry. Please. I'm sorry."

"I don't understand," she wails, "I really don't."

"It's okay. It's okay." The crate is starting to slide back. "I just wondered why you're, well, so suddenly interested in Colin. Why you want to know where he is, why you're taking his side. That's all."

"I don't know. I was just talking." Janine is wiping her face with a rag.

The crate has stopped sliding, but Claudine feels precarious all of a sudden, hands pressed against ancient glass, watching the cars below. There's something on the tip of her tongue. She closes her eyes, opens them. "You slept with him, didn't you?"

"How can you say that? How can you even think that? I can't believe what I'm hearing."

"He told me."

"He's lying. He's the liar."

"I don't believe you."

"I'm going," Janine says. "I'm not staying here one more minute." She goes into the bedroom. Marie-Ange doesn't want to leave. "Five more minutes," she pleads.

"Five more minutes and that's it," Janine says. "I mean it."

Janine comes back. Claudine can feel her rummaging around, putting her cleaning supplies together. But she can't move, can't say a word. Her hands press against the glass, which suddenly feels flimsy, a thin brittle membrane that could crack and send her crashing down. She is trying to manoeuvre herself out of her bent position without pushing the crate back and losing her balance, but it's impossible.

"Janine," she says quietly.

"What?"

"I can't move."

"What?"

"If I let go of my hands on the window, the crate will slide back."

Claudine can feel her sister's hands wrapping around her knees, can feel the warmth of her forehead on her calves.

"Okay," Janine says, "you can start straightening up." Claudine lets go of the glass, straightens up, steps off the crate with shaky knees. Janine gives her a hand to help her down off the table, and then turns away from her. But Claudine won't let go of her hand. "Please," she says. "Please look at me."

Turning, Janine tries to stare her down with stubborn, dead eyes. "I'm looking at you. Are you satisfied now?"

This face, Claudine thinks, this face with their mother's eyes, their father's lips, this face she's looked at forever, in bedrooms, in cars, in boats, in fields, in parks, behind couches, under covers, in all kinds of weathers and terrors, this face is as close to her as it is closed to her.

"You're okay now," Janine says.

"Please."

"What?"

Claudine lets go of her hand. Janine takes it again. "I'm sorry," she says. "I'm sorry."

Its the oddest thing, Claudine wants to be angry, but her face feels hot, flushed with life. The truth, for once, has surfaced. And it feels good, like removing a splinter.

Marie-Ange bounds into the room covered in Claudine's jewellery. She has fake gold around her neck, bangles around her thin arms. "I want to make soup," she says.

"We have to go," Janine says.

"No! No! No!" Marie-Ange screams. "I want to make soup for my babies."

"What babies?" Janine says.

Marie-Ange points all around her. "There, and there and there."

Claudine fills a pot with water and takes out a ladle and some bowls. She spreads a teatowel on the floor and places the soup things around it.

"Oh god, I'm so sorry," Janine says.

Claudine looks up at her. She's not going to feel sorry for her feeling sorry. Janine can suffer a little bit. "I don't know what I want," Claudine says. "But I don't want sorry. I'm going to go up to the roof and check on my plants. Marie-Ange can play for as long as she wants."

She fills her big red watering can with water and leaves the front door open behind her.

*E*very day she'd been back from Quebec City, she'd thought about it, thought about going up and watering the plants, but it's been like a tug that she's deliberately ignored.

She didn't want to see it. Didn't want to see the state the little roof garden would be in after weeks of neglect. When it rained yesterday, she was so grateful she almost cried. The skies can look after it, she thought, the skies can do it. I can't go up there. Everything I start ends up a mess. I can't take care of anything.

The late August sun is still hot, but the wind from the lake is cool. Stepping onto the deck, she can smell the fall coming in. She likes that. She is sick of the intensity of summer, she's ready for a new season, even if it pulls the long winter in its wake.

She expected everything to be dead, the earth in the planters to be cracked, the plants hollow, yellow sticks. But the tomatoes, while pale with thirst, have grown way beyond their stakes, and would have fallen over onto the deck if it hadn't been for the morning glory vines that wrapped themselves around them. The morning glories never went up the strands of string she'd stretched onto the trellis. They grabbed the nearest thing, and now their vines are thick and wiry and hardy. The blooms are stretched tight, almost transparent, like china cups full of sky.

Claudine kneels, and in the dark shadow beneath the fragrant tomato leaves and the heart-shaped morning glory leaves, she sees the red glistening skin of tomatoes. "Oh," she says, feeling foolish with delight, and slips her hand inside the darkness and twists a tomato off the vine, and then another and another. She lines them up on the deck, six of them, and then stands back to look at them so red and luscious on the white pine. She stretches her arms up to the sky, picks up the tomatoes, gathering them in the front of her green T-shirt. But she's forgotten something. She holds up her T-shirt full of tomatoes with one arm, picks up the watering can and waters the plants.

The roof door bursts open. "Claudine. Claudine."

"I got some tomatoes, look, I got some tomatoes," she says to Janine.

"God, she's uncanny. Come, quick. C'est Maman, on the phone. She says she wants to come and visit."

"Maman? You're kidding."

Hugging the tomatoes to her belly, Claudine walks down the metal stairs and meets Marie-Ange halfway. "Granny," Marie-Ange says. "Granny."

"Yes, it's Granny," Janine says, and rolls her eyes at Claudine. Then she reaches over to pick up Marie-Ange and carry her down.

Claudine sits cross-legged on the floor, folds her T-shirt over her tomatoes. She picks up the phone.

"Hello?" she says.

"Allo, Claudine?"

"Oui, c'est moi."

"Je t'endends pas, Chérie. Parle plus fort."

"Maman, Maman," she shouts, then pauses. "Can you hear me now?"

Acknowledgements

Many thanks to Layne for his patience, forebearance and loving support. I would also like to thank my sister for her insights; Nicky and Robin for their generosity; Sarah, Anne, David, Don, and M.A. for editorial guidance; Maureen and the crew at Flying Colours for their ongoing encouragement.

And I thank the Ontario Arts Council and the Explorations Program of the Canada Council for their support.